KING SHOES
AND
CLOWN POCKETS

D0112279

By the Same Author

Mighty Close to Heaven
Some Glad Morning

KING SHOES
AND
CLOWN POCKETS

FAYE GIBBONS

For Logan —
Happy reading
to you !
Faye Gibbons
11-16-00

Originally Published by

MORROW JUNIOR BOOKS / *NEW YORK*

ACKNOWLEDGMENT

The inspiration for this book came from my brother, Jerry Junkins, who held me spellbound and dizzy with his account of being "frozen" on a quarry wall back in 1956. Thanks, Jerry.

Copyright © 1989 by Faye Gibbons

All rights reserved.
No part of this book may be reproduced
or utilized in any form or by any means,
electronic or mechanical, including photocopying,
recording or by any information storage and retrieval system,
without permission in writing from the Publisher.
Inquiries should be addressed to
William Morrow and Company, Inc.,
105 Madison Avenue,
New York, NY 10016.

Printed in the United States of America.
1 2 3 4 5 6 7 8 9 10

Library of Congress Cataloging-in-Publication Data
Gibbons, Faye.
King shoes and clown pockets / Faye Gibbons.
p. cm.
Summary: Two ten-year-old boys from rural Alabama, each with his
own personal problems, become friends who face the vicissitudes of
life together.
ISBN 0-688-06592-9
[1. Friendship—Fiction. 2. Alabama—Fiction.] I. Title.
PZ7.G33913Kl 1989
[Fic]—dc20 89-33429
CIP
AC

Cover art by Mike Wimmer © 1989

To the three wonderful men in my life:
my husband, Benjamin,
and my sons, Ben and David

CONTENTS

1

THE PROMISE

"Raymond, get the field glasses," sang out Jasper Brock, squinting at the view through the windshield of his antique truck, Old Lizzie.

On the passenger side, his ten-year-old grandson bent to sweep his hand under the ragged seat until he caught hold of a familiar black strap. "What is it?" the boy asked excitedly, swinging around to his window. "A bluebird?" Lately his grandfather had been keen on spotting bluebirds. A few months ago it had been red-tailed hawks, and before that, barn owls.

The old man shook his head and pointed. "Down there! Across the field and just the other side of them trees. What do you see?"

Eager to please, Raymond trained the field glasses in the direction indicated, examining the familiar meadows, trees, and hills of his grandfather's Tennessee farm. Frowning, he lowered the glasses.

Jasper Brock swerved to miss a large mud hole in the

dirt road and laughed. "Hang on there, Butch!" he hollered out the window to the big red dog in back. "You're gonna fall out again!"

Barking a reply, Butch reared up on the side of the truck bed, tongue flapping in the warm August breeze, and nosed his way as close as he could to the cab.

"What a dog!" the old man said affectionately, punching Raymond. "We got us some dog, ain't we?"

Raymond smiled. "Sure do!" He wouldn't have allowed his fifteen-year-old sister, Jackie Lee, to claim part ownership of his dog—nor would he have shared Butch with his thirteen-year-old brother, Vance. But Grandpa Brock was his best friend—maybe his only real friend. Raymond was shy at school, and at home—in a house on his grandfather's large farm—there were no near neighbors. As for his family, they were all busy with their own interests. Just making a living seemed to take most of his parents' time, while his sociable, outgoing brother and sister found all kinds of school and church groups to join and lead. Sometimes Raymond included himself in their activities, but mostly it was Grandpa with whom Raymond spent his free time.

"Look again, boy!" Grandpa said. "See the pond?"

Raymond nodded. "I see little bits of it through the trees."

"Well?"

Raymond shrugged. "I don't see anything but water."

Grandpa braked to a sudden stop, and Butch, who was still reared up on the side of the truck, tumbled off into the dirt. He was up immediately, however, prancing around, barking and panting and shaking off dust.

"Well, don't say I didn't warn you!" Grandpa told him in an affectionate kind of fussing that Butch did not take seriously. "Ain't you never going to learn?"

Butch barked happily.

"Now, you ain't going down to the pond with us," Grandpa told him firmly. "Me and Raymond got business that don't include you."

Butch lowered his ears and drooped his tail. He was accustomed to being told this when the old man and the boy were off to seek birds or deer or some other wildlife that a dog might frighten off, but that didn't mean he had to like it.

"You stay," Grandpa told him. Then he softened. Pulling from his pocket one of the peppermints he always carried since giving up chewing tobacco, he unwrapped it and tossed it to the dog.

Watching the dog gobble down the offering in one gulp and lie down in the shade of the truck, Raymond said, "Mom says candy's not good for Butch."

Grandpa grunted. "Yeah, just like she thinks it's not good for an old man and a boy to spend so much time together! I don't reckon a piece of candy now and then is going to hurt. Let's go."

Raymond looked at Butch's reproachful eyes and then patted the dog on the head. "It's all right. We'll be right back," he whispered before heading across the field after his grandfather.

Despite the more than sixty-year difference in their ages, their kinship was apparent. Raymond and his grandfather both had the same wiry bodies, the same look of concentration on their round faces, and what was left of the old man's hair was as brown and curly as the boy's.

Grandpa stopped and turned back as they neared the trees. "Don't you tell Cecil and Millie about what I'm going to show you."

"I don't tell Mom and Dad our secrets!" Raymond said, indignant. How many times did he have to repeat that he had not been the one to tell his parents that Grandpa let him drive Old Lizzie around the barn that day? Vance, who had been mad that he had not been allowed to drive, had been the one who told.

"Don't get me wrong," Grandpa went on. "We're gonna tell 'em once we get it all worked out." His voice dropped. "But not yet."

"I couldn't tell Dad today anyway," Raymond said, still a bit offended. "He's gone to Alabama to see about that job, remember."

Grandpa grunted and frowned. Raymond's father had been laid off from a paper mill a couple of months before and had not yet been able to find a new job.

"Sh-h-h-h!" said Grandpa Brock a few moments later. He was walking crouched over now, moving silently through the trees and bushes that grew thickly around the pond. Raymond took in quick glimpses of the pond as he crept along behind his grandfather, wishing he could dive into its dark-green depths and swim to the little island that dotted its center. But he knew better. His city-raised mother was convinced that any water outside a chlorinated swimming pool would drown him like her third cousin once removed, or at the very least give him an ear infection that would require a doctor the family could ill afford right now.

"There!" Grandpa whispered, pulling aside a bush and pointing.

"Ducks," murmured Raymond, watching nearly a dozen of various sizes glide across the water, making soft chicken-like cluckings as they moved.

Grandpa grinned broadly. "White Pekins. I bought 'em yesterday, one drake—that's him in front with the curled-up tail—six females, and three or four young'uns. I got more coming next week."

Raymond eased forward and reached to separate the thick grasses right next to the water. A startled frog sounded an alarm with a plop-splash that quickly set off others. All around the pond, radiating circles within circles announced the arrival of intruders.

"Tattletales!" Raymond said, reaching for a bit of down that had detached itself from a willow limb and floated downward like a snowflake.

The ducks were not disturbed. Acting as if unaware of being observed, they glided, circled, dipped their heads into broken reflections of blue sky and white clouds.

"Took-took-took-took," Raymond whispered, imitating them.

One of the larger birds lifted an orange webbed foot from the water and scratched its head almost exactly like a dog. Another spread its wings to unbelievable length and shook them out. Several paused to run flat orange beaks through ruffled feathers on necks, backs, and chests.

"Preening," Grandpa explained. "Getting themselves all duded up."

As the ducks moved on, Raymond noticed one that was different from the rest. Not only was it the smallest of the young ducks but it had a yellow beak instead of orange. It floated along to the rear of the flock, doing the same things they did, paddling in the same direction, but always alone and behind.

"Get on up there with the rest of them," Raymond muttered under his breath. Unheeding, the duck dipped its head and came up looking a bit silly with a string of slimy debris dangling from its beak. Meanwhile, the other ducks moved off toward the opposite bank. Yellow Bill, debris still dangling, finally noticed and paddled furiously to catch up, only to have one of the large ducks turn on him with squawks and outspread wings. The small duck retreated. Raymond was so mad he forgot to keep his voice down. "Get on up there! Don't let him scare you off!"

Alarmed now, the ducks headed for the safety of the far bank, and as they departed, Raymond felt his grandfather's hand descend on his shoulder. "It's all right," he said. "That little fellow will learn to take care of himself soon enough."

Raymond nodded, though he was not at all sure that his grandfather was right.

"Well, what do you think?" Grandpa asked presently.

Raymond shrugged. "They're okay."

The old man grunted with impatience. "I mean, what do you think of 'em as a business idea?"

Raymond was puzzled. "Business idea?"

"Yeah. Don't you see? Them ducks are going to lay eggs and hatch more ducks. Your father can sell duck eggs, he can sell ducks for meat, he can sell feathers for pillows. I'll drive my car and let him use Old Lizzie until he can get a truck of his own. Don't you see? There could be money in this for Cecil!"

He knew his father was not going to like this idea any better than he had liked Grandpa's suggestion that he take up farming. Raymond knew his father wanted a job with a salary and health insurance, but he also knew Grandpa did not want to hear this. "I . . . I don't know," Raymond finally said.

Grandpa exploded. "You don't know! Listen, boy, you better start thinking positive! Do you want your father getting a job way off somewhere and taking you where I wouldn't see you but about once a year?"

Of course, Raymond didn't want that. He shook his head.

"Well, then, you and me better come up with something fast. Cecil's gonna move if we don't."

Raymond knew he was right. Eager to escape farm work, Jackie Lee and Vance were willing to move anytime and his mother, who had been talking about getting a job, would not mind moving to a place where this would be more likely.

"The way I see it, this idea can work," Grandpa was saying, "if Cecil will give it a chance. 'Course he'd need to work at a few other things besides the ducks." Grandpa started back toward the truck and Raymond followed.

"Maybe raise a few hogs, a few chickens. He could grow them fancy houseplants. You and me could build him a dandy greenhouse."Good with tools and carpentry projects, Raymond had helped his grandfather build birdhouses, a house for Butch, and even a small shed during the past year.

The old man turned to face Raymond. "Don't you think Cecil could make a living right here?"

Raymond was used to pretending when things were not the way he and his grandfather wanted them to be. Besides, he wanted this as much as his grandfather did, so he nodded his head.

It was all the encouragement Grandpa needed. All the way to the truck, he made plans for enlarging the flock and improving the pond.

Grandpa lowered the tailgate for Butch and then studied his truck keys. "Don't see what it'd hurt for you to drive, long as we're on our own land," he said. Then he shook his head and swung around toward the cab. "Don't guess we better, though."

"I guess not," Raymond reluctantly agreed. If only Vance hadn't caught them last time. If only he hadn't told.

In the truck, Grandpa gave Raymond a peppermint and turned to happier subjects. "The hummingbirds might come today," he said, swinging the truck around and heading for home. "They'll likely hang around long as them mimosas at the edge of my porch are blooming."

"Yeah," Raymond replied, cheering up at once. "Did I tell you that one came yesterday while you were taking your nap?"

Grandpa rapped his knee in disgust. "He didn't!"

Raymond laughed with delight. Usually it was his grandfather who saw such sights. "I was lying on your porch— you know where that mimosa branch hangs over the bannisters?"

Grandpa nodded.

"Well, that hummingbird acted like he didn't even see me. He flew in there right over my nose and stuck his bill in those blossoms pretty as you please."

Grandpa rounded a curve and his big farmhouse and the barn behind it came into sight. Raymond's eyes swept over them and then across the overgrown pasture to the small white house where his family lived, trying to determine through the obscuring trees and shrubs whether his father had returned.

"I tell you what we're gonna do this afternoon," said Grandpa, slowing as they neared his house. "We're gonna set us up a table out on the front porch and while we wait for Mr. Hummingbird, we'll just have us a domino game. What do you say?"

Raymond did not answer. His family's yard had finally come into full view and he saw not only his father's familiar blue Plymouth there but something else that made his heart sink—a large U-Haul trailer. Grandpa Brock's smile faded as he, too, discovered the trailer. Solemn now, he headed Old Lizzie in that direction.

Laughter greeted them as they pulled to a stop and got out. On the porch, Raymond's father, mother, sister, and brother all seemed to be laughing and talking at the same time. Raymond looked at them standing together. Except for himself, Raymond thought wistfully, they all matched. From their black hair to their long legs, they looked alike. Even in their happiness, they mirrored each other.

Cecil Brock turned around as Butch ran up to greet him. He stepped off the porch all smiles. "Hello, Dad, Raymond!" He put an arm around Raymond's shoulders. "Glad to see you, son. Well, I got the job on the dam construction project in Fuller, Alabama. They want me right away, and the pay's good."

Grandpa Brock turned to look at the U-Haul, his shoulders sagging. "You're moving then?"

"Yep!" said Raymond's father. "Couldn't find a house to rent. But I found a secondhand house trailer we can afford."

"A trailer!" Grandpa said, disgust clear in his voice. He didn't approve of what he considered makeshift excuses for houses on postage-stamp-size lots.

Cecil Brock refused to be daunted. "That's right. It's a nice one, Dad. And I found a trailer court outside of town and right close to the dam."

Raymond had seen trailer courts with their lines and lines of metal structures on wheels. He didn't like the idea of living in such a place.

"The trailer has gas heat, Grandpa," Vance chimed in. "I don't have to cut wood for heaters anymore."

"And it has two bathrooms!" Jackie Lee said, shaking out her long hair.

"Bet it don't have no garden space!" grunted Grandpa in a voice that had begun to quiver. His hand reached for Raymond. "How you all gonna raise peas and corn and tomatoes?"

Raymond's mother stopped smiling. Stepping off the porch, she put out her hand to her father-in-law. "We'll come back every chance we get. And you have Claude and Otis here close by."

"That's right, Dad," Cecil Brock agreed. "It's not like you'll be left here all alone." Everyone stood around in awkward silence for a few moments. Then Mr. Brock opened the door of the Plymouth and pulled out some boxes. "Guess we better start packing."

Soon Raymond and his grandfather were alone in the yard. "I can't stand it," Raymond said, throwing his arms around the old man's waist. "I can't leave you."

It seemed like a long time before Raymond felt his grandfather's hands on his shoulders and heard his muffled words. "Yes, you can, boy. You got to. You wouldn't want them to leave without you."

It sounded as if it was meant to be a question, and Raymond answered it in his head. No, he really did not want his family to leave without him. He loved them. But his grandfather was the one to whom he could talk, the one with whom he could share things. "What I wish is that we could keep on staying here where we belong," he said into his grandfather's shirt.

Grandpa broke free from Raymond's grip, and, taking his arm, turned to the porch with a heavy step. "So do I, boy," he said. "So do I. But wishing ain't getting. And when we don't get what we wish for, we have to make the best of what we get." He tilted Raymond's face up. "Promise me you'll do that."

Raymond promised, but he had never felt more alone.

2
TROUBLE

Butch did not make the move to Alabama. After a lot of discussion, Raymond's parents had decided that a crowded trailer park was no place for a country dog used to a big territory to call his own. When Raymond protested, they reminded him of how lonely Grandpa Brock was going to be, and he could argue no more: Butch would stay.

Raymond had promised he would make the best of things, and he tried, but it was not easy and it was lonely. While his new home was crowded with people, none of them was his age. Raymond was thinking of this very thing one hot and humid day two weeks after the move. Trying not to really see his surroundings, he jogged through the park with his grandfather's field glasses bouncing out a comfortingly familiar rhythm against his chest.

Pulling his blue cap down tight, he whirled around until the two dozen or so trailers and the big pasture that wrapped around them on three sides blurred into the woods across the road. If it had not been for droning air conditioners all around him and the sound of traffic on the county highway in front of the park, he could almost imagine himself back home in Tennessee.

"Bad boy! You quit that right now!" a voice ordered.

Raymond stopped to find Mrs. Katie Frances Clendenin, the grouchiest old lady in the park, lumbering down the steps of her double-wide trailer. To his relief, she was not looking at him but at her white poodle, Tosche, which she was trying to take for a walk. The dog pulled his stout mistress along at a waddling trot that set her large body to bouncing.

Raymond watched as the dog ran beneath Mrs. Clendenin's purple lawn chair, wrapped his leash around her pink birdbath, and knocked over one of her plastic flamingoes. It didn't seem fair to him that she could have this dumb dog while he had not been able to keep Butch. The argument that this was an inside dog didn't carry much weight with him.

Suddenly Raymond saw something that made him forget Mrs. Clendenin's dog and his own family—a new trailer. It was being set up on the empty lot next to the Brocks. This might mean a boy his age was moving in. The idea excited Raymond but scared him a little, too. Two weeks in a trailer park filled with strangers had not eased his shyness.

He dusted off the grubby shorts he had inherited from Vance, before moving forward for a closer inspection. The trailer was nicer than the Brocks' secondhand model and it was longer—perhaps that meant a large family. Toward the near end, its flat roof peaked in what Jackie Lee elegantly referred to as a "cathedral ceiling." Raymond wrinkled his nose. Lately his sister was always trying to be fancy.

He stopped on the gravel drive just short of three trucks that apparently belonged to the workmen swarming around the place. The men looked very smart and very busy, joining pipes here and connecting wires there. Raymond studied their tools from a distance, identifying several of them before moving on around the trailer.

The air conditioner was running, he noticed. That must mean the new people would be here soon. The Brocks usually didn't run their air conditioner at all. It was expensive, and too many bills were stacked up from when Mr. Brock had been out of work.

One of the workmen was tall, slender, and black-haired like Raymond's father. Raymond smiled at him and the man grinned back, showing a mouthful of nice straight teeth. "About finished up," he said, picking up his toolbox and heading for the nearest truck. Raymond followed, wanting to ask whether a boy would be moving in. Why could he never think of the right thing to say to strangers as Vance and his father could?

The man swung his tool chest into the back and grinned again. "Y' like trucks?"

Raymond nodded. "We have one." He pointed to the red pickup at the end of the Brock trailer. "It's my grandfather's," he rushed on, "but he let us borrow it to move our things in, so it's sort of ours, too."

"I noticed it," the man replied, looking at Old Lizzie. "A valuable antique that is. It's a nineteen-fifty Ford, isn't it?"

Raymond nodded proudly and lifted the field glasses around his neck. "These are my grandfather's, too." He looked quickly toward home and lowered his voice. "But I use them sometimes."

The man turned away as a fresh eruption of barking came from the Clendenin yard. Now untangled, Tosche was dragging his mistress in the direction of an overloaded green car that had entered the park and was backing up to this new trailer.

The car stopped and the engine shut off. Raymond

watched eagerly as a slender black woman in a white uniform slid from behind the wheel. Then a skinny black girl jumped out on the other side and Raymond went heavy with disappointment. This scrawny girl sure wasn't the pal he'd had in mind.

When the girl leaned back into the car and came out lugging an overweight red cat, Tosche went crazy. "Behave!" Mrs. Clendenin ordered, but she did not sound as if she really meant it.

"There, there, Chester," the girl crooned, trying to smooth the cat's upraised fur. She cast a baleful look at the tiny poodle. "The dog can't get you." Chester arched his back and hissed his disbelief.

Meanwhile, the uniformed woman had made her way to the trailer steps, where she was trying to hold a box she had taken from the car and open an overloaded purse at the same time. "Didn't I tell you that cat would go wild, Henrietta?" She dug in the purse. "Now where are my keys?" At that moment her purse dropped, scattering its contents all over the ground around her white shoes. "Darn!"

Henrietta waited in grim silence with both arms full of yowling, snarling cat.

"You should have left that tom with your father," the woman snapped, throwing down the box and squatting to shovel loose change, tissues, cosmetics, combs, and wrinkled papers of all sizes and colors back into the purse. "Frank Lazenby and that cat are two of a kind. He got the house; let him keep the cat!" She grabbed the keys and the box. "Serve him right!"

Henrietta frowned fiercely, hugged her cat closer, and turned away. Her gaze swept around the park and stopped on Raymond. She looked at him with curiosity for a few moments before heading for the door her mother had finally managed to open.

Raymond started toward the Brock trailer. It looked

dingy, shabby, and small next to the shiny new one. Its wooden steps were a little crooked, the screen door sagged, and the underpinning was badly in need of paint. None of this bothered Raymond, but it sure bugged his sister, who had wanted something much nicer; and the fact that she still had not been able to find space to unpack everything was driving his mother crazy.

A swell of organ music greeted him as he entered the yard and headed toward Old Lizzie. Raymond rolled his eyes upward. Jackie Lee was watching a soap opera again. He could make out the hum of his mother's sewing machine, too. Mrs. Brock was still working on back-to-school sewing. Hurriedly, he opened the truck door and slid the field glasses into their old place beneath the passenger side of the seat.

"Guess what?" he said to his sister and mother moments later when he burst into the sweltering trailer.

"Sh-h-h-h-h-h!" hissed Jackie Lee from the family area, holding up a red-nailed finger to scarlet lips. Her hair was wrapped in a towel from its second shampoo of the day. Her eyes had a new coat of makeup and her cheeks blazed with a brownish-pink rouge that seemed to clash with her lips.

Mrs. Brock looked up from her sewing machine on the clothing-strewn kitchen table. She did not like sewing and her whole body showed it. Her sweat-beaded face was tight and frowning under her cap of damp black curls, and her shoulders seemed to sag under the burden of a limp yellow tape measure.

"I want you to try on these pants I just hemmed," she ordered, biting off a thread. She pointed to a pile of jeans on the floor beside her. They were Vance's castoffs, as usual. Raymond usually did not mind, but these were the baby type with reinforced knees.

Raymond frowned. "Mom!"

"Not a thing wrong with those pants." Mrs. Brock

sniffed, fumbling with a box under the table near her feet and pulling out a shiny pair of leather dress-up shoes. "Try these, too, while you're at it," she said, eyeing several holes in his ragged sneakers.

Raymond backed away, horrified. Everyone at the new school would laugh at him if he had to wear those things.

"I got these for next to nothing at a closeout sale," Mrs. Brock went on.

"I can see why," said Raymond, scowling at the wide brown laces and the gleaming patches of leather on heel and toe. "Nobody in the world wanted them."

"You can make out with these until I can get a job and earn a few paychecks," she replied.

Raymond snorted in disgust. "Mom, those aren't school shoes! Nobody wears shoes like that to school! They . . ." His voice trailed off as he looked at his mother's strained face. He might as well save his complaints for his father, who usually understood such matters better and didn't worry about money as much. Raymond leaned on the table and went back to his earlier subject.

"Guess what?"

Mrs. Brock pushed a strand of hair off her forehead. "Mmmmmmm?"

"Hush, Raymond!" said Jackie Lee. She was setting up an ironing board in front of the television set.

Raymond glared in her direction. Just because he was the youngest in the family, they all tried to boss him around. He defiantly raised his voice louder. "There's a new trailer next door!"

"Uh-huh." Jackie Lee shoved her ironing board closer to the screen, where a girl with long blond hair and false eyelashes was crying and talking to a dark-haired man with a beard.

"Yeah! And it's a big one!"

Jackie Lee nodded. "We saw it pull in—cathedral ceiling, bay window, and all."

Raymond was crestfallen. He had figured they had been too busy to notice. He loved to be the first to tell something. "You did?"

Jackie Lee did not answer but turned to Mrs. Brock instead. "Make him keep quiet, Mother!" She had stopped calling her parents Mom and Dad as Raymond and Vance did. "I think Angelique is about to tell Colin that she has regained her memory."

At that moment Vance burst through the front door. His face was flushed and angry and his fists were clenched. He looked around the dim room and then zeroed in on Raymond. "You dummy! You miserable little creep!"

Mrs. Brock put down her sewing. "What on earth . . ."

"Mother-r-r-r!" Jackie Lee wailed, pointing to the screen where the blond woman and bearded man were entwined in each other's arms.

Vance paid no attention to his mother's question or his sister's complaints. He leaned over Raymond and shouted, "Don't you ever, ever come around again when I'm with my friends!"

Mrs. Brock pushed back her chair and turned to Raymond. "What did you do?"

"I'll tell you what he did," Vance answered for him, stomping the floor so hard that the trailer vibrated.

"Mother, make them keep quiet," Jackie Lee called again, turning the volume on the TV up.

"Can't you see, Colin?" The woman on the screen was sobbing. "Can't you see, I had to?"

"He sneaked along after me and my friend Bunky over to Glenda and Brenda's house," Vance continued. Glenda and Brenda Hinkle were pretty twins who lived across the road and down the highway a bit in one of the area's few houses.

"I did *not* sneak—" Raymond began, but Vance did not allow him to finish.

"When we got to their house and went in, you'd think

he'd get the hint and go home. But no-o-o-o-o! Not Raymond! He used those field glasses and inspected their whole yard."

"Tattletale!" said Raymond, using the taunt his brother so often used against him. But apparently Mrs. Brock saw nothing wrong with older brothers telling on younger ones, for Raymond was the one she turned on.

"Raymond Brock! Didn't I tell you to leave your grandfather's field glasses alone? When he comes after that pickup, I want everything in it exactly the way he left it. Your father isn't even driving the truck except when he has to."

"He kicked in fire anthills all around the edge of the Hinkle yard." Vance continued his report.

"So what's wrong with that?" Raymond demanded. Ever since he had moved to Alabama and found out how awful this kind of ant's sting was, he broke up their huge mounds wherever he found them.

"Then he pressed his big nose up against the storm door in their den"—Vance mashed his nose flat to demonstrate—"and just stood there, staring at us."

"My nose isn't as big as your ears," Raymond said, bringing up the feature about which he knew his brother was most sensitive.

"He looked exactly like a pig, didn't he, Bunky?" Vance asked, turning to a tall lanky boy who had slipped inside unnoticed and now leaned against the wall next to the door. As usual, Bunky Potter was quick to agree with his hero. Nodding his shaggy head, he covered his mouth and most of his face with one big hand. The part of his pimpled face still showing was very red and his cheeks were puffed out. Every time he looked at Raymond, his face got redder.

Raymond looked from Bunky back to his brother. "I was only looking in, trying to find you!" he protested, refusing to believe he had looked as silly as Vance and Bunky were trying to make out.

"Glenda and Brenda fell on the floor laughing at you."

"They did not! They only smiled at me, friendly like."

But now Raymond wondered. Had he looked as foolish as his brother said?

"—and their mother finally said for Raymond to come on in before he got nose prints all over her door."

"Did not! She said—"

In the family room, Jackie Lee let out a loud sound of disgust and began pulling the ironing board toward her room at the other end of the trailer. The blond-haired woman now had the bearded man by the shoulders. "Can't you see that it was my only chance, Colin? My only chance? I was so vulnerable, so very vulnerable."

Mrs. Brock grunted with impatience. To Raymond's relief, she seemed at least as much irritated with his brother as with him. Maybe Vance would see this and shut up. But he didn't. He plowed right on.

"Just wait, Mom," he said grimly. "You didn't hear the worst. Then he started telling embarrassing things about me."

"He-he-he," Bunky sniggered from the doorway, but he managed to control himself when Vance turned to glare at him.

"I only told them how you can do those funny burps anytime you want to," Raymond said, defending himself.

Vance's face blazed with fresh fury. "Big mouth! I don't do that anymore."

"Do so! Only day before yesterday, you—"

"Did not, you little liar! But even if I had, I wouldn't want Glenda and Brenda to know about it."

"And I told them about those cookies Vance baked the other day," Raymond continued. "Even Jackie Lee liked them," he said, looking toward his sister for support. But she was too busy crawling behind the as-yet-unpacked cardboard boxes that blocked the electrical outlet where the television was plugged in. As the screen went blank and the organ music died, Raymond turned back to his mother, to find her face going from impatience to anger. He speeded up. "I only told them how Vance and me were going to learn to cook and do housework on account of you getting a job, Mom."

Bunky sniggered aloud once more, but at the sight of Mrs. Brock's face, he turned quickly to stare at Jackie Lee. She had grabbed up the heavy TV set and was walking stiff-legged toward her room.

"Then I went outside," Raymond finished.

"Yeah," said Vance, "he went outside all right. That's when he really showed himself. He started jumping on their trampoline right in front of the biggest window in the den."

Raymond ignored the fresh burst of giggles from Bunky and rushed to defend himself again. "Mrs. Hinkle said I could!"

"And then he ripped his shorts."

"He-he-he-he-he!"

Raymond looked down at the jagged shorts' leg he had caught on a sharp edge as he had pulled himself up. "So what? That ain't nothing! They're old, and Mom can fix them."

Vance laughed angrily. "Yeah, but what about the hole in the seat?"

Raymond's hands flew to the seat of his shorts and for the first time he realized that the entire rear end seemed to be missing. The seam must have split. He was so astonished and humiliated that he could think of nothing to say. A convulsion of laughter came from the doorway and then Bunky threw open the door and stumbled down the steps, holding his sides.

"There the little moron was, jumping up and down, with his whole rear end hanging out for the world to see!"

Raymond pictured himself as he must have looked to those girls and his cheeks blazed hotter than Vance's.

"I'll be ashamed to ever show my face over there again!" Vance declared. "They think—I mean, they *know* that I have an idiot for a brother!"

At that moment the entire trailer seemed to vibrate with a deafening crash and Mrs. Brock jumped up with a yelp. All three of them turned to see a horrified Jackie Lee standing over the shattered remains of the television set.

"Now I'll never know what Angelique told Colin!" she wailed.

Mrs. Brock threw up her hands. "Can't you three ever get along? Can't you ever stop arguing? I can't have a thing! Not a blessed thing. I have to live in this scroungy little trailer where I don't have room for anything, sewing on rags that anyone else would use for dust cloths! I have to walk around boxes that I don't have room to unpack. And all you three can do is fight like the beginning of World War Three!"

The front door opened and in stepped Mr. Brock with the cheery smile he almost always wore since getting his new job. "How's my happy family?" he asked.

3
MORE TROUBLE

"Oops!" said Vance in mock apology as he bumped against the bucket of water his brother was carrying. Warm suds dripped down Raymond's legs and into the leather shoes he had put on in a vain attempt to convince his father how awful they were.

"That's all right!" said Raymond, slinging some of the water at his brother. He gloated at the sudden dark stains on Vance's favorite red T-shirt.

A warning sound came from Mr. Brock, who was working on the TV set just inside the front door, and the boys returned to their chores.

It was Saturday afternoon. It was also the last weekend before school started next Friday: the weekend Mrs. Brock had declared to be clean-up, fix-up time. Because they were mad at each other, Raymond and Vance worked separately. Raymond was washing the family's old Plymouth while Vance was painting the underpinning and making a terrible mess of it. Raymond had helped his grandfather with painting, so he could have told his brother he should keep his strokes up and down instead of side to side and that more careful wiping of the brush would prevent all those runs and drips. But he said nothing. Let know-it-all Vance do it his own way.

Feeling mistreated by his entire family, Raymond began to scrub the car furiously. He had just started on the hood when Bunky arrived and began a whispered conversation with Vance. Laughing and gesturing as they always did when planning something big, they looked in Raymond's direction and then moved to the far edge of the yard.

It was probably something to do with Bunky's motorbike, which Raymond was never allowed to get near, much less ride. Raymond couldn't help rejoicing in the fact that, unlike Bunky, Vance had not reached the magic age of fourteen, when he would be able to get a license. For now he had to content himself with operating the bike along bumpy margins of fields and on the miles of abandoned roads behind the Hinkle house. Of course there was the less-glorious privilege of being a passenger hanging on behind Bunky.

Deliberately, Raymond turned away and pretended great interest in a slow-moving truck out on the highway. He had seen the dilapidated black pickup sputter its way past several times in the past two weeks. Once when headed home from the supermarket with his mother, he had seen it parked by the trash dumpster next to the country store about a mile down the road. Loaded with junk, it was as worn and scruffy-looking as the man slouched behind its wheel.

PEAVY MANIS FLEE MKT, the crudely lettered sign on its door announced. In the back of the truck, between an old cedar wardrobe with a cracked mirror and the remains of an iron heater, was a boy with wild blond hair and strange deep-set eyes.

They must live somewhere nearby, Raymond thought, beginning to scrub the car again. For the first time, he wondered exactly where. Except for this park, which was filled mainly with dam construction workers and their families, and the remnants of houses that seemed to confirm Bunky's tales of ghosts, there were very few houses in the area. The countryside was mostly pasture, overgrown meadows, and woods, crisscrossed here and there with washed-out dirt roads. Of course, there was the pink house next to the creek where all the wrecked cars were, but he had heard Bunky talking about the weird woman who lived there alone.

Stealing a glance in his brother's direction, he found that Bunky was gone and Vance had returned to his painting. When Raymond gave the car its final rinse a short while later and wandered off toward Old Lizzie, his brother was still hard at work. What could he do with the rest of the morning? Raymond wondered.

He climbed into the cab of the truck and forgot his troubles. Even when he had rolled the windows down, the air inside it was fragrant with tobacco, fertilizer, and peppermint: the smells of his grandfather, the smells of home. From the Clendenin yard where a boy Jackie Lee's age was mowing, the fragrance of fresh-cut grass added to the illusion. It might have been Grandpa Brock's hay field, newly cut and baking under a Tennessee sun.

Taking in a deep contented breath, he stretched out across the wide front seat. Horsehair peeking through a torn place in the worn upholstery scratched against his hot cheek with a comfortable familiarity. His hand trailed through the dust on the floor and, as if by accident, swept under the seat and found the field glasses. Then in the nest of wadded papers and oily rags behind them, his fingers found something else, something wrapped in crinkly plastic.

"A peppermint!" he whispered, pulling himself over the

edge of the seat to look, but there were no more. There was only this one, left like a gift from his grandfather for him to find. Grandpa Brock was always doing things like that for Raymond. He touched the field glasses again. Maybe they were a gift, too. Perhaps they had been left on purpose. He pulled them out and sat up. He looked toward the trailer and then defiantly hung them around his neck.

Surely it wouldn't hurt to wear the glasses in the truck. He unwrapped the peppermint and slipped it into his mouth. With the fresh sweet taste strong on his tongue, he scooted behind the steering wheel and stretched his legs to reach the round pedals on the floor.

"Clutch and brake," he said, suddenly feeling like a grown man. He pushed both pedals hard and pretended to insert a key in the ignition. "Varoom! Varoom!" he whispered, and then a little louder, "Voooooo-den!" He reached for the gear stick and pretended to shift into reverse. Stretching upward, he checked the rearview mirror.

"Voo-den," he said, forgetting to be quiet. He shifted gears again. *"Vooooo-den!"* He could almost feel the truck moving. He saw himself pulling out of the graveled drive, leaving the trailer park behind, heading for home and his grandfather.

Suddenly a dark head appeared at the window of the passenger side and the motor sounds died in Raymond's throat. He was deeply embarrassed. The new girl next door had caught him acting like a little kid. He waited for her to laugh as Vance would have.

"Hi!" she said. "What you doing?"

Raymond could not raise his eyes. "Nothing!" he muttered. "I'm not doing nothing."

"You mean you're not doing *anything*," she corrected him primly.

Pulverizing what remained of his peppermint, Raymond

began inspecting the strap on the field glasses with great diligence. "That's what I said."

"No, you didn't," she contradicted in a schoolteacherly tone. "You used a double negative."

"I know that," he cut her off. "I *like* double negatives."

She decided to let the matter drop. Smiling determinedly, she said, "My name is Henrietta Lazenby. I don't like to be called Henry. Henrietta is a perfectly good name."

"I didn't say it wasn't," he countered.

"My mother doesn't approve of silly names like Brandy, Tiffany, and La Donna."

Something to agree on. Raymond wrinkled his nose and looked at the girl at last. "I can't stand Angelique myself."

She nodded comfortably. "Mama is a nurse in a hospital and she hates those dumb names people hang on poor little babies when they aren't old enough to defend themselves."

Personally, Raymond didn't see that "Henrietta" was any big favor for a little baby, but since the girl had been nice enough to ignore his motor sounds, he decided to keep this opinion to himself.

"I hope you aren't Chad or Kevin or Sean," she continued in a tone that conveyed her mother's low opinion of those names.

Raymond shook his head. "My name is Raymond Brock."

She gave a slow, approving nod. His name had apparently met her standards. "How old are you?"

"Ten."

She smiled. "Me, too. So we're both going into fifth grade."

Before Raymond could confirm this, Henrietta swung around to watch a car pull into the park. "Daddy!" she squealed, heading for home. "I told Mama you would come!"

Raymond climbed from the truck in time to see a red car stop in front of the Lazenby trailer and Henrietta's mother throw open the front door. The woman stood there, holding what appeared to be wet laundry away from her pale-blue dress, and glared at the big mustached black man who leaped out and raced to meet Henrietta.

"Baby!" he yelled, lifting her up and swinging her around and around.

"Henrietta," Mrs. Lazenby called in an icy voice, "I just took your shirts out of the dryer, and I'm about to put your jeans in. How about some help?"

Henrietta appeared not to hear, but Henrietta's father did. Looking over his daughter's shoulder, he smiled up at the woman and said in a loud voice, "I brought your stereo, Henrietta baby. Just like I promised. Get the door for me and I'll carry it in and set it up."

Henrietta ran to obey while her mother turned in a huff and stalked away. Mr. Lazenby pulled a huge plastic-lidded stereo from his car and started for the steps. Raymond moved forward for a closer look at the car. "The kind Vance likes," he murmured, looking around and suddenly realizing that he had not seen his brother in a good while.

At that moment a wild cacophony of motor sounds, thumps, and yowls made Raymond swing back toward the Lazenby trailer. Stereo in his arms and right foot hunting for the first step, Mr. Lazenby seemed to freeze. "What in the . . ." he began.

Henrietta's eyes grew large. She dashed up the steps as the motor and the thumping clicked off, reaching the threshold just in time to collide with a screeching, hissing ball of fur.

"Chester?" she cried, but the wild-eyed creature did not respond. Hurtling past her and landing on the ground at least six feet away, he tore past the car, clawed his way spitting and hissing across the gravel, passed Raymond at breakneck speed, circled the end of the Brock trailer, and was gone.

As Henrietta took off after the cat, Mrs. Lazenby cried,

"How was I to know the fool cat would crawl into the dryer?"

The cat was nowhere to be seen. Raymond helped Henrietta and her father search the Brocks' yard. With them, he looked up into trees, under trailers, and behind bushes until Mr. Lazenby finally decided they should split up. "You keep looking in the trailer park," he ordered Henrietta. "I'll search the woods, and you," he went on, turning to Raymond, "look along the edge of the highway."

Privately, Raymond thought it was a dumb idea. He doubted a terrified cat would go near the traffic sounds of the highway, but he didn't have anything better to do. Besides, as he started off, the man yelled after him, "There'll be a reward if you find him!"

A reward! By the time Raymond reached the pavement, he had already thought of ten things to spend reward money on. He looked up and down the highway. There was nothing much to see in either direction other than trees and pastures, but to the right, just around the distant curve, was a store. He turned in that direction.

"Maybe the reward will be five dollars," Raymond said to himself, looking eagerly in the ditch and at the pasture to his right. Boy, wouldn't that burn Vance up if Raymond got a big amount of money. However, as the minutes passed without any sight or sound of the cat, his hopes of gaining a reward dwindled. They had about faded away entirely by the time he passed the long driveway between pastures that led to the big brick house where the Hinkle twins lived, but he kept walking. He decided he would go as far as the country store. He had been wanting to see it anyway.

Suddenly he remembered the field glasses hanging around his neck. How could he be so stupid as to forget he had them on? He turned back toward home for a moment. The last thing he needed was more trouble with his parents. They would never be willing to listen to his explanation.

On the other hand, how would they know? Mr. and Mrs. Brock were both occupied and Vance was probably over at the Hinkles'. Raymond told himself he would sneak the field glasses back to the truck as soon as he got home. Satisfied, he started on.

A slow-moving Jeep pulling a covered trailer passed him. It caught his attention at once, not only because it was so old but because it was weaving right and left. The driver was craning her neck to peer intently at first one and then the other side of the road.

Curious, Raymond looked, too. At this particular place, there were pastures on both sides. Except for the kudzu draping the older fencing on the left, Raymond saw nothing. The Jeep snaked its way around a bend and disappeared, but when he rounded that same curve a few minutes later, he saw the vehicle parked beside the store where he was headed. The driver—a big muscular woman with short-cropped graying hair—was just getting out. With the air of a policewoman, she stared at several boys collected around two helmeted motorcycle riders until the group scattered and moved around to the far side of the store. She watched until they disappeared and then began an inspection of the pasture at the back of the building. Raymond turned his eyes back to the store.

An ancient two-story wooden structure badly in need of paint, Messer's Store was located just short of Dozier's Crossroads. The building seemed to sag against the patch of trees separating it from the meadow. A huge oak pressed up against it in back and spread branches protectively over its roof. Fading signs along its side advertised soft drinks from another time and fertilizers from an era when this must have been more prosperous farming country. A brown-and-white dog sniffed along the weeds that bordered the near side of it.

Raymond looked around the parking lot. He didn't see

Henrietta's cat, but he did see a vehicle he recognized. Near the trash dumpster was the black truck he had seen passing the park earlier, and as he drew nearer, he saw its two passengers. The unkempt man was pulling soft-drink cans from the dumpster, crushing them with his foot, and dropping them into a bag held by the blond-headed boy. The boy was dressed in a shirt at least two sizes too large and ugly green pants that had strange-looking patch pockets with snap-down flaps.

"I guess that's all, Bruce," the man was saying to the boy as Raymond passed. From the corner of his eye, Raymond saw the man tie the bag, throw it into the truck, and shove another bag into the boy's hands. "I'll go on to Elmore. You pick up 'tween here and home. I figure the scrap-metal people will pay fifteen to twenty dollars on what we got." The man got into the truck and the boy named Bruce turned toward Raymond.

"Whatcha looking at?"

Raymond swung around only long enough to take in the boy's too-large shirt billowing around his bony frame and then he turned back to the store. "That dog," he said, pointing to the hungry-looking animal that now sniffed his way toward the front of the building.

The dog turned sad eyes toward them. One of his ears stood up and one flopped down mournfully. Despite his ragged coat, he somehow looked like a dog that had seen better times. He sniffed the Jeep in passing, sprinkled one of the tires, and then pushed his way between two trash cans near the front door, circled around, and lay down. Something in his eyes reminded Raymond of Butch.

"Yeah," Bruce said, and then dismissed the dog with a wave of the hand. "Dump dog."

A fat man in overalls looked at the dog as he started up the front steps. "See you got another stray, Mr. Messer," he hollered.

From inside came a snort of disgust. "Yeah, and I'm about to get rid of another stray, too."

"Maybe you could sell it to Junior Elrod. He's always on the look out for a good dog."

"Not likely. Junior wants coon dogs. That 'un don't look like he hunts anything more'n a biscuit."

The door of the store opened again moments later. A woman and a little girl came out. The woman with her grocery bag headed toward the fanciest car in the lot, while the little girl trailed along behind, lugging a huge stuffed bear and a small bag of her own. Her mouth was full of candy. She stopped at the sight of the dog, dropped everything, and reached out her hands. Giving his tail a tentative wag, the dog stood and sniffed in her direction.

"Kimberley, you come on this instant!" the woman shouted as she started up the car.

"But, Mama . . ."

"Right now!"

Sniffling, the little girl gathered her belongings and ran to obey.

The car was rolling away when Raymond saw the dog moving toward what he suddenly realized was spilled candy and bubble gum from the little girl's bag.

Bruce saw it, too, and pounced on it. "Finders keepers," he sang out. Then his eyes met Raymond's and his face flushed. Slinging his hair from his eyes, he shoved the candy bar and gum into his shirt pocket and raised his chin defiantly. "Ain't nothing wrong with me getting it."

Raymond shrugged and turned toward the store, but the boy wasn't satisfied. "Well, there ain't."

Raymond felt his own face go hot. "I didn't say there was."

"Yeah, well . . ." The boy looked him over. "That's some getup you're wearing!" he finally said. Laughing, he slowly unwrapped a piece of gum and popped it into his mouth.

"Them shoes look like what Old King Cole wears in the cartoons! You got king shoes, man!"

The words confirmed Raymond's worst fears about how awful the shoes looked. Why hadn't he taken them off after showing them to his father? "Look who's talking," he said without taking time to consider his words or their consequences. "Your pants look like something a clown would wear, with those big pockets."

Bruce jostled him with his elbow. "King shoes!"

Heart pounding in his throat, Raymond elbowed him back. "Clown pockets!"

"Yeah, well, I got money in these pockets instead of balloons and scarves," Bruce said, pulling out a twenty-dollar bill and waving it in front of Raymond's face.

Raymond was impressed in spite of himself. "Wow!"

The boy seemed mollified. His eyes dropped to the field glasses. "What you got there?"

"Field glasses," Raymond said, grabbing the strap with one hand and reaching around the boy to take hold of the door with the other. "Just field glasses." He ran up the two steps and half-fell into a long high-ceilinged room filled with wonderful smells. The fragrance of apples, tobacco, and freshly sliced bologna rose from the cluttered aisles like a fog. Then unpleasant smells mixed in, too—sweat from the fat man, cigarette smoke from the man to whom he talked, and pungent perfume from a woman in hair curlers who was laying out grocery items on the counter next to the cash register.

An aproned man, who must be Mr. Messer, glanced at Raymond with a face that looked like it would crack if he smiled. "Can I help you, sonny?" he asked, beginning to ring up the purchases in front of him.

"No, sir," Raymond said. "Uh, I mean, yes. Have you seen a big red cat?"

Mr. Messer shook his head and the fat man laughed. "No,

Mr. Messer is fresh out of cats," he said, almost losing his breath. "How 'bout a dog?"

The door squeaked open again and Bruce entered, closely followed by the driver of the Jeep. When Bruce looked back and saw the woman, he wasted no time getting out of her way. She stomped her way toward the back. Mr. Messer nodded at her. "Morning, Miss Autrey. You about ready for school to start?"

"Just about. You seen my bull? He's out again."

This broke the fat man up. He bent over gasping and wheezing for breath. "Cats, dogs, bulls! Messer, what you running here? A zoo?"

Bruce laughed longer and louder than anyone else at this joke. Miss Autrey glared at him.

Mr. Messer grunted. "You don't have enough cows to keep that bull at home. You're either going to have to sell 'im or get more cows."

"Couldn't sell Buster," Miss Autrey said. "He's just an old pet, and he was my father's pride and joy." As the woman discussed with Mr. Messer where the bull might have gone, Raymond watched Bruce edge his way toward the cash register.

"Have you got any boxes to spare, Mr. Messer?" Miss Autrey finally asked.

"Sure do, ma'am. Help yourself to any that are empty. You know where I keep 'em." Mr. Messer turned back to the woman in curlers, who was tapping her foot impatiently, and began to bag her purchases. Bruce leaned across the counter to whisper something in the man's ear and then moved back to stand by the racks of candy.

"You come back, now!" said Mr. Messer, handing the woman her groceries.

Raymond walked past shelves of chili and soup and stared at a glass display case covered with a thick layer of dust. Then he circled toward the front.

Mr. Messer pulled a long file box from beneath the counter and turned to Bruce. "Want to pay twenty dollars on your account, eh?"

Raymond looked just in time to see Bruce give a barely perceptible nod.

"You been helping Peavy with the flea market this summer?" Mr. Messer boomed. "Good. Good. Ever hear from your mother?"

This time Bruce spoke out loud and clear. "No, I ain't heard nothing, and I don't want to."

"And you gonna pay for that candy bar in your pocket, or do you want it on your father's bill?"

The store grew quiet. The fat man, who had been working his way—still talking—to the front, stopped and turned back. From the door, Raymond could see Mr. Messer was pointing his pencil toward the pocket where Bruce had put the candy bar he had picked up outside.

"I already had this when I come in," Bruce replied.

"You did?"

"Yes, I did!" Suddenly the boy didn't look so tough anymore. In fact, he looked as unsure of himself as Raymond felt most of the time lately. Without stopping to think, Raymond spoke up.

"He did, mister. I saw him with it before he came in." Raymond made himself look straight into the man's eyes.

"Just checking," Mr. Messer said at last, bending over the pad.

Raymond went out the door and almost walked right into his brother. Motorbike between them, Vance and Bunky had joined the crowd collected around the motorcycles, or perhaps they had been there earlier and he had not noticed. Raymond jerked the field glasses off and thrust them behind his back just as Vance turned and saw him.

Vance's face went red. "Hey! What are you doing here?"

Raymond would have retreated into the store, but the

way was now blocked by the fat man. He had no choice but to back his way around the store.

"I got as much right here as you," he said, inching his way toward the corner of the building. Now, too late, the fat man left the doorway and headed for his car. Bruce came out right behind him. His face lit with a grin when he saw Raymond.

"Thanks," he said, and then broke off. He looked from Raymond to Vance and then moved down the steps to stand by Raymond's side. "What's going on?" he whispered from the side of his mouth.

"My brother," Raymond whispered back. "He—"

"I told you not to follow me anymore," Vance said, "and you're not riding Bunky's motorbike, if that's what you're after."

"I told you I didn't follow you!" Raymond answered. "And I don't want to ride that old motorbike."

"Ha!" said Vance, stepping forward. He knew as well as Raymond did that that was not true. "What are you hiding behind you?"

Raymond lifted his chin. "Nothing!"

Bruce looked behind Raymond's back and seemed to size up the situation. "Thanks for keeping my stuff for me," he said loudly, grabbing the field glasses from Raymond's hands. He thrust them under his shirt and zipped around the corner of the building.

"Hey!" Vance yelled, rushing forward, but by the time he got past Raymond, who was trying to block him, and rounded the corner of the building, Bruce was returning empty-handed. This made Vance angrier than ever. "You go home!" he ordered Raymond.

"I don't have to," Raymond replied.

"No, he don't have to," agreed Bruce. "You can't boss him around!"

Vance's face grew redder than ever. "You'd better!"

"I won't!"

"Atta boy!" cheered Bruce. His hands were now doubled up into fists.

Vance glanced at him and hesitated. Finally he shrugged. "All right then, stay. Just keep out of my way." He turned on his heel and walked back to where his friends stood.

Bruce leaned casually up against the building and pulled the candy bar from his pocket. "You want some candy, King Shoes?"

"Don't mind if I do, Clown Pockets," said Raymond, enjoying this rare victory over his big brother. He could tell by the set of Vance's shoulders and the way his thumbs were clamped into his belt loops that he was seething with anger. Raymond finished his candy and squatted to pet the dog that had moved over near him. The dog drew back warily. Raymond wished now he had thought to save some candy for the dog.

Presently, Vance and Bunky moved around to the back corner of the store. Raymond was tempted to follow but held himself back. He wasn't going to give Vance the satisfaction of saying he'd followed him again.

Eventually the cyclists revved up their motors, zoomed from the side of the building, and took off down the highway. Moments later, Vance and Bunky followed on the motorbike.

Bruce clapped Raymond on the back as they moved out of sight. "Boy, we got him!"

Raymond laughed. "We sure did! Where're my field glasses?"

"A place they'll never look!" Bruce ran between the gas pumps and the front door. "I hid 'em in the back of old lady Autrey's Jeep." He rounded the corner and slid to a stop, with Raymond close on his heels. Then Raymond let out a groan. The Jeep was gone.

THE SEARCH

"This is it!" Bruce yelled back to Raymond, stopping at a dirt road cutting off from the highway. He shook the plastic bag he still carried in the direction of the road. "This is the way to old lady Autrey's house."

Raymond reached Bruce's side moments later and took in the narrow washed-out road while he caught his breath. The afternoon sun glittered off a thousand pebbles along its stretch of dusty red dirt. There was no sign of the Jeep, or any houses, either, except for the ghostly remains of a distant chimney. Raymond licked his lips. "You sure?"

"Positive. You can't see her place from here. I told you, my old man drives all these back roads looking for aluminum cans and stuff. I know this road like the back of my hand."

Raymond was still doubtful. He looked back in the direction they had come. It must have been three miles. The trailer park, the store—all of the landmarks he knew were far away.

"I didn't mind bringing you over here," Bruce said, just

as if Raymond had thanked him, just as if it wasn't Bruce's fault they had to come over here to begin with. "Glad to help out. Anyway, I can probably get a few aluminum cans from that trash pile over there on our way out."

Raymond swallowed the hateful answer he wanted to make and started down the road. Bruce trotted happily after him. "Here's the plan," he said after a few moments. "Miss Autrey's had time to get home, right?"

"If she went home," Raymond muttered, picking up a stone and slinging it toward a NO DUMPING sign tacked to a pine tree next to the rubbish. Naturally, it missed and hit a rusted-out washing machine instead. "So?"

"So," Bruce said, lowering his voice as if someone might be eavesdropping, "we sneak up to her house, find the Jeep—it's probably parked in one of those two dozen outbuildings of hers—and—"

Raymond stopped. "*Two dozen* outbuildings!"

Bruce nodded impatiently. "Well, nearly that many. I told you a while ago—she's got one of them old-type houses like you see in movies. Anyway, we find the Jeep, sneak and get your glasses, and—"

"And get arrested," Raymond finished up for him. "No, thank you. *I'm* not going to sneak. I'll—I'll just go up to her door and explain." Raymond liked to stay out of trouble when he could.

"Yeah, like them Valley Point sixth graders of hers explain!" Bruce laughed. "Boy, I'm glad I ain't in sixth grade yet. They don't call her Alligator Autrey for nothing!"

Raymond was very glad for himself, too. He'd never seen anybody he would want less for a teacher than Miss Autrey.

"That woman's as mean as the devil," Bruce continued, "and she don't never forget nothing."

All the more reason, it seemed to Raymond, not to risk getting in her bad graces. "Well, I'm gonna knock on her door before I look for anything."

Bruce shrugged and headed for the woods that were just ahead. "Suit yourself," he called over his shoulder. "It's your funeral."

The trees closed over the road like a tunnel. As the land dropped into a steep descent, the cool shade wrapped about the boys' sweating bodies and the damp leaf-layered road cushioned their feet. Time seemed to stand still in the shadowed quietness of the huge oaks, tulip poplars, and maples. Even Bruce seemed to sense the spell of it, for he slowed his steps and walked quietly along beside Raymond.

As the road went back uphill and leveled, the woods began to thin out, and then, up ahead and off to the right, Raymond saw a house—or the ghost of one. Half-hidden behind a wall of hedges and shrouded by tall and ancient oaks, the building rose like something out of a ghost story. Built partly of brick and partly of wood, it sprawled over a large expanse of yard. It had chimneys of several different heights and styles. Its windows, too, varied, and what he could see of the ones on the first floor were shaded by awnings that made them look like half-closed eyes that watched and followed, daring them to come closer. Several green shutters hung askew. A fluttering at an upstairs window drew their attention upward.

Bruce laughed nervously. "That's just a curtain flapping through an open window." He started on, though more slowly than before.

They paused at the opening in the hedge through which the driveway passed. Peeking through, they found a lawn that needed mowing almost as much as the house needed painting. Only the strip of worn-down grass that was the driveway showed recent signs of human activity. It snaked its way toward the rear of the building. Raymond was inching forward to see where it led when a glimpse of movement off to the right made him suck in his breath and spin around.

"Chickens!" he said with a nervous laugh. There were three of them in variations of black, gray, and white, moving through the grass and pecking at the ground. Still another headed for an inky black opening in the brick underpinning that Raymond only now noticed through a gap in the shrubbery.

"You still going to the front door?" said Bruce.

Raymond detected amusement in the innocent question. "Sure," he said quickly. Then he looked toward the front of the house and instantly regretted his words. He couldn't even *see* the front door. The porch was too heavily shadowed by wraparound awnings and overgrown shrubbery to allow much more than a glimpse of the steps. Raymond gulped.

"Well, then, let's go," said Bruce.

Raymond had no choice. He moved through the grass just ahead of Bruce, grasshoppers zinging to the right and left with each cautious advance. It seemed like twenty minutes before he reached the steps and looked up at the porch looming above him.

It had a front door, of course, faded and ancient behind a rusty screen, but it looked as if it had not been opened for a thousand years. Bruce nudged him. "Spooky, ain't it?"

Raymond shrugged and began to inch his way upward. A sudden high-pitched hum made him swing to the right. It was only an ordinary dirt dauber building a nest on the wall behind three rockers. Raymond headed toward the door with an upraised fist.

Rap-rap-rap-rap! The sound his knuckles made was as timid as he felt. He knocked again, more boldly, and this time called out—for Bruce's benefit more than anything else—"Anybody home?" He looked at Bruce and knocked again, even harder.

As if in answer, the door gave a sudden lurch and began to creak slowly open. Raymond fell back, his eyes fixed on the doorway. A musty, moldy smell of old houses with very old furniture and very old people wafted out.

"Yes?" said someone from inside.

He swung back to see Miss Autrey standing there. She filled the doorway. "I'm Raymond," he gulped. "Raymond Brock. Uh—my friend here hid something of mine in the back of your Jeep a while ago at the store. I want to get it."

"There's nothing of yours in my Jeep," she said. "I just emptied it out."

"But it has to be," Raymond said. "It was field glasses, and—"

"They weren't in there," the woman replied and closed the door.

"She's lying," Bruce said when they were out of earshot. "Has to be. I know I put 'em in there. I know what we'll do. We'll just look in that Jeep for ourselves. It's bound to be parked in back."

Raymond's eyes turned back toward the house doubtfully. The side yard was in full view of a whole line of windows down the length of the house.

"We won't go that way," Bruce said, following the direction of his gaze. "We'll act like we're leaving and then find a way to get through the hedge and into the backyard."

They found no gap, but they did discover that by crawling up under the curtain of prickly vines, it was possible to squeeze through the hedge. This they did and found themselves in a village of sheds that looked like miniature houses. Though obviously never painted, the buildings had gables and balconies and were decorated with carved wood along the eaves, windows, and shutters. There must have been a dozen of them, but luckily the ones that served as garages for various vehicles were easy to spot—not only because they were bigger and had larger doors but also because of the tire patterns leading to them. Unfortunately, their doors were all chained and padlocked.

"It's this one," Bruce whispered a few minutes later, peeking through a crack of a building with no windows. "I can see the Jeep. She unhitched the trailer."

Raymond looked, too, and then circled the building in a run. "How are we going to get in?"

"Maybe we could pull off some boards," suggested Bruce, who was right behind him. "Or maybe we could break the lock."

Raymond shook his head. It was on his second trip around that he found the answer. Centered in the triangular space inside a balconylike projection in front was a small door, and the door was partway open. He pointed it out to Bruce.

"Good job!" Bruce said.

At that moment a sound Raymond did not expect split the air. A train whistle. It sounded as if it was in the yard with them.

"The railroad tracks must be right back behind here," Bruce said.

Raymond had no interest in the train. He was looking up at the window again. "We need a ladder."

"I'll be your ladder," Bruce said, dropping his plastic bag and grabbing one of the posts of the overhang. "You just climb up on my shoulders."

Raymond hesitated only a moment, then he was clambering up the boy's skinny back and shoulders and hoisting himself to the balcony. "I'll keep a watchout," Bruce whispered as Raymond crawled toward the small door.

Raymond hardly heard him. The noise of the train wheels and the roaring of the engine grew louder by the second. Inside, he paused a few moments to catch his breath and get his bearings. There were only unceiled rafters to walk on and he had to cover six before he reached the part of the Jeep on which he could drop down. Shafts of sunlight cutting through numerous cracks gave the place an eerie quality. Spiderwebs festooned the rafters and hung down from the underside of the roofing. They seemed to dance to the vibrations of the passing train. He brushed one of them away from his face and began to duck walk from beam to beam.

"One, two, three, four, five, six," he whispered, only he hardly heard himself above the clackety-clacking. Silently he lowered himself to the back of the Jeep and jumped to the ground. He raced to the back of the vehicle and leaned inside through its open window.

Even in the dimness, he could see that except for a tool-box and a bag of animal feed, it was indeed empty. The field glasses were nowhere to be seen!

"They have to be here," he whispered, leaning farther inside and shoving the toolbox to one side.

At that moment he heard a noise that could not be the train. This noise was too close. It came again and paralyzed him with fear. Someone was opening the door! He could hear the chain rattling.

Escape! He had to escape! He darted a glance at the rafters, but it was hopeless. There was not enough time to climb up on the Jeep and swing himself up there. Desperately, he cast about for another way out, knowing full well that there was none.

Even as he looked, the door swung open and sunlight flooded the darkness. Raymond crouched against the Jeep as a shadow fell across the dirt floor.

Easing up, he peeked through the front windshield. It was Miss Autrey, her face angrier and meaner than ever. Had she seen him?

"Wasn't expecting you this soon," she was saying to a man Raymond only now noticed behind her. "Don't hurt him. Buster is just a big pet. If you call him by name, he'll come."

Raymond moved forward around the other side of the Jeep as the woman and man entered, careful to stay low and keep the Jeep between them and himself. When he heard the Jeep door opening, he tore through the doorway and made for the hedge where he saw Bruce's head sticking out.

Raymond threw himself under the curtain of prickly vines and elbowed his way along behind Bruce's worn sneakers. He heard Miss Autrey's voice as he squeezed himself through a gap Bruce had found and pulled himself out onto the road, but he could not make out her words nor could he tell to whom they might be directed.

"Did she see me?" Raymond whispered.

"This way!" Bruce hissed, tearing out across the road and into the woods on the other side. Raymond followed blindly. When Bruce jumped over stumps, he jumped them, too. He waded through the same briars and crawled through the same fences. Finally he dropped beside Bruce in a field of grass next to a dirt road very similar to the one they had just left.

"Did she see me?" Raymond gasped.

Bruce shook his head and took in several ragged breaths. "Why didn't you get outta there when I gave the signal!"

Raymond swept an arm across his sweating forehead. "What signal?"

"*What* signal!" Bruce almost screamed. "You must be deaf! I nearly scraped the skin off my fists knocking on that post when I saw Autrey coming! I whistled. I called you as loud as I could without taking a chance of the old bat hearing me!"

"The train must've blanked you out," Raymond reluctantly admitted. "I guess it wasn't your fault."

"Hey, where're the field glasses?" Bruce asked.

"That's what I'd like to know!" Raymond replied. "They weren't there. I looked through everything."

"Had to be. I slid 'em right down in the back. Between two boxes."

Raymond shook his head emphatically. "They were gone and so were the boxes."

"You sure?"

"I'm positive." Raymond's anger over the signal or lack of one was now becoming overshadowed by a far bigger problem. All he could think of was the fact that the field glasses were lost beyond recovery. Eventually his parents would discover their absence and his grandfather would have to be told.

"They had to be there," Bruce said again. "I know where I put 'em."

"And I know they weren't there! It was a dumb place to hide them to begin with."

"I was trying to help you out," Bruce reminded him. "It isn't my fault if old lady Autrey decided to steal 'em!"

There was an angry silence in which both boys glared at each other. Then Raymond climbed down from the bank and looked around. The sun was low and red in the sky. Long shadows fell across the tree-dotted meadows and the woods were growing dark. Above the tree line off to the right, the jagged face of a strange sliced-away mountain rose against the sky.

"Do you know where we are?" Raymond asked abruptly.

Bruce laughed. "Ought to! I live right up there." He jerked his head to the left. "You remember. I showed you the road a while ago."

Raymond nodded. He vaguely recalled Bruce pointing out a road.

"And that's the quarry," Bruce added, indicating the sliced-away mountain. "You ever been over there?"

"No," Raymond replied and turned away. Any other time, he might have been interested. But not now.

"I go over there all the time," Bruce bragged. "In fact, that's where I plan to have my hideout." He paused as though to allow for questions, but Raymond was too dispirited to offer any.

"Every place we move to, I always have me a place to

go to when the old man is on the warpath. I ain't had time to get me one here yet."

Curiosity finally penetrated Raymond's misery. "You move a lot?"

Bruce shrugged. "Two or three times a year, is all."

Raymond was appalled at the very idea. Two or three new places a year, two or three new schools?

"I'm usually in the same school," Bruce went on as if reading Raymond's thoughts. "The old man likes this side of Fuller better. He don't get along too good with a lot of people and there ain't as many folks out this way for him to fuss with. Lots of good garbage dumps here, too." Bruce broke off and stood. "You want to go home with me?"

"Can't," Raymond answered. "My mother'll be expecting me for supper. What's the quickest way for me to get to the trailer park?"

"Easy," Bruce said. Pointing off across the meadow, he explained how Raymond should go through the woods, cross Indian Creek at one of the narrow places, and follow the back edge of Rosanna Garmon's place. "Madame Rosanna, the fortune-teller."

Raymond nodded. "The pink house with all the wrecked cars and the big hand with the diagram drawn on it."

"You'll come to that big pasture and then you'll see the trailer park on the far side," Bruce finished.

Raymond started slowly in the direction Bruce had indicated, but his doubts must have shown on his face, for the boy called out, "You need me to go with you?"

"Heck, no," said Raymond. "I can find the way."

Bruce smiled. "Good. I got to rustle up some aluminum cans before the old man gets home."

Raymond swung off through the woods, thinking about the boy he had left behind. For some reason, Bruce seemed to like him, to want to be friends. And yet, Raymond wasn't sure *he* wanted to be friends. He was more than a little afraid of Bruce Manis. Besides, he didn't feel safe around people who didn't go by the rules.

Raymond found the creek without any trouble. He was crossing it by jumping from rock to rock when he spotted the woman on the tree-shadowed far bank.

A short plump woman in a big flowered shirt with loads of beads hanging around her neck, she had a headful of black curly hair that somehow did not match her middle-aged face. She seemed to be asleep, since her eyes were closed and her back was propped against a tree. Several feet away, a fishing pole was stuck in the ground, its line dangling in the water.

Looking back over his shoulder and then toward the strange house off to his left, Raymond crept up the bank and into the field, making sure he stayed clear of the wrecked cars that must mark the beginning of the woman's property. Then suddenly he wasn't walking anymore but falling, falling down the nearly vertical bank of a ravine. Before he could get to his feet, he heard a wild spitting and hissing, and twisted around to find a cat looking at him from behind a curtain of kudzu and briars only a few feet away.

"Chester!" he whispered.

5

MADAME ROSANNA

" 'I'm on my way—the way to heaven's door,' " Mr. Brock sang out from the family room, starting again on the song he had been stuck on since Sunday services let out an hour before.

In the tiny bedroom he shared with Vance, Raymond could hear his sister's sigh of irritation. Already angry because her parents had refused to consider her lunchtime idea of changing her "country" name to a fancier one that might impress the kids at the new school, Jackie Lee was getting worn out with her father's determined high spirits. Mr. Brock ignored her as cheerfully as he had overlooked his wife's earlier hints and sang on. " 'Oh, I'm on the upward bound road!' " The song almost drowned out Mrs. Brock's sewing machine.

Raymond tugged the sheet over the corner of his mattress—one of the jobs his mother had told him he must do before he could go outside. He eyed his brother.

Through with cleaning his part of the room, Vance was

combing his hair at the mirror over their chest of drawers, getting ready to go to town to see a movie with Bunky. Raymond suspected that meeting girls was part of the plan, too, from the way his brother was preening and splashing himself with aftershave cologne.

"Whew!" Raymond said. "Something stinks!"

Vance laughed. "You sure do! Maybe it's from that dirty cat you claimed you found yesterday!"

"You're just mad because I'm the one that'll get a reward!"

Vance grunted sarcastically. "You'll probably get enough to buy a package of gum, if you're lucky!"

Raymond made no answer to that. Late yesterday when he had finally found Henrietta and told her where her cat was, she had not said how much the reward would be.

"Grandpa's not here to make everything turn out right for his pet!" Vance said. Before Raymond could reply, a horn sounded outside. "The Potters!" Vance said, and was gone.

Suddenly the room was empty and Raymond could no longer put off thinking about the lost field glasses. He had tossed about half the night, imagining ways to find, or replace, them. But there were no answers—or at least none that were possible. Groaning, he grabbed up his dirty clothes, tossed them into the closet, and slid the door closed.

His mother looked up from her mending when he passed through the hall on his way to the back door. "Through cleaning?"

"Uh-huh," he answered.

"You sure?"

Raymond nodded and ran down the steps, headed for Old Lizzie. He found Henrietta waiting for him.

"Here," she said, handing him a dollar. "Your reward."

Raymond took it. It wasn't as much as he had hoped for, but more than he knew he had really earned. After all, he had happened upon the cat only by accident, and he had not been able to get his hands on the hissing, clawing animal to bring it home.

"Chester wasn't where you said," she went on. "But then I heard him crying real pitiful and I found him in one of those old wrecked cars."

"He musta moved after I left," Raymond said, defending himself. He dodged around her and headed for the cab of the truck.

Henrietta followed. "I would've found him myself."

"Huh!" Raymond grunted.

"I would've, because I'd already made up my mind that the next thing I was going to do was visit Madame Rosanna."

Raymond turned back. "Why would you go to see her?"

"Because Madame Rosanna's supposed to be psychic, and—"

"Psychic?"

"You know, have powers."

Raymond laughed. "You believe in that kind of thing?"

Henrietta shrugged. "I'm not sure. But when you have something valuable as Chester lost . . . well, it's worth taking a chance."

Raymond's laughter faded. "Yeah."

Henrietta lowered her voice. "You know, people like her know things. The police get them to help locate missing people. And sometimes they have visions of the future."

Raymond looked around to see whether anyone was listening. "You sure she could tell you things like that?"

"If she's really psychic, she could." There was a long silence and then Henrietta spoke again in a near whisper. "I'm still going to go. There's something else I need to know." She looked toward home. "Something about . . . about my mama and daddy."

"How much you reckon she'd charge for something like that?" Raymond asked.

Henrietta shook her head. "I don't know. But I've got nearly five dollars saved up."

Raymond thought of the dollar in his pocket. It was all he had. "You think she'd charge that much?"

Henrietta shrugged. "I'll have to ask." She had started walking away.

"You're going now?" Raymond asked, trotting to catch up.

"Yes, I am," Henrietta said, as if she'd just that moment made up her mind. "You want to go, too?" When Raymond hesitated, she grinned. "You afraid?"

Raymond shuffled about. "Heck, no."

"You're going with me then?"

"I would, if you'd ask her something for me."

"Why don't you ask her?"

"Because I don't have enough money. But if I give you my dollar, maybe you could ask her one thing in with yours."

Henrietta thought it over as she walked toward the end of the trailer park. She stopped at the fence and looked across the pasture to the bit of pink and dark roof showing above the grass. "All right," she agreed. "What do I have to ask?"

Raymond gave her the dollar and after swearing her to secrecy, told her that the field glasses were lost.

"Where?"

"That's what I want to know," Raymond answered, taking off through the grass. He wasn't going to tell her a thing more than he had to.

A few minutes later when they were approaching the Garmon yard, Henrietta insisted on stopping to clean the cockleburs and beggar-lice off her socks and jeans before going on. While she picked and pulled, Raymond impatiently moved on ahead.

"Come on," he said, creeping up to the remains of a wrecked Cadillac. Beyond that was a truck that advertised potato chips and a Volkswagen with weird swirls of color painted down its sides.

"Over there's the one Chester was in," Henrietta said moments later when she ran to catch up. "That red one."

They threaded their way through wrecks that must have been there for years. Some were draped with vines and hemmed in with bushes and even small trees. As they neared the house, Henrietta stopped dead still and pointed to a long gray vehicle that had to be a hearse. The draped curtains were still in place, though the front was smashed in and the sides dented.

Raymond swallowed hard and then managed to say, "So what? It's just another wreck." Beyond the hearse and the edge of the house was the creek, and on the far side of the stream, he could glimpse what looked like a white bus. Next to it was a black truck.

"Back door or front?" Henrietta asked as they went closer.

"Front," Raymond decided, looking in that direction.

Raymond paused at the front porch, which was covered with junk. An old washing machine, several stacks of cardboard boxes, and a haphazard pile of lumber allowed only small trails across it. A sagging clothesline hung with laundry was strung between two posts.

Suddenly the door banged open and the woman Raymond had seen on the creek bank the day before burst out of the house brandishing a broom and yelling at the top of her lungs. Henrietta gasped and fell back against Raymond and both retreated to the corner of the house.

"Get out of here, you sorry freeloaders!" the woman shrieked, heading for a pecan tree a few yards away.

Henrietta giggled. "Squirrels." She pointed out two furry shapes scampering along a tree limb.

Beads swinging and print dress billowing, the woman pounded the tree. "You rascals think you're going to get every last pecan before they hit the ground!" The squirrels chittered and scurried higher in the tree. "Well, I got news for you. I'm gonna have some nuts to eat myself—or I'll have me some squirrel meat!"

As if in response to the threat, the squirrels leaped out one after another and made for the trees along the creek bank. The woman pursued them only a few feet and then stopped. Turning back, she grinned in satisfaction, showing yellowed teeth with several obvious gaps between them. She saw Raymond and Henrietta and smiled bigger. "Well, well. Company!"

Gathering courage from her cheerful face, Raymond stepped forward to introduce himself and Henrietta. The woman hugged them as if they were long-lost relatives. "I'm Rosanna Garmon, sometimes known as Madame Rosanna," she said, heading for the porch. "Come on in."

Raymond followed Madame Rosanna and Henrietta into a small darkish room and practically felt his way to the chair the woman offered. It was an uncomfortable chair with a spring trying to push through the quilt that covered its sagging upholstery and two bricks replacing a missing leg. On the wall over the chair was a mounted deer head complete with antlers on which hung several caps.

"Grady's work," Rosanna explained. "My late husband earned his living on cars, but stuffing animals was what he loved."

The room had two windows, but dingy gray lace curtains kept much light from entering either of them, and the light from the cluttered kitchen off to Raymond's right helped but little. Henrietta took a chair next to a closed door with stuffed hawks on either side.

Rosanna sighed. "Grady's been gone a year, but it feels like he's still here." She chuckled. "And in a way, I guess he is." She threw open the closed door and reached inside to produce a tall vase. "At least his ashes are. His family had a fit, but it was what he wanted."

As the door creaked fully open, Henrietta sucked in her

breath. Then Raymond saw what she was staring at. On the floor of the room Rosanna had just opened was a casket! Rosanna saw the direction of their gaze and laughed. "Don't worry. It ain't occupied. Grady wanted a regular funeral service before he was cremated, and the funeral home wouldn't rent me a casket for 'im. Said I had to buy one. So I says, 'Well, if I have to buy it, I'll sure keep it!' I use it to store blankets and stuff in."

She returned the vase to the back room and, to Raymond's relief, closed the door. Taking a seat on the sofa, which seemed to sink beneath her bulk, she propped her feet up on an upturned paint can. "Well, what brings you over this way?"

Raymond and Henrietta looked at each other, each waiting for the other to speak. Madame Rosanna leaned toward them encouragingly. "Well, what can I do for you?"

"I need to find out something," said Henrietta at last.

Punching Henrietta, Raymond cleared his throat and mouthed the words, "Test her!"

"Huh?" Henrietta mouthed back.

Madame Rosanna looked from one to the other until Raymond finally spoke.

"How do we know . . . " he began. "I mean, are you psychic?"

She laughed. "I leave that to other people to decide."

"And, uh, how much do you charge?"

"It depends." She winked. "For you, a good price."

"I only have four—I mean five dollars and seventy-five cents," Henrietta said.

"Well, I guess I could give you young'uns a discount. Who's ready to hear what the future holds?"

"Me," said Henrietta, running across the room.

"Don't forget that special thing you were going to ask," Raymond reminded her.

Henrietta nodded and gave her hands to Madame Rosanna.

Rosanna hardly had time to glance at them before someone began banging on the door.

"Rosie, you home?"

Turning, Raymond saw Bruce Manis pressing his face against the screen wire.

Grinning, the boy threw open the door and stepped inside. His feet were bare and his jeans wet to the knees. "Hey, Raymond," he said before turning to Rosanna. "Rosie, you got a deal. The old man said he'd pick up that stuff and sell it for you if you'd go fifty-fifty on the profit!"

"Later." Rosanna motioned him to silence and bent over Henrietta's hands once more. Bruce shrugged and pulled a chair up next to Raymond's. "Look!" He pulled out a pocketknife with an elaborately carved white handle and flicked out three blades, a can opener, and a nail file. "Ain't that fancy? I found it at a flea market last year." He returned it to his pocket and pulled out a plain pocketknife. "This 'un is for everyday use."

"You are very intelligent," Rosanna was saying in a voice different from her regular one. There was almost a foreign accent to her words. She traced several lines with an index finger. "Very intelligent, indeed."

Henrietta nodded and Bruce sniggered. Raymond was on the verge of laughing himself. "You are creative and artistic, too," Rosanna went on. The girl smiled. "Yes."

She turned Henrietta's hands over and was examining nails that had been chewed short and ragged. "But you have worries too. Big worries. Yes?"

Henrietta nodded, her eyes growing large and solemn. "My daddy and my cat."

"Your father and your cat?" Rosanna encouraged her.

"Yes," Henrietta whispered, "Mama and Daddy are getting divorced and my cat ran away after my mother ran him in the dryer."

Bruce burst into laughter. "Your mother ran your father in the dryer!"

Henrietta turned furious eyes on him. "My cat, stupid!"

Bruce elbowed Raymond. "Her cat's named Stupid!"

Rosanna straightened her shoulders and swung around to face Bruce. "Young man, if you don't behave, I'll tell your daddy about a certain bunch of aluminum cans he doesn't know about."

Grinning, Bruce held up his hands in surrender. "Okay! Raymond and me'll just look at all of your stuffed animals while we wait. You won't even know we're here." He jumped up and crossed the room to examine an owl perched on a limb next to the window. Raymond followed.

"Raymond found my cat," Henrietta was murmuring. "But Chester's still nervous and unhappy, and I'm worried about my daddy, too. He and Mama . . ."

The rest of her words were lost to Raymond as Bruce began to tell him about the owl he had seen the week before. "It was just like this one," he said, moving to see it from different angles, "only bigger. It was sitting on this dead tree over close to the quarry. It turned its head nearly all the way around looking at me."

". . . troubles, but great happiness, too . . ." Madame Rosanna was saying.

"Then after a while it flew off so quiet you couldn't hear it," Bruce said, lifting his arms to demonstrate.

Minutes passed. Bruce moved to a raccoon that stood on a table next to the front window and began telling about the time he had spotted one of these at the creek. Raymond edged closer to the sofa, trying to keep up with Henrietta and Rosanna's conversation. When was the girl going to mention his field glasses? Or had she completely forgotten?

Then something moving in the yard caught Raymond's eye. Something was stealing from car to car, from bush to bush. He nudged Bruce.

Bruce pulled the curtains to one side. "A dog."

"The dog from the store," Raymond said with sudden recognition.

Even as they spoke, the dog darted from behind a bush and took off toward a squirrel creeping along the edge of the yard. The squirrel saw the dog and made a mad dash for the trees along the creek, reaching one just ahead of the dog's snapping teeth. Barking, the dog reared up against the tree as if to climb it, but it was too late. The squirrel leaped from that tree to another and then another until it had disappeared.

The boys moved across the room to the door as the dog made his shamefaced return to the yard. He did not see them, though he was moving warily in the direction of the porch. He was too wrapped up in checking out the line of flapping clothes. Presently, he jumped up onto the porch and began sniffing behind and between stacks of boxes.

All at once a horsefly zoomed by and the dog was instantly alert. Pulling back, he growled low in his throat and turned his head this way and that in a vain attempt to keep a bead on the enemy, snapping his teeth at thin air again and again while the horsefly escaped to zoom-dive from a different direction.

Suddenly the dog bared his teeth and leaped high off the porch, crashing into the line of flapping clothing and then into a stack of boxes. The boxes trembled and then slammed into the stack next to them. Dozens of fruit jars and old dishes shattered against pots and pans.

"*Yip-yip-yip-yip-yip!*" cried the terrified dog as he fought his way out of the mess of fallen boxes, glass, and clothing. "*O-o-o-o-o-o!*" he howled, taking off across the yard, dragging the clothesline with several items of clothing still attached.

"Good Lord, have mercy!" said Madame Rosanna, leaping up from the sofa and running to the door. "Is it an earthquake?"

Bruce was laughing too hard to answer, but Raymond managed to gasp, "I-i-i-i-it was a dog!"

Rosanna saw nothing funny. She stepped out onto the

·porch, surveyed the damage, and then spotted the dog and her clothesline heading across the yard toward the highway.

"My best blouse!" she shrieked. "Catch that varmint!"

Bruce and Raymond took off in pursuit and found the line and the clothes halfway to the highway. They had just picked up the last item when a screech of brakes and a honking horn caught their attention. The boys looked at each other, their smiles now gone, and started back toward the house.

"Well, I guess the varmint got run over," Rosanna said when they stepped up onto the porch. She reached for the clothing and handed them a broom. "You two clean up this mess for me while I finish up Henrietta's fortune."

The boys said very little as they swept up glass and refilled the boxes, but their eyes drifted frequently toward the highway. "It was just a stray," Bruce finally said. "They get run over around here all the time."

"Yeah," was all Raymond could think of to answer.

A few minutes later when Rosanna pronounced Henrietta ready to go, she motioned Bruce to come in. "The porch'll do. Me and you have got business to talk over."

Henrietta and Raymond said their good-byes and started back the way they had come.

"Well?" said Raymond as soon as they were out of hearing. "What did she say?"

"I'm not going to tell you my fortune," said Henrietta. "It's private." There were tears in her eyes. She ran by the last of the wrecks and started out across the field, paying no attention now to the cockleburs and beggar-lice.

Raymond hurried to catch up. "What did she say about my field glasses?"

Henrietta looked blank and for a moment Raymond feared she had forgotten. Then she said, "Oh. They are in a place you wouldn't think of. A dark place, she said. Madame Rosanna said she sees a place with stone around it."

"What else?"

"Nothing else. That's all."

"That's all I get for a dollar?"

Henrietta took off running once more and her voice came back to him on the wind. "Yes."

6

FIRST DAY
OF SCHOOL

The lingering fragrance of bacon and coffee hung in the morning air like a mist, and Raymond, who had been able to force very little breakfast past the lump in his throat, could smell it in the bathroom with the door closed. His chest was heavy with dread. Today was Friday, the first day of school.

There was a pounding on the bathroom door. "Let me in!" Vance demanded.

Raymond grunted in reply and plunged his head under the faucet. Then, attacking his hair with Vance's stiff-bristled brush, he raked every curl until his scalp stung. Yet when he allowed himself to look into the mirror, he still saw defiant curls and waves all over his head.

The pounding came again. "I said, let me in!"

Then his mother joined in. "Hurry up, Raymond," she called from the kitchen. Her voice was sharp with anxiety, though Raymond could not for the life of him see why. What did she have to worry about? She didn't have to go to a new school today. She was only going into Fuller to look for a job.

Throwing down the brush, Raymond pressed both hands on top of his head so hard his ears rang. He glimpsed his full-length reflection in the mirror on the door and dropped his hands in despair. "What's the use?" he muttered. From his slicked-down hair to his leather shoes, he found himself unsatisfactory. He would wear his blue cap to hide as many curls as possible, he decided, if he could find it in his closet. But the shoes were impossible to either hide or disguise.

Raymond threw open the door and Vance nearly fell into the bathroom. "About time," he grumped.

"Shut up, elephant ears!" Raymond said, pushing past him.

"Stop using my hairbrush, you little creep!" Vance yelled, slamming the door.

From the kitchen table where she was bent over the want-ad section of the newspaper, pencil in hand, Mrs. Brock sighed loudly.

In his room, Raymond dove into the closet and began tossing things out of first one box and then another until he spotted the cap on the floor on Vance's side. He fitted it down over his curls.

"Hey, Vance!" Bunky called from the steps. "Time to go!"

The message came like a blow in the stomach. Raymond wondered whether he could pretend to be sick. He started for the kitchen with one hand clutching his stomach.

"Mother-r-r-r," Jackie Lee called from her room before Raymond could get out his first groan. "Couldn't you take me to school just this one time?"

Mrs. Brock shook her head and circled an ad. "Your father didn't arrange to ride with Mr. Harris so I could chauffeur you to school, dear." She turned to Raymond but took no notice of his hand on his stomach. "Your day to cook supper."

Raymond's groan was real. What little enthusiasm he had originally felt for cooking had evaporated with the worries of the last few days. He had only half-listened to the instructions she had been giving.

"You'll have plenty of time. You'll get out early on the first day. Now, here's your last year's report card to turn in."

"Do I have to?" he asked, fingering the frayed corners of the envelope and wishing he could make its contents disappear. Although none of the grades were failing, neither were they the excellent marks that Jackie Lee and Vance usually brought home.

Vance chose that moment to make his appearance, a cocksure look on his face. "Where's *my* report card?" he asked, glorying in the fact that he had nothing below a *B* on it.

Raymond longed to wipe away his brother's smug expression. "Shut up, big mouth," was all he could think of to say.

Mrs. Brock threw up her hands. "Raymond! For heaven's sake!"

At that moment Jackie Lee made her grand appearance and Raymond almost gasped. He had seen his sister in some weird getups but this one took the prize. She had tortured her hair into the cover style on the latest issue of *Teen Scene Magazine*. Her spiky eyelashes and violet-colored lids looked too heavy to hold open. "I've got it!" she said.

Vance howled with laughter. "I hope you get over it."

Jackie Lee ignored him. "My new name just came to me, Mother—J'Lee! Well, what do you think?"

"I thought we settled the matter of your name," Mrs. Brock said.

Raymond sniggered. "Urp!"

"Jelly?" shrieked Vance.

"J'Lee, stupid! It rhymes with Marie."

Mrs. Brock shook her head at Vance until he threw open the door and went to join Bunky. Then she turned back to her daughter. "Use your real name. And don't you think you need to take off a bit of makeup and brush your hair?"

"Yeah," Raymond agreed. He was so unhappy that he wasn't too particular about anybody else's feelings. "Your hair looks like a bird nest and your eyes look like two greasy spiders."

Jackie Lee's face crumpled and her shoulders sagged. She disappeared back into her room.

"Raymond!" Mrs. Brock reproved. "Can't you be nice to your sister?"

Raymond dropped his eyes. He was ashamed but he wasn't ready to admit it. After all, he told himself, nobody seemed to care about *his* feelings.

Mrs. Brock began tucking in Raymond's shirt. "I told Jackie Lee to stay with you today until you're registered."

He jerked his shirt back out. "I'm not a baby," he said for the benefit of whoever might be overhearing the conversation. Actually, he could not help being relieved that he would not be completely on his own.

Mrs. Brock hugged him and then returned to the paper. "I'll see you this afternoon. Everything'll be fine."

"Huh!" Raymond grunted as he trudged toward the door. It was easy for her to say, he thought. Outside, he forgot his problems for a moment at the sight of Henrietta leaving her trailer on tiptoe. Casting frequent glances over her shoulder, she hugged something to her chest. It wasn't the cat, Raymond was sure. Chester was too wild to be held with one hand or even very easily with two. Besides, the thing she held was white. Henrietta looked around and then suddenly, to Raymond's puzzlement, headed across Mrs. Clendenin's yard. Curious, Raymond followed.

Sticking close to the shrubbery and flower beds, she rounded the end of the double-wide trailer and headed straight for the trash cans in back. Just as she lifted the lid, she turned and spotted him.

"What do you mean, spying on me?" she demanded, shoving the bundle she held into the can. She clamped on the lid and backed up against the can as though to defend it. "I guess you're going to tell," she said in a voice that trembled near tears. "Well, I don't care. I couldn't let Mama find the curtain Chester clawed up. She's already mad at him. My window doesn't need but one panel of sheers anyway. And Daddy will buy me one to replace it before she finds out."

Suddenly the back door of Mrs. Clendenin's trailer banged open and the stout woman appeared, hair disheveled and chenille robe askew. "What are you doing in my yard?" she said. "I'm going to speak to your parents!"

Henrietta's eyes grew large. She edged away from the trash can. "I—I—" she began. Raymond was surprised to see the usually talkative girl at a loss for words.

He cleared his throat. "We were picking up some trash and putting it in your cans."

The woman looked surprised. "And I guess you're wanting to get paid?"

"No, ma'am," Raymond said, edging away. "We don't want nothing."

"Anything," Henrietta said as they ran for home. " 'Don't want nothing' is a double negative."

Raymond frowned at the girl until she had entered her trailer, and then he headed slowly out the driveway toward the mailbox. Jackie Lee flounced by as he passed the back corner of the Clendenin lot. Glancing quickly at her, Raymond noticed that she had rubbed off some of her makeup and her hair appeared to have been brushed a little. Her eyes were red.

"You look better," he said, trying to make amends. "I mean good. Real good."

"Humph!" she replied, giving her head a toss.

"I mean it," he said. "You look—pretty."

Jackie Lee looked at him gratefully. "Do you really mean it?"

"Sure," Raymond said, surprised that his opinion mattered. Could it be that she was afraid to face the new school, too?

"Bus!" Bunky shouted from the mailboxes, where he, Vance, and several young children waited. Raymond was the last one to get on. Even Henrietta made a breathless dash that put her on the bus ahead of him.

About twenty minutes and fifteen stops later, the bus reached Valley Point School. It had barely lurched its way onto the potholed pavement separating the brick junior and senior high school building from the stucco elementary school when Jackie Lee was hustling Raymond off the bus.

"Come on!" she said sweetly for the benefit of some girls and boys her age. Raymond watched Vance and Bunky saunter off through the noisy mob as Jackie Lee hurried him along. "Got to hurry so I can register myself," she was saying.

Just ahead of the buses, in a chained-off playground area, Raymond saw Miss Autrey. If possible, she looked more severe than when he had last seen her. From her broad shoulders down to her stumplike legs and no-nonsense lace-up shoes, she was the very image of a person accustomed to issuing commands—and having them obeyed. Her broad face showed not the slightest trace of either cosmetics or humor. Raymond automatically began detouring around her.

"Come on!" Jackie Lee urged him needlessly. On the way up the steps, Raymond glimpsed two boys fighting in the shrubbery. As he entered the building, Raymond realized that the one on top was Bruce Manis. It had been five days since he had seen the boy, but Bruce was wearing the same clothes that he had worn at Madame Rosanna's.

Inside there was a long line of children and parents at a door marked NEW STUDENT REGISTRATION. Jackie Lee shoved Raymond into the line and turned to go. "See you after school," she said.

Raymond wanted to run after her, to remind her of their mother's instructions, to beg, to do anything to keep from being left alone. But he only stood there watching her leave while the lump in his throat swelled to boulder size.

The hall grew noisier. Old students milled confidently about, yelling and laughing with friends. Several adults who must be teachers passed by. One—a slender black woman in high heels and a pretty print dress—stopped to talk to a child who called out to her, and then entered a room marked MISS ROBBINS—FIFTH GRADE. Raymond hoped she would be his teacher. She reminded him of his third-grade teacher, whom he had especially liked.

A boy in a blue shirt stopped at the door the woman had entered. Grabbing a sheet of paper from a boy nearby, he scrawled a sign in big red letters saying DOWN WITH SCHOOL! and hung it on the doorknob. The way all the kids collected around laughing—as if it was funnier than it really was—told Raymond the boy was popular.

A boy who was laughing harder than the rest said, "Hey, Wade, I dare you to hang a sign on Miss Autrey's door!" Wade withered him with one scathing glance and looked around for something else to entertain his admirers.

A commotion broke out in the hallway and the crowd surged forward. "Miss Autrey!" someone said. "She's got Bruce Manis and Kelvin Thomas!" Raymond looked through the crowd and saw Miss Autrey dragging Bruce and the other boy along on either side.

"Well, boys," she was saying, "I think it's high time you learn you are not running this school."

If Bruce was learning this, he didn't show it. Undismayed and unrepentant, he was managing a kind of jauntiness as he hurried along beside her. He spotted Raymond and grinned. "Hey, King Shoes!" he called before disappearing through a door marked OFFICE.

Raymond tried to fade into the wall.

Time passed and Raymond inched slowly forward. He was sixth in line when the bell rang and a flood of students poured in from outside. Across the mass of bobbing heads, he caught sight of Henrietta walking along with a tall red-headed girl. He saw Miss Autrey pass, too, and then moments later, Bruce. "That dog didn't get run over like we thought," the boy yelled. "I seen him the other day."

It was like a ray of sunshine on an otherwise bleak day. Raymond smiled as he moved forward to find a new place to lean against the wall.

The noise in the hallway subsided. Finally Raymond reached the head of the line and a brisk young woman was looking over his report card and firing rapid questions at him. "Come with me," she said at last, ushering him down the hall at a trot. She chattered faster than she walked, and Raymond was so busy listening and answering that he almost plowed into her when she suddenly stopped at an open door.

"We'll send for your cumulative records. Meanwhile, we'll have to assign you to a classroom, and I think Miss Autrey has the smallest class."

"But she has sixth grade," Raymond managed to croak.

"Not this time," she whispered. "This year we modernized sixth grade. We have different teachers for each subject. Miss Autrey didn't—well, she decided to take fifth grade, where students still have one teacher all day." She shoved a paper into his hand and nudged him into the doorway. "Go right in. She doesn't like students to be late."

Raymond stood paralyzed on the threshold while the

woman's steps echoed down the empty hallway. In quick glimpses, he took in the crowded room. The walls, the counters under the two bulletin boards, the bookcases, the teacher's desk, and the space beneath it were all littered with what appeared to be the accumulation of years. Yellowed test papers with faded hundreds inked on them, ragged books in tilting stacks, and rolled-up maps were scattered carelessly about the room.

Four lines of student desks and the oversized teacher's desk seemed to take up every inch of floor. Raymond's eyes swept over the crowd of strangers and made out Henrietta's black hair in the first row, Wade's blue shirt in the third, and Bruce's wild blond head near the front of the second. Miss Autrey was nowhere to be seen.

The class was restless. Wade was turned slightly sideways, casting furtive glances at a boy who was mouthing a silent message. Seeing the class favorite thus distracted, Bruce leaned over to Wade's desk and in one smooth motion swept the red pen from its place. Only one other person besides Raymond seemed aware of what had happened: the girl who sat in front of Bruce. Her eyes lit up and she shot up her hand.

A desk drawer shut with the impact of a pistol shot and the class snapped to attention. Wade swung around and the girl in front of Bruce jerked her hand down. Beyond the stacks of books on the teacher's desk, a gray head arose like a monster emerging from the deep.

"There," Miss Autrey said, brushing off her hands and looking directly at Bruce, who busied himself nonchalantly slipping Wade's red pen into his pocket. "The pocketknife is mine. You know better than to bring that kind of thing to school, young man."

"I got another at home," he said. "And it's a lot better than that one."

"You won't have it if you bring it to school," she replied, running her eyes around the room as though to make sure the lesson was not lost on the other students. Then she caught sight of Raymond in the doorway and suddenly every head in the room was turned in the same direction. Miss Autrey glowered at him as if he had done something wrong by merely being there. Raymond quaked, wondering all over again whether she had seen him the day he had escaped from her garage.

Henrietta flashed him an encouraging smile, but it did not help. He considered running. He pictured himself tearing down the long hallway, leaping out over all the steps, bounding across the playground, and racing down the highway toward home. Old Stumplegs would never be able to catch him. His heart raced as if he was actually doing it.

Miss Autrey's voice brought him back. "Come here, young man."

Tearing his eyes away from the hall, Raymond moved forward, but not quickly enough to satisfy her. She met him halfway and snatched the cap from his head. "Gentlemen remove hats indoors," she informed him. She took the paper from his hand and skimmed over its contents. "Raymond Brock," she read, heading back to her desk. Raymond followed, wishing he had the courage to grab the cap.

"Well, let's see," she said, looking out over the rows of desks. "I believe I'll put you up front." The place where she would put a troublemaker, Raymond thought. And he hadn't done anything! Miss Autrey pointed to the squinty-eyed girl in front of Bruce. "Justine Weaver."

"Yes, Miss Autrey?" Justine said in exactly the kind of overly polite voice Raymond would have expected.

"Move to another desk so Raymond can have that place."

"Yes, ma'am!"

Miss Autrey turned to Raymond and held out his cap. He took it quickly, afraid she might change her mind. "You'd best see that cap stays off your head and out of trouble in my class unless you want to lose it."

"Yes, ma'am."

She paused for a moment while Raymond made his way to his assigned place. "As I was saying before I was interrupted," she said, "my sixth-grade students were always ahead of the other sixth grades. And that's how I intend to have it now that I'm teaching fifth. Furthermore, my students always behaved themselves. When you are out on that playground, you are to act just as if I were out there supervising." She paused. "Most of the time I will be."

Raymond placed the cap on his desk with both hands. He smoothed all the wrinkles and rubbed a soiled spot, convincing himself that Miss Autrey was responsible for them all. Sliding one hand underneath, he pushed out a dented-in place. He snapped and unsnapped the straps in back. Then he became aware of a deep silence and looked up, to find Miss Autrey staring at him. He dropped his hands to his lap just as a knock sounded at the door and saved him.

"I need to see you for a moment, Miss Autrey," a young woman in shorts said. She wore a whistle around her neck and carried a clipboard in one hand. Glowering with displeasure, Miss Autrey lumbered slowly to the door. As the low-pitched conference dragged on, Miss Autrey moved farther and farther out into the hall. The students grew bold enough to whisper and shift about in their seats. "The Phys Ed teacher," one student informed them. "No, just a parent," another argued. Justine's little eyes were darting about, making note of each and every misdeed.

Wade leaned across the aisle. "Hey, let me see that," he whispered, sweeping the cap off Raymond's desk without waiting for permission.

"Give it back!" Raymond said, grabbing too late.

"I'm not hurting your dumb cap!" Wade said. "I just want to see it."

"Give it back, I said!" Raymond leaned out over the narrow aisle so far that he felt his desk beginning to tip. He tried desperately to right himself, flailing his arms and legs about madly, but it was too late. The desk crashed to the floor, taking Raymond with it, and a swell of laughter echoed around the room. Wade threw the cap to the floor just as Miss Autrey stormed back inside.

"What is the meaning of this commotion?"

"Raymond was only trying to get his cap back," Henrietta volunteered.

Miss Autrey scooped up the cap and headed to the front of the room. "I see I'm going to have to add this to my collection."

Raymond jumped to his feet. "That's not fair!"

A desk drawer opened and slammed. "If you behave yourself," she said, "you may get it at the end of the school year."

"But it's mine!" Raymond sputtered. "It wasn't my fault—"

"He's telling the truth," Bruce Manis said. "I seen it all and—"

"You *saw* it all," Miss Autrey corrected him.

"That's what I said, and he was just trying to—"

"I don't want to hear about it," she answered. "Raymond, set your desk upright and have a seat. Now, before I give out the student information cards and the school lunchroom sheets, I need to go over our class rules. . . ."

Setting up his desk, Raymond slid into it and stared at the initials cut into its top. From the corner of his eye, he could see Justine trying to ease up her hand each time Miss Autrey paused for breath.

Presently, he felt a sharp jab in his back and turned to glimpse a red ink drawing Bruce was sliding toward him. It was a picture of a heavyset devil with chunky legs. Wielding a paddle in one hand and a pitchfork in the other, the devil scowled out at the world, while flaming letters announced: "Miss Autrey!" The identification was unnecessary. The likeness was too close to miss.

Raymond suppressed a gloating smile and turned around

as Miss Autrey ended her talk and began handing out student information cards and other beginning-of-school paperwork. Justine could stand it no longer. Popping her hand up again, she burst out, "Miss Autrey, Bruce Manis took Wade Ellis's pen!"

Wade looked at the empty slot on his desk and leaned across the aisle. "Hey! Gimme my pen!"

Behind him, Raymond heard a scuffling and a scrunching of paper. "Blabbermouth!" Bruce hissed.

Justine smiled. "And Bruce drew—"

Miss Autrey held up her hand for silence. "You remain in your seat when the dismissal bell rings, Bruce."

Bruce grinned slowly. "I'll miss my bus. My old man brought me to school this morning, but he said I had to ride the bus home."

"I won't keep you very long," she answered. "And you are to see me at recess Monday. I may have other people to keep you company." Feeling her gaze shifting in his direction, Raymond dropped his eyes to the area beneath her desk, where numerous boxes, books, and even some rocks were stored. Then at a back corner, Raymond spotted something between the largest of the rocks—something black with a dangling strap. He could not help recalling Madame Rosanna's words. The field glasses were in a place where he wouldn't expect them, a place with stones. He leaned this way and that, trying to get a closer look, but when the dismissal bell rang a few minutes later, he still was not positive it was what he thought it was. He had to know.

While other rooms emptied noisily into the hall, Miss Autrey assigned them homework—an essay, minimum length, one page—and then ordered the class to line up by rows. They had to do it three times before she was satisfied. Then, like a general, she squared her shoulders and marched to the head of the line to lead them out. She paused and fastened her eyes on Bruce one last time before departing. "You sit right there until I get back."

Raymond found himself about halfway back in line, his eyes on the object beneath the teacher's desk. He was still trying to decide what to do. When the line began to move, he hung back barely inside the room. He couldn't leave without knowing.

Bruce leaned toward him eagerly. "Whatcha doing?"

Raymond only shook his head. As soon as the last student left, he made a mad dash for the front, squatted behind the desk, and swept his hand beneath it. As heavy steps sounded at the back, he pulled out what he suddenly realized was a leather camera case!

"I might have known," Miss Autrey said. Looking up, Raymond saw his teacher and just behind her, Justine.

Raymond slid the camera case back beneath the desk and jumped to his feet. "I thought . . ." he began and faltered.

"You thought incorrectly," the woman said, reaching his side faster than he would have believed possible. She reached for the biggest of her desk drawers, jerked it open, and took out Raymond's cap. Stuffing it into her oversize bag, she slammed the drawer hard. "I'll keep this at home until the end of the year," she said.

"But—" Raymond began, and then stopped. It was useless. She was not going to believe him no matter what he said. Swinging around, he ran for the door. Behind him, he vaguely heard her order him to stop running in the building, but he did not slow. He felt an overwhelming urge to escape.

7

SPAGHETTI AND OTHER DISASTERS

Bruce Manis arrived on the Brock steps late that afternoon just as Raymond, worn out with watching for his mother to drive up in the Plymouth, dragged himself to the kitchen to start the job Jackie Lee had been nagging him about since lunchtime: cooking supper.

"Hey there, King Shoes!" Bruce said, entering the trailer without invitation. There was no one in the kitchen except Raymond. Vance, as usual, was off somewhere with Bunky, and Jackie Lee was in her room, writing a story to enter in a *Teen Scene Magazine* short story contest.

"I guess you noticed I didn't ride your bus," Bruce said, touching the sofa and the afghan hanging over one arm. "That's 'cause I had to ride my old bus to the place we lived last year. Had to help the old man with a job over there."

Raymond could have told him he had been too upset to notice who was or was not on the bus, but he said nothing.

Bruce pushed his feet into the carpet. "Fancy place!"

Raymond shrugged. It didn't look so fancy to him.

Bruce sauntered on into the kitchen. "Boy! I thought Miss Autrey was going to bust a gut today! I guess you showed that old bat!"

Of course, big-eared Jackie Lee heard this and came on the run, pages of notebook paper clutched in her hand and head bristling with hot rollers. "What?" she demanded from her bedroom doorway. "What are you talking about?"

"Nothing," Raymond answered quickly, "nothing at all." He tried to signal Bruce to shut up, but Bruce wasn't paying attention. He clapped Raymond on the back.

"King Shoes ain't afraid of nothing."

Desperate to change the subject, Raymond darted across the room and snatched several notebook pages from his sister's hand. "I was just telling Bruce about your story," he said, ducking to one side and running backward across the room. " 'Love Came Riding by J'Lee Brock,' " he read.

"Shut up!" Jackie Lee yelled, chasing after him while Bruce laughed. "Give me back my story!" Several rollers came loose and fell from her hair and Bruce laughed even harder.

" 'The midsummer-night sky was filled with a thousand stars and reflected silver off Angelique's golden blond hair and Kevin's handsome profile. . . . ' " Raymond read between giggles.

Jackie Lee trapped him next to the sofa and forced the pages from his hand. "Give that back to me!" she ordered. She hugged her manuscript to her chest and grabbed up her rollers. "I'm going to tell Mother."

"Keep quiet about what happened at school," Raymond whispered to Bruce when Jackie Lee was back in her room. Then, loudly enough for her to hear, he added, "I wish I didn't have a sister."

"I'm glad I ain't got none myself," Bruce agreed, mopping an arm across his sweating face. "Whew! It's too hot to stay in here. Let's go outside and do something."

Raymond had no interest in doing anything except waiting for his mother and somehow convincing her that he had to get into another teacher's class. Besides, he had to start supper or he'd get in trouble. Before he could think of an acceptable way to explain this to Bruce, Jackie Lee saved him the effort.

"Raymond can't go anywhere," she came out of her room to say. "It's his turn to cook."

That made up Raymond's mind. "I'll go if I please." He turned back to Bruce. "It won't take me any time to be through in here."

Jackie Lee laughed. "Sure! Like you'd ever done it before! I bet you don't even remember what Mother said for you to fix."

As a matter of fact, he didn't, but he wasn't about to admit it. "Huh! I bet you don't know yourself."

The trick didn't work. "All I know is you're in trouble if you don't get your job done." She went back to her room and closed the door, but she continued peeking out frequently to keep up with what Bruce and Raymond were doing.

Bruce examined the bookshelves that divided the kitchen from the family room, running his hand over a ceramic bird of Mrs. Brock's. "I do just about all the cooking at our place. Whatcha gonna fix?"

That question again. Raymond groaned inwardly. Why, oh, why hadn't he paid attention when his mother had given him his instructions? Today of all days he didn't need trouble with his mother. He jerked open the refrigerator door for ideas and a plastic pitcher of lemonade on the overcrowded top shelf tumbled to the floor with a splat and a splash that set Jackie Lee off again.

"*Raymond-d-d-d!* What have you done now?"

"Nothing," he yelled, throwing a couple of dish towels over the mess and tossing the pitcher into the sink.

"Particular, ain't she?" said Bruce, tracking through the

lemonade and throwing himself down on one of the kitchen chairs. The chair squeaked ominously. "Whatcha gonna cook?" he asked again.

Raymond threw open the door of the pantry and spotted a box of noodles. It was as if a light had turned on in his head. "Spaghetti! That's what Mom said for me to fix!" Sure enough, he found a package of hamburger in the refrigerator.

Bruce leaned his chair back at a precarious angle, using one arm to brace himself on the table. "Guess what?"

"What?" Raymond asked with no real interest. He rose on tiptoe to get the box of noodles from the shelf. "Bring water to rapid boil . . ." the directions on the side instructed.

Bruce walked the squeaking chair back and forth across the linoleum on two legs. "I got me some wheels!"

Raymond tore open the box of noodles. "Some what?"

Bruce fumbled in his pocket and produced a key on a tarnished chain. "Wheels! Something to drive. A car."

Raymond's interest was finally caught. "A car?"

"Yep!" Bruce smiled expansively. "A seventy Camaro. That's what I helped Pa with today. We changed the tires so we could tow it home. The old man bought it for next to nothing from the man he used to work for. He says he's going to overhaul it and do some body work."

"And he's gonna let you have it?"

"Not exactly," Bruce admitted. "But I figure he can't drive it and the truck at the same time. So I'll just drive it."

"I drove my grandfather's truck," Raymond said, and then instantly regretted his bragging. What if Bruce offered to let him drive the Camaro? Hastily Raymond added, "But that was just around the farm. We're not old enough to drive out on the highway."

Bruce shrugged this off as a matter of no consequence,

and then conceded, "Only thing I've drove so far is the old man's truck—when I could get away with it. Mostly I've done my driving on that old dirt road that goes out to our place."

Raymond pulled out a skillet and a deep pot from a cabinet and ran hot water at the sink to fill the pot. The sound of a car just outside made him slosh water over the counter and down to the floor in his rush to look out the window, but it was only Mrs. Clendenin coming home. There was a man with her. A tall slender man with a beard.

"I got it up to fifty-five one time," Bruce was saying.

"Huh?" Raymond said.

"The truck," Bruce said. "I got it up to fifty-five."

Raymond stared at the boy in disbelief.

Bruce grinned and held up his hands in surrender. "Okay, okay! Thirty-five."

"Your father doesn't miss the gas or anything?" Raymond asked, setting the pot on the range and turning the dial to High. He knocked a can of grease drippings over in the process and had to grab for the paper towels.

"Not yet, he ain't. 'Course the gauge don't work and he's been saying for a long time that he thinks the tank leaks." Bruce was now concentrating on balancing the chair on one shaky leg. "He works for this one man every now and then who picks him up. When he goes off with him, I ride."

Raymond emptied the box into the water. Some of the noodles spilled on the stove and down to the floor. He swept them aside with one foot and reached for the hamburger.

"I figure what he don't know ain't going to hurt me!" Bruce said, giving up on the one leg trick and letting the chair crash on all fours. "I mean, he whups me enough the way it is." He pulled up his pants leg to reveal a long purplish bruise.

Raymond caught his breath. His parents had spanked him, but they had never left marks. The two boys' eyes met for a moment and Bruce jerked his pants leg down.

"Aw, but it ain't nothing. It didn't hurt hardly none."

Raymond dumped the wad of hamburger into the skillet and set it on High. Now what? Tomato sauce, he remembered. He opened the pantry and took out the six cans he found there. There was a line of spice jars, too, the kind his mother used in spaghetti sauce. He read the labels. Garlic, cinnamon, allspice, chili powder, cloves, and thyme. He would use a tablespoon of each, just to be sure.

"Once you find out that whuppings won't kill you, why, you don't have to be afraid no more," Bruce said. "Guess that's why I ain't afraid of old lady Autrey."

Raymond recalled that Bruce had not seemed much braver than he at the old lady's house a few days before, but he kept the thought to himself. He jerked open a drawer to look for a can opener, only to have the drawer come completely out and rain spatulas, knives, and other utensils around his feet.

"You better clean up what you mess up!" Jackie Lee yelled.

"Don't she never shut up?" Bruce said.

There was no time to answer. The hamburger was already sizzling and popping and Raymond didn't have the tomato sauce in yet. Several minutes later, the sizzling was replaced with a *plop-plop-plop* when all the tomato sauce and spices began to bubble up around the wad of meat and splat out on the stove. By this time the pot of noodles on the back burner was beginning to hum and steam was rising like a heavy fog from the layer of foam on top.

The kitchen grew hotter and hotter. Bruce grabbed up a *Teen Scene Magazine* from the table and fanned himself so vigorously that the cover began ripping away from the spine. Raymond said nothing.

Bruce strained sideways to look toward Jackie Lee's closed door, and then said in a low voice, "No, sir, I ain't afraid of old lady Autrey. I guess me and you are the only ones in the room that ain't."

Me, not scared? Raymond thought. He almost laughed.

Bruce chuckled. "Boy, was she mad today when you went up there to get your cap back!"

Now was the time to tell the truth. "I didn't—" he began, but he broke off when the pot of noodles began to boil over. He pulled the pot to one side and began to mop up the cascade of water.

Bruce slapped his knee with Jackie Lee's magazine and the cover ripped off and fluttered to the floor. "And then when old lady Autrey hollered 'Stop' and you kept right on running, I thought I'd die!"

"Quiet!" Raymond said, pointing to his sister's room. His stomach tightened with worry. He knew that even if she heard nothing to report to his parents, he was still in trouble with Miss Autrey.

At that very moment, Jackie Lee threw open her door. "What is that awful smell?"

Only then did Raymond realize that something was burning. He swung around to see the sauce boiling up like lava around the clump of meat and streaming over the side of the pan to the red-hot coils of the burner. Even as he looked, dark smoke was beginning to rise and drift around the kitchen. He rushed to pull the pan to one side. An avalanche of the red liquid sloshed out and streamed down the cabinets beneath the stove.

"What are you doing?" Jackie Lee screamed, running across the room and sliding down in the lemonade. Noodles and kitchen utensils skimmed across the floor in front of her feet, the pile of crumpled towels went flying, and the two pieces of her magazine cover floated up in the air and then drifted down on the indented marks Bruce's chair had made in the linoleum.

"The lemonade was Vance's fault," Raymond said

quickly, gathering up knives and spatulas and dumping them into a drawer.

Bruce grabbed up the magazine, wrapped its damaged cover around it, and presented it to Jackie Lee. "Sorry."

"Vance left the jug right on the edge of the shelf," Raymond went on, scooping up the drippy towels and the soggy wedges of lemon and dumping them into the sink. "It was bound to fall as soon as . . ."

Jackie Lee wasn't listening. Her attention had shifted to the stove. "Good heavens!"

Raymond looked at the stove, seeing it through his sister's eyes. It did look awful. The foam from the noodles had dried and baked brown and the red from the sauce had polka dotted the entire stove, the counter, the wall, and the floor. He grabbed up the noodle box. "The directions said, 'Bring to rapid boil'! That means High." He pointed to the hottest control setting.

Jackie Lee looked up at the ceiling as though asking for help. "Dummy! You don't cook *anything* on the high setting!"

"Yes, you do! See right here? It says, 'rapid boil.' And I guess the tomato sauce must've sort of boiled over."

This gave Jackie Lee fresh fuel. "Sauce? You cooked sauce? I don't believe this!" She jerked open the pantry door and pulled out a large jar plainly labeled SPAGHETTI SAUCE. "Mother told you that all you had to do was cook the noodles and heat this!" She thrust the jar at him.

Raymond looked at the sauce and then up at his sister. She was right. But he wasn't going to admit it. He shrugged. "I just decided to fix my own, like Mom does."

"Some recipe!" Jackie Lee jeered, grabbing up a fork and punching at the wad of meat. Only now did it occur to Raymond that he should have broken it up.

"Ah, it's all right," Bruce said, pushing his way past them to pull out a clean pan. "I burn things all the time. It's no big deal." He took the fork from her hand. "All you have to do is rake out the top part into a clean pan, like this"— he skillfully dumped off the sauce and meat from the blackened ruins in the bottom and dropped the scorched pot into the sink—"and you're back in business. I bet it's good, too."

Jackie Lee snorted her disbelief. "And on top of everything else, you used the meat for tomorrow night's hamburgers! Well, you can just get to work and clean up this kitchen and heat up the sauce Mother told you to use. And I mean right now!"

"I will not," Raymond declared, making up his mind. He punched the Medium control button. "You're not the big boss around here. I'm going to finish cooking *my* sauce."

Bruce grinned. "Then we can go. Raymond's going home with me."

"Yes." Raymond didn't take his eyes off his sister. "That's right!"

Jackie Lee turned on Bruce. "You can just run on home by yourself. Raymond is not going anywhere. He's going to clean up the kitchen and finish supper."

Raymond planted himself directly in front of his sister and faced her down. He hadn't really given any thought to whether or not he *wanted* to go with Bruce, but he knew he was not going to let her win this time, especially in front of Bruce. "You can't tell my friends to go home, and you can't tell me where I can go."

Jackie Lee blinked. "Mother put me in charge."

"You're not in charge of me."

"But, but supper—"

Raymond cut her off. "You can't tell me how to cook supper, either, and as for cleaning up, I'll do that when I please."

To Raymond's surprise, Jackie Lee burst into tears. "Yes, you do as you please. Everybody in this family does as they please except me. But I'm the oldest and I have to be in charge. Then when you and Vance get in trouble, I get in trouble, too. It's, 'Why did you let them do this,' 'Why did you let them do that,' and I'm tired of it!"

Raymond had never thought of it like that. To him, it had always seemed that being the oldest in the family had no disadvantages. He could see that he himself would not want to be in charge, but he wasn't about to say so.

Looking embarrassed and uncomfortable, Bruce moved over to the window and acted as if he had suddenly found something interesting about the trailer next door.

"Being the oldest is not fair!" Jackie Lee finished up. Turning, she ran to her room and slammed the door. Moments later, she came out and headed outside, her pencil in one hand and her notebook paper in the other.

She had given up. Raymond was now free to do as he pleased, but somehow he couldn't, not now. "I guess I'll clean up this mess before I go anywhere," he said to Bruce.

Bruce shrugged. "That's okay. I gotta do some things anyway," he said. "I'll be back after a while."

Raymond had cleaned up the worst of the mess by the time his mother arrived home. He could hear her talking about her job to his father, whose ride had dropped him off right after her. Jackie Lee ran to meet them. All their voices blended in chatter about school and Mrs. Brock's job at a textile mill.

Jackie Lee made a point of ignoring Raymond when she came in moments later. "We're having something very unusual for supper," she said to Vance, who came in behind her and headed for the bathroom.

Vance laughed. "You can bet on it!"

Raymond pretended not to hear either of them. He returned his parents' greetings when they came in, and hurriedly set out the last of the food while everybody washed up. The plates of spaghetti didn't look too bad, if everyone overlooked a few flecks of scorch, he decided; and when his mother sat down at the table, she did not seem to notice. Neither did Mr. Brock, until Jackie Lee slipped into her chair and made a big show of fishing out a black speck.

"Supper's ready," Raymond called down the hall to Vance.

"Ready for what?" asked Vance, running to jerk out his chair and fall into it. The chair gave one loud groan and then splintered and crashed. Vance hit the floor with such a yelp of surprise that Raymond almost laughed out loud.

"This is all Raymond's fault!" Vance bellowed, leaping to his feet. "Jackie Lee told me about that friend of his who was walking this chair all over the kitchen on two legs."

"Raymond!" Mrs. Brock said.

Raymond turned on his brother in a fury as Vance pulled over another chair. "Everything's always my fault. You sit down like a ton of bricks, but it's my fault when the chair falls in!"

At that moment, Mr. Brock made a choking sound and dropped his fork. "What's wrong with this spaghetti?"

Jackie Lee smirked. "Raymond didn't use the store-bought sauce."

Mrs. Brock punched at a large chunk of meat on her plate. "Is this tomorrow's hamburger?"

Jackie Lee nodded. "And I think he used every spice you have." She pointed to the collection of jars that Raymond had neglected to put away.

"Yuck!" said Vance, spitting a mouthful of spaghetti into his napkin and pushing back his plate.

Mrs. Brock took one cautious taste and then reached for the bowl of chopped-up lettuce and tomato. Vance went to the pantry and took down the crackers and peanut butter and returned to the table.

Raymond leaped up from his chair. "Well, my spaghetti is as good as Jackie Lee's concrete meat loaf yesterday and Vance's half-raw baked potatoes the day before that, and nobody made fun of their stuff!" He ran for the back door. He did not cry until he was stretched out across the seat of Old Lizzie.

It was a good while later when Mrs. Brock opened the door on the passenger side. "Aren't you hungry?"

Denying his empty stomach, Raymond shook his head and stared through the windshield. His father had come out to play touch football with Vance and Bunky in the backyard. The three of them were laughing and yelling.

She turned her eyes to where he was looking and slipped onto the seat. "Nobody said you couldn't join them, you know."

Raymond shook his head again.

Mrs. Brock sighed. "All right, don't play!" she said. She paused a moment and then made a fresh start. "So you messed up supper. You'll do better next time." When Raymond still did not answer, she touched his shoulder. "What's bothering you? Still miss your grandfather?"

Raymond nodded. "But it's more than that. I—I have this awful teacher!" he blurted. "She . . ." he faltered. How much could he risk telling? He longed for his parents to be proud of him—the way they were proud of Jackie Lee and Vance. Why did he have to be the one to get into trouble? "She just hates me, that's all."

Mrs. Brock sniffed her disbelief. "Don't be silly. She only met you today."

Raymond decided to let that pass.

"So how could she hate you this soon?"

"Miss Autrey does! You don't know her. That old lady probably hates people she's never even seen."

"What did you do to make her hate you?"

"I—well, nothing."

"So she can't hate you."

Raymond grabbed his mother's arm. "Make them put me in another class! Please!"

Mrs. Brock shook her head. "They wouldn't do it even if I asked. Anyway, you're going to have to learn . . ."

Raymond closed his ears to his mother's lecture on getting along with difficult people. The touch football game was drawing nearer and Jackie Lee and a girl from the other end of the park had joined in. The sight made him feel sorrier for himself than ever. "It's not fair," he said. "Jackie Lee and Vance always have things their way. They have good teachers . . ."—he hesitated—"and they have friends."

His mother's face softened. She rubbed his hair with one hand. "You'll make friends, too. It just takes time, and practice—which is something you didn't get much of when you had your grandfather right next door."

Before she could say more, Raymond heard someone calling his name. He jumped from the truck to see Bruce Manis coming around the corner of the trailer at a gallop, swinging a paper bag in one hand, his blond hair blowing in the breeze.

Mrs. Brock got out of the truck. The football game broke up and everybody gathered around Bruce.

"Can Raymond come spend the night with me?" he panted.

Mr. Brock laughed. "Hey, whoa! Who are you and where do you live, son?"

"This is Bruce Manis, a boy in my class at school," said Raymond.

Jackie Lee elbowed her mother. "He's the one who was here this afternoon."

Bruce smiled at her as if she'd paid him a compliment and then turned back to Mr. Brock. "Yeah, and I live down on the other side of that bridge. You can't see our place from the highway but you just take that dirt road to the left a little piece on the other side of Indian Creek. Can Raymond come?"

Mr. Brock glanced at his wife, who hesitated a moment and then asked, "Your parents know he's coming?"

"Sure!"

Mrs. Brock nodded and Mr. Brock smiled. "Well, why not? Tomorrow's the weekend."

Bruce grinned big enough to show his back molars. "Great!"

"He hasn't had supper," Mrs. Brock reminded her husband.

"He can eat at my place," Bruce offered eagerly. "There'll be plenty."

"It's his turn to do dishes!" said Jackie Lee.

"I'll swap turns with him," Mr. Brock volunteered, giving Raymond a nudge. "You go on and have a good time."

Raymond went.

8

A NIGHT
UNDER THE STARS

The trees along the creek were dark and indistinct and a
few fireflies were beginning to flicker in the grass and
bushes by the time Raymond and Bruce neared the bridge.
Madame Rosanna's house was as dark as if it had been
abandoned.

Ignoring the honking of a passing truck, Bruce stopped
on the middle of the bridge to gaze down into the murky
stream. "I'm fixing up a canoe that I found at a dump," he
said. "When I get it finished, you and me could paddle to
Fuller in it."

Raymond looked at the dark water doubtfully. He could
just hear what his mother would have to say about that
plan. "Maybe," he hedged.

Bruce chose to ignore the lack of enthusiasm. "It'll be
great," he said, moving on. He cut off the highway well
ahead of the dirt road and scooted down a vague path in
the steep embankment. "Shortcut," he called to Raymond
over his shoulder.

At the bottom was a ditch over which a plank had been laid to make a bridge. Bruce walked across it backward, talking all the while. "Pa likely won't be home till late to-night," he said. "Me and you will have the place to our-selves."

They climbed a steep hill and pushed their way through some thick-growing bushes. "There it is," Bruce said as the underbrush at last began to thin out. "That's where I live." He said it with a trace of embarrassment and when Ray-mond leaned around him for a view, he understood why. It was the white-painted school bus visible from Rosanna Garmon's house. Only an electric line connecting to its front, an air conditioner hanging out the back, and makeshift cur-tains over the windows gave it some semblance of a dwelling place. This explained why the boy had thought the Brock trailer was fancy.

Raymond cast about for something complimentary to say, but before he could think of anything, Bruce began backing up. "Hey! Somebody's here!" he whispered.

Raymond looked where he pointed and saw a pink con-vertible parked off to the edge of the clearing. At that moment a slender blond-headed woman in a western shirt and tight jeans walked from behind the bus and headed toward the car, her long blond hair floating behind her as she turned her head this way and that.

Bruce crouched low in the bushes. "Rita?" he whispered.

As though in answer, the woman began calling "Bruce! Bruce! Mama's here!"

Raymond turned to Bruce in surprise. The woman didn't look like anybody's mother, least of all Bruce's. Mothers were supposed to be a little plump like his own mother and their hair wasn't supposed to be long and flowing.

"You ain't my mama!" Bruce muttered under his breath. "A mama don't run off and leave her kid for two whole years!"

The woman reached into the car and pulled out some kind of package. She waved it in the air. "Come on, Brucie. I've got you a present."

Bruce bolted through the bushes. "Let's get out of here. If the old man comes home and finds her, there'll be trouble and I ain't going to be caught in it this time."

Raymond's thoughts must have shown on his face, for when Bruce looked back moments later, he forced a laugh. "Oh, don't worry. He won't kill her. They'll just fight, like they always do. Then Rita'll leave with whatever she can get out of him in the way of money. Then he'll be sore for a month."

Raymond glanced about and changed the subject. "It's nearly dark. Where are we going?"

Bruce laughed softly. This time it sounded real. "To my place. Over at the quarry. I finished fixing it up last week." He paused at the dirt road, looking both ways. "We'll have to be real quiet," he whispered, stepping out on the road. "If you hear anything, jump into that thick grass along the right side and lay low till I give you the word."

He was off and running before Raymond could express the doubts he was feeling, and there seemed no choice but to follow. Their feet made hardly a sound in the soft dirt. Bruce was hugging the paper bag against his chest to quiet its rattle.

Suddenly a thrashing erupted in the underbrush and sent both boys diving into the field on the opposite side of the road. Before they could catch their breath, the barking began. Peeking out from the grass, they saw a vague dark form outlined in the broomsage across the road. A dog.

Bruce cursed. "Rita's going to catch us, all because of a stray mutt!" He found several pebbles and threw them, one after the other. The dog howled as if he were dying before retreating into the shadows.

Bruce leaped up and ran for the road. "Let's get out of here!"

They covered a good distance before they dared slow long enough to look back. The road was empty. "You reckon that was the same dog that was at Rosanna's last week?" Raymond asked when he had caught his breath.

The question seemed to bother Bruce as much as it had Raymond. He stared hard at the road, and finally shook his head. "Nah! This dog was a whole lot littler."

The road narrowed and the trees closed in, but as Raymond's eyes adjusted, he found he could still see well enough. The twittering of birds going to roost on limbs and in bushes all around added a homey note. They passed over a stream and climbed up and around a hill. It was when the road leveled out and the trees thinned that the quarry burst into view again, looming five times as high as it had appeared from a distance. Raymond gazed up, up, up at its vertical sliced-away face, now stained red by the last rays of the dying sun. He caught his breath at how far away the dark-etched trees on its summit appeared.

Bruce looked upward, too, but his face held a kind of excitement. "It ain't that high. I climbed it."

"Why?" Raymond blurted. "Why would you want to do that?" The very thought of climbing to such heights took his breath away.

"I . . ." Bruce began, and then hesitated. "Well, I just did."

The red was already fading from the sky by the time they reached the high chain-link fence that surrounded the quarry area, but here where it was fairly open, there was still enough light for Raymond to make out two big gates, both chained shut, that must have once let traffic in and out. Now pines and grass were taking over the graveled roads that led to them, as well as the grounds beyond. Like decaying remnants from a lost civilization, the remains of pieces of machinery and long-abandoned buildings showed here and there among the trees.

While Bruce took off through the grass alongside the

fence, Raymond paused at a weather-beaten sign warning, NO TRESPASSERS! VIOLATORS WILL BE PROSECUTED. Another sign, equally bent and rusted, informed him that this was the property of the United States Government. Bruce looked back and saw Raymond staring at the signs. "Don't worry. That don't mean nothing. They don't use this place no more. They ain't used it since they got the rock here for that first dam."

"You sure?" Raymond couldn't help asking.

Bruce grunted with impatience. "Look at them pines. Trees that big take a while to grow! Besides, Rosanna told me this place hadn't been used since she was a little girl. Lord knows, *that* was a long time ago." He laughed and disappeared behind a clump of bushes growing against the fence. "Come on. This ain't the best way in, but it's the closest."

Raymond followed and worked his way under the same washed-out place that Bruce used. He was getting to his feet and brushing himself off when a sound seemed to stop his heart in mid-beat. It was only a slight rustling—like someone moving stealthily through the underbrush.

"What was that?" Bruce whispered.

Raymond hunched his shoulders and, half-crouching, pushed back against the fence. Bruce moved back with him and they huddled there for what seemed a long time, turning their heads and straining their eyes for the source of the noise. Then Raymond saw it. Off to the right a bit and just ahead—it was a skunk! He punched Bruce and pointed.

"Just what we need!" Bruce whispered. "Listen, we better run that thing off before it sprays us." Easing to the left what they judged to be a safe distance, they found stones and sticks and began throwing, not actually trying to hit the animal, and shouting at the top of their lungs. For a while it looked as if they were doomed to failure, for the skunk only looked at them and stood its ground. Finally, however, it moved away, following the line of fencing until it reached an unusually large gap, where it exited.

When the skunk had disappeared into the semidarkness, Bruce led the way through the rusting pieces of equipment, piles of stone, and bits of building. Raymond had just spotted what seemed to be a kind of tent made of canvas draped over several ropes stretched between trees when a distant bark caught their attention. The barking almost immediately turned into a *yip-yip-yip* of surprised anguish and then a howl that grew fainter and fainter and then seemed to fade away in the night.

"Guess that skunk found itself something to spray," said Bruce, laughing. He bent over and entered the tent. "Welcome to my place!"

Curious, yet cautious, Raymond stuck his head in. He couldn't see anything, but he could hear Bruce fumbling about in the darkness.

"I thought about setting my tent up inside one of the buildings here," he was saying. "But I was afraid it'd fall in on me."

Raymond privately suspected the tent might do the same. The ropes that supported it seemed none too steady to him and neither did the pine saplings to which they were attached.

The interior of the tent suddenly lit up as Bruce struck a match to a candle stuck in a bottle. By the wavering light, Raymond could see that a mattress covered almost the entire floor of the shelter. In one back corner, there was a rickety chair and in the other, some shelves made of boards supported by bricks. Unopened cans and closed jars of various foods lined the shelves.

"Emergency food and water," Bruce explained.

Raymond fingered a rip in the canvas and looked at the opening in the far end. "Won't you freeze in cold weather?"

Bruce shrugged. "I guess I'll have to fix me a better place before it gets cold."

Raymond decided not to ask how. Instead, he said, "Where did you get all this stuff?"

Bruce looked around, his face glowing with pride. "Garbage dumps mainly. Things people throw out along the road. Brought the heavy stuff over here in the truck." He patted the chair. "It's hard to believe people throw away good things like this, ain't it?" He picked up a bottle. "You want a drink of water?"

Raymond shook his head just as his stomach rumbled. Bruce laughed. "Me, too," he said. "We'll have supper in a minute."

Raymond's eyes returned to the shelf. "Peanut butter and crackers?"

"Nope!" Bruce dumped the contents of the paper bag he had been carrying out onto the mattress. There were wieners, marshmallows, two candy bars, and what looked like a large leather change purse.

Curious, Raymond reached a hand toward the purse, only to have Bruce snatch it away and dump it back into the bag. "We're going to build us a little fire and have a weenie roast," he said. "And if that ain't enough, we'll use some of my emergency grub."

By the time they had cleared a place for a fire and gathered up enough twigs and sticks to feed it, full darkness had fallen. Together they pulled the mattress out to sit on. "We'll just leave it out here and sleep on it tonight," Bruce decided.

Soon they sat side by side, spearing wieners on long sticks and holding them over the fire to roast. Raymond ate his first two before they were warm clear through and found them delicious. They were, in fact, the best he'd ever had. By this time the sky was spangled with stars and a whippoorwill was calling through the darkness.

"How'd you get money for this food?" Raymond asked after his third hot dog had comfortably filled his stomach.

The question dropped into a pool of silence. All Bruce's laughing chatter halted instantly. His face turned grim in the dancing firelight and he rolled the plastic wrappings around the leftover wieners as if to smother them.

"We'll save the candy for breakfast," he said, scooping up the two bars and dropping them into the bag along with the wieners. Ripping open the bag of marshmallows, he took a handful and offered the bag to Raymond.

Raymond couldn't help remembering what had happened at the store the week before. Could Bruce be stealing stuff, as the storekeeper had suspected?

"Heck!" Bruce burst out suddenly. "I guess I can trust you." His voice was muffled from the untoasted marshmallow he had just stuffed into his mouth. "I collect more deposit bottles and aluminum cans and stuff like that than the old man knows about. I take 'em to stores round about. Sometimes I hire Rosie Garmon to take me to the grocery store with the bottles or to the recyling place with cans. I buy a little emergency food, but I save the rest."

Relieved, Raymond lay back on the mattress and looked up at the Big Dipper, which seemed to hang just above his head. "What're you saving for?" he asked idly.

"I'm not sure, exactly," Bruce said slowly. "Something different from the way things are now. That's for sure."

Raymond wanted things to be different, too. He wished saving money would solve his troubles. It would help. It would get new shoes, for example. Far more important, it could replace his grandfather's field glasses. "Here," he pictured himself saying to Grandpa Brock, "take this hundred-dollar bill and buy some better field glasses."

The whippoorwill called out again, and then in the distance there was another sound—a train whistle. Though not nearly as distinct as it had been at Miss Autrey's house that day, it didn't seem too far away. Bruce cocked his head attentively for a few moments and then he threw himself back on the mattress. "I guess I'm saving for when I take off from here."

Raymond raised himself up. "You mean, run away?"

"No, I mean take off. Kids like you run away. Kids like me take off."

Raymond didn't get the difference. Running away was running away, wasn't it?

"You know," Bruce said in a voice so low that Raymond could barely make out the words, "I got this uncle—Rita's brother—he owns a big farm over in Georgia. Melvin Holland's his name. Got horses. Bet he's got twenty of 'em. He's got cows, dogs, chickens, ducks—all kinds of animals. We used to go over there when I was little. One time Uncle Melvin even offered the old man a job. Boy, was I ever wanting him to take it! And he might've, too, if it hadn't been for Rita. She made fun of the whole thing from the word go. Said Melvin's farm was in the sticks, out in the boondocks. Said she wasn't going to turn into a cook and field hand like Aunt Agnes." He was silent for a few moments, and then added, "But I liked it. I liked it a lot."

The train whistle sounded again, closer this time. Raymond yawned. "So you're wanting to live on a farm?" He could understand that.

"Heck no," Bruce replied. "Don't you see? It's the whole thing—having land that's yours forever, and . . ." He rolled over on his stomach. "Why am I trying to tell you about all that? It's a dumb idea anyway. I'm just going to save up and go off on my own when I get a little older."

The train whistle came again, sounding lonely and sad in the night. Bruce turned his head and listened. "If the old man decides to stay on here, the railroad'll be real handy when the time comes. You ever seen the siding they have over that way?"

Raymond yawned again. His eyes were growing heavy. "No."

Bruce wadded up the paper bag and stuffed it under the corner of the mattress. "It ain't far. Trains pull off onto it all the time, waiting for other trains to go through, and . . ."

Raymond was no longer listening. Stretching out, he looked up and up at the darkness that was the quarry wall until it touched the stars, and then he closed his eyes.

9

FLOPPY

Raymond woke to a soft crunching and an unpleasant smell. He rolled over, blinking in the pale light of early morning, saw Bruce's sleeping form, and closed his eyes again. He pressed his nose against the mattress, but sleep would not return and the unpleasant smell would not go away. He tossed about to reposition himself on the lumpy mattress. That didn't help, either. The smell grew stronger by the minute. It was the smell of skunk.

"Sniff-sniff," went something close by. *"Crunch-crunch."*

When Raymond raised himself up on one elbow, looking over Bruce's shoulder, he discovered the source of the odor. It was a dog—the dog from the store, the dog with one ear standing up and one ear flopping down! The animal looked at him, pulled back for a moment, and then eased forward once more. The rattling came again, louder this time, and suddenly Bruce was awake and jumping up.

"Hey!" he bellowed as the dog took off with a paper bag in his mouth.

Raymond sat up. "So that's what that noise was!"

Bruce turned on him, his hair bristling in every direction and his face still dazed with sleep. "Dummy! You mean you watched him steal the bag with my food and my money in it?"

"Don't call me a dummy!" Raymond yelled back at him. "Who left the money in a paper bag to begin with? Anybody with sense would have had it in their pocket! Besides, I didn't know what was going on till just now!"

Bruce let out a sound of disgust and took off after the dog, which was disappearing behind one of the decaying buildings.

For a few minutes Raymond was angry enough to be glad that the dog had gotten the money. He sat down on the mattress and watched with grim satisfaction while the dog evaded every maneuver Bruce could devise.

"Hey!" Bruce called after a while. "I'm sorry, okay? How about helping me out!" He hesitated a moment and then added, "Please."

Raymond relented.

They chased the dog until Raymond was ready to drop, but each time they thought they had him cornered, he found a way to slip away. Finally he found a hole in the fence and clawed his way through, the bag still clutched in his teeth. Since the hole was too small for Raymond and Bruce, they had to go back to the place where they had entered the night before. By the time they were outside, the dog was halfway across a meadow.

"After 'im," Bruce hollered, taking off in pursuit. The dog stayed well ahead of them and when he entered the woods at the far side of the meadow, they lost him completely. They ran on for quite a distance anyway, looking this way and that, turning about at each noise, but the dog was gone.

Finally they came to what appeared to be an old roadbed. Shadowed by trees and carpeted by years' worth of leaves and needles, it cut a corridor through the land. The boys looked both ways and shook their heads. There was nothing to see or hear except the multitude of birds overhead.

"Which way?" Bruce asked.

Raymond hunched his shoulders. "I guess we could split up and check both directions. That skunk spray ought to make him easy to find."

"Good idea," Bruce said, heading off to the right. "I'll go this way. Signal if you find him." His footsteps soon faded.

Hungry and thirsty, Raymond didn't run anymore. The road curved around one small hill after another and he followed it at a walk, looking at the road banks with their mysterious burrowed holes and mossy overhangings. At last the road rose sharply, and just off to the right and up the hill, he spotted something interesting enough to make him speed up: pear trees. There were two of them and they were heavy with fruit.

Forgetting the dog for the time being, he scrambled up the bank and fought his way through the brambles to the nearest of the trees. He chose a pear, wiped it on his shirt, and took a bite. It was neither too soft and mushy nor hard and chewy, he decided. It was just right. He polished it off in hurried bites and picked another just as a breeze stirred the branches around him.

Tap-tap-tap-tap-tap! went a sudden noise.

Startled, he looked around and noticed for the first time a chimney up ahead and off to the left. Composed of uneven stones fitted together like a puzzle, it rose out of a sea of pines and underbrush and supported a multitude of vines.

He took another bite of pear and climbed down the bank just as the tapping sound came again. At a creep, he moved forward until he came to a break in the plant growth where he could see the fallen timbers that had once been a house. Gray and weather-beaten, they lay around the chimney, their rusty tin roofing still attached. Even as he looked, the breeze stirred slightly, and one sheet of the roofing rose and fell with a mournful *tap-tap!*

Raymond cut off the road and edged around the remains of the house, finding remnants of outbuildings scattered behind it. Familiar with his grandfather's homeplace, he could guess the functions of some of the structures by their location, size, and design. He found the well by almost falling in it. After he had stilled his pounding heart, he got on hands and knees to crawl to its edge. His face was reflected back to him against a background of blue sky.

He jumped up at a slight noise and discovered the dog a short distance away. He was lying down by the remains of a paper bag and shredded candy wrappers, licking his chops contentedly.

"You no-good hound!" Raymond muttered, starting toward him. The dog was on his feet at once, slipping into the underbrush and yelping as if he was being killed. Then Raymond spotted the change purse, undamaged except for being a little moist. He picked it up, but before he could open it, he heard Bruce calling him from the road.

"Hey, King Shoes! Where are you?"

"Over here," Raymond replied, waving the purse in the air.

"I didn't find the dog," Bruce yelled, running around the remains of the house. "But guess where this road comes out? Nearly right at the quarry! Only you can't hardly tell it's a road there. Trees and grass grow right over it. . . . Hey!" he said, spotting the change purse at last. "How'd you get that?"

"I just ran down the dog and took it away from him," Raymond replied, stretching the truth a little.

Bruce slapped him on the back. "Good work!" He looked around. "Where's the mutt?"

"Down that way," Raymond said, pointing off in the direction the dog had taken when Bruce ran up. Suddenly

Raymond spotted another building—this one intact—halfway down the hill. Bruce saw it, too, and started toward it at the same moment Raymond did.

The dog reached the building first and stood waiting on its porch, for all the world as if he had come home; but he moved off as they neared and peeked at them from the safety of a clump of blackberry brambles that grew thickly in the area.

"I ain't going to do nothing to you," Bruce told the dog. "I know how it is to be out on your own. You musta been hungry." The dog whined and lay down, stretching his head out on extended paws.

The boys turned back to the building. It was small, too small, Raymond decided, to have been a dwelling. Besides, it had no windows, at least on the two sides they were viewing. Thick blackberry vines on the far side and back discouraged circling around. The land immediately in front of it was level but dropped abruptly past the porch. The building itself was perched on a stone foundation that became higher and higher as it neared the back.

The dog stood and crept closer as they approached the stone porch. He sat down while the boys stared at the wide-board door and argued softly about who should lift the outside latch. At length, it was decided and Bruce lifted the latch while Raymond pushed the door. Both jumped back while it began creaking open with much the same sound as Miss Autrey's front door.

Raymond was the first to step forward and lean into the small dark room. "Looks like some kind of toolshed," he said when his eyes had adjusted enough to make out a small rough table crowded with bits of wire and metal, a rusted hammer, and a vise. Beyond that were several small barrels with corroded bands, a hoe, a wagon wheel, and a length of chain. On the floor to his left were piles of burlap bags.

"I believe you're right," said Bruce. "It used to be a toolshed, all right. But it ain't no more. It's going to be my new place." He looked at Raymond and amended himself. "I mean, *our* place. It'll be our hideout."

Raymond was immediately caught up by the idea. He was seeing all kinds of improvements he could make with only a little wood and a few tools. "We could put some shelves in here, and fix us places to sleep!" he said.

"We've already got a window," said Bruce, running across the room to where bits of daylight showed through between boards that had been nailed over the glass. "And none of the panes are even broken."

"We have pear trees up by the road for food," Raymond remembered, "and a well to get water from."

A snuffling drew their eyes to the door. The dog had gotten enough courage to stick his nose inside. Bruce grunted. "What you looking at, Flop Ear? I don't have no more candy and wieners if that's what you're after, and you stink too bad to come in."

The dog whined and pulled back a bit.

Raymond looked at the dog. The animal returned his gaze, head cocked to one side. His large eyes, so much like Butch's, were brown and liquid. His sides were sunken in even after he'd devoured the wieners and candy. "You know, we could use a watchdog," Raymond heard himself saying. He wondered even as he said it to which one of them the dog would really belong. Of course, if he were his dog, there would be the problem of getting his parents' permission. "When the stink wears off of him, he'd be a good watchdog," Raymond repeated.

Bruce grunted. "Yeah, he could watch himself eat up all our emergency grub," he said, but he didn't sound as if he meant it. After a few moments he added, "You know, tomato juice is supposed to take skunk stink off, and the old man has plenty of that at the house."

Raymond stepped outside and got as close to the dog as

the wary animal would allow. "He barked at us last night," he said, getting down on one knee and whistling softly. The dog gave one tentative wag with his tail. It was like a question.

"Yeah, well," Bruce relented, squatting beside Raymond. "I guess we wouldn't have found this place without old Floppy." He held out his hand and eased forward, clicking his tongue. The dog wagged his tail and grinned a doggy grin, but it was a few minutes before Bruce was able to get his hands on the animal and really pet him. "I'm going to stink to high heaven," he said, wrinkling his nose. The chase through the woods forgiven, the dog was beside himself with joy. He could hardly lick the two boys enough. His tail never stopped wagging, and when they went back inside the building, he followed. He even discovered the trapdoor.

It was just inside the front door and off to the left. Floppy uncovered it when he began sniffing and scratching in the pile of burlap bags.

"Wow!" said Raymond, taking hold of the strap and lifting. It was heavier than he expected and when he pushed the door back, it fell heavily against the wall. Dust rose like a cloud and sifted slowly on a steep descending stairway lit by a greenish light.

Both boys fell back. "Reckon where that light's coming from?" whispered Bruce.

Raymond shrugged. Then he eased forward, lay down, and leaned his head slowly into the opening. His eyes followed the stairs to a tablelike landing next to a stone wall and on down to a brick floor. High in the back wall was a window with leaves covering its outside.

"We got us a cellar with an escape hatch," said Bruce, who had lain down beside him. "You wanna go down and look around?"

Bruce went first, placing one foot at a time on the first several steps until he was sure they would hold his weight.

Raymond followed while Floppy whined and paced the floor above.

Step by step, they descended into the stone-walled, brick-floored room. They turned about in the green light with a mixture of relief and disappointment. There was only an old dusty basket, several cobwebbed boards, and a few farm implements. As they squatted to examine these, Floppy let out a mournful howl that set them both to laughing.

When they were back upstairs a few minutes later, Floppy danced about them as if they had been gone for a month. The dog was their shadow while they closed the trapdoor and concealed it with the burlap bags, then latched the door to the building.

"You want me to help you bring all your stuff over here before I go home?" Raymond offered as they stopped to gather pears for breakfast.

Bruce instantly agreed it was a good idea and all the way to the quarry road they planned what they would take and what they could do to the hideout that day. But they never had a chance to carry out any of the plans, for as they neared the quarry, Peavy Manis drove up.

"Where you been!" he called to Bruce with hardly a nod for Raymond. "I've been looking for you all over the place. You and me got a job over in Chatsworth that'll take us at least two days to finish. Git in here, and let's go."

Bruce hesitated only a moment before vaulting into the back. As the truck rolled away, Floppy took off after it, whining loudly. Then just as the truck started downhill, he gave a mighty leap that took him into the truck bed with Bruce.

Bruce's smile was so big, his face seemed to glow. He grabbed the dog in such a tight embrace that Floppy's eyes appeared to bulge. "Me and Floppy'll see you later, Raymond," he yelled as the truck disappeared from sight.

Now Raymond knew whose dog he was.

10

BACK TO SCHOOL

Raymond strained for a view of the Manis place when his family passed by on their way to church Sunday morning. However, he could not even see the bus, much less anything else. He decided against the idea of going to the hideout alone. So he stayed home and watched boring television shows on the black-and-white set Mr. Brock had bought to replace the one he could not fix. He also spent a little time looking at field glasses in a mail-order catalogue. They were expensive. But no matter what else he was doing, the dread of returning to school and facing Miss Autrey after what happened Friday was in the back of his mind like a black cloud.

All too soon it was Monday morning; his parents had left for work, and he was hunting for the notebook paper and pencils his mother had given him the week before. He had already searched the floor of the closet and under the chest of drawers—two of his favorite places to stash things in a hurry—and had found his new notebook binder, but he could find no supplies to go with it.

"Aw, come on, Vance," he begged when his brother swept into the room to grab up his things. "Let me borrow some of your paper and a pencil until . . ."

Vance was unsympathetic. "No way."

"Just for today!"

"Tough luck!" Vance called over his shoulder. "You ought to keep up with your own stuff for a change."

Raymond headed for his sister's room. He heard her hair-dryer roaring in the bathroom and decided not to ask her permission this one time. He knew exactly where neat and responsible Jackie Lee kept her hoard of notebook paper. He would repay her when he found his.

Eyes on the doorway, Raymond hastily cracked the top drawer of her desk and swept in his hand. Sure enough, he found pencils and also a red felt-tip like Wade's, which would be perfect for writing his name on his notebook. Easing open the second drawer, he grabbed a handful of paper and shoved it into his waiting notebook.

On the bus a short time later, Henrietta plopped down beside him. "Chester and I went to visit my father this weekend," she announced.

Raymond nodded. Now that he thought of it, he hadn't seen her since Friday.

"He bought some new curtains for my bedroom and a scratching post for Chester and he helped me write my essay for Miss Autrey."

"Uh-oh," said Raymond, thinking of the essay for the first time since Friday. He was going to be in enough trouble already without failing to do his assignment. He jerked a sheet of paper from his notebook. He allowed himself several seconds of thought and then began scribbling in his biggest handwriting while Henrietta leaned over him, alternately reprimanding him for not having done his assignment earlier and advising him on how to improve it. He ignored her on both counts and kept writing.

"If you hadn't gone off with that Manis boy on Friday,

you'd have done it already," she said. "Bruce Manis is nothing but trouble. Emily Edwards told me he had to go to the office all the time last year. You'd better stay away from him."

Raymond made no answer. Several children seated immediately around him were from Miss Autrey's class, too. One of them, a scrawny boy called Little A because he was unfortunate enough to share the name Al with a heavyset boy whom the kids called Big A, was practically falling out of his seat to hear what was going on.

Henrietta persisted. "Where did you and Bruce go anyway?"

Raymond chewed on his eraser for a moment and began writing again.

Henrietta refused to give up. "I figure he must live somewhere over there close to Madame Rosanna."

Feeling a loyalty he didn't fully understand, Raymond wasn't about to tell her Bruce lived in the bus and risk her comments on that. He finished filling the last line on the page, wrote "the end," folded the page lengthwise, and stuck it into the back of his notebook. Not a moment too soon either, for the bus was already pulling into the drive at Valley Point School.

Miss Autrey was waiting when he stepped off the bus. Her big hand closed over his arm like a vise. "I want to see you in private, young man," she said, rushing him across the sidewalk and up the steps. "And I think you know what about!"

Yes, Raymond knew. How could he explain that he had not been trying to get the cap? What he had been trying to get would be equally bad in her eyes, if she even believed him.

"Never," she said a few minutes later in the echoing silence of her room, "never in twenty-eight years of teaching have I permitted disrespect or disobedience." From the corner of his eye, Raymond glimpsed several familiar faces at the open windows. He recognized Justine and Big A.

"And I don't intend to start permitting it now," she continued. "Do you understand?"

Raymond backed away from the big finger that the woman jabbed at him. "But I didn't—"

"Do you understand?"

"Yes, sir," Raymond muttered. There were titters from the window and then a rustling in the shrubbery, but by the time Miss Autrey turned to look, there was no one to see.

"Sir?" she said, swinging back around and drawing herself up indignantly. She looked seven feet tall. "*Sir?* Do I look like a man?"

"N-no, sir, I mean, no, ma'am!"

She glared down at him for a long moment. Squeals and laughter from the playground seemed directed toward him.

Miss Autrey cleared her throat. "Do you have anything to say for yourself?"

Raymond tried to think of something she would accept as an excuse, but could not. Finally he only shook his head.

"When I told you to stop running in the hall Friday, I wasn't talking just to hear myself talk."

"No, ma'am."

"And you'd better not ever let anything like that happen again."

"Yes, ma'am."

"And as for trying to get into my desk, well, nothing like that had better happen again, either."

"Yes, ma'am."

She stepped behind her desk, shifted tilting stacks of books, and set down her purse. It clanked. She stared out the window for several moments before turning back to Raymond. "Starting tomorrow, you will report to my room each morning as soon as you get off the bus. You will"—

she looked around, frowning—"do clean-up jobs—erase and wash chalkboards, sweep, dust, and that kind of thing."

"Yes, ma'am," Raymond said again, staring at a spiderweb in the right-hand corner of the room. It had been there so long that a large amount of droppings had collected beneath it.

The bell rang and by the time the students began to pour in a few minutes later, Raymond was already at his desk, busily decorating his notebook with Jackie Lee's pen.

The morning passed in a blur of checking out textbooks, taking up information cards, enrolling students who had not shown up for the first day of school, and asking after those such as Bruce who were absent.

It was afternoon and everyone was drained by the day and by the humid heat when Miss Autrey thought of the essays she had assigned. "I need someone to take up papers," she said, looking around the room as if everyone wanted the job. However, there was only one eager hand-waving volunteer—Justine Weaver. Miss Autrey's eyes skimmed right over the girl and stopped on Little A. "Al Goforth," she said.

Raymond wasn't the only one who sniggered when Justine let out a dramatic groan of disappointment, but he seemed to be the only one she heard. She glared at him with pure hatred.

"Make sure you have folded your papers once," Miss Autrey was saying, holding up a sample paper correctly folded, "and write your name and today's date right up here at the top."

"I already did, Miss Autrey," Justine said, making a face toward Raymond, who was pulling his notebook from beneath his seat. Several papers came out with it and joined other litter on the floor. Feeling the girl's eyes on him, Raymond grabbed the folded paper from the back of his notebook and scrawled his name and the date in the proper place just as Little A reached him. Raymond handed over his essay and shot Justine a triumphant look, only to find her gaze directed at the floor. Looking down, he saw that one of the scraps of paper had a red drawing on it. A drawing of a devil. Justine smiled and shot up her hand even as Raymond grabbed for the paper.

"Miss Autrey, Raymond has a bad picture," she said.

"Blabbermouth!" Raymond hissed at her as Miss Autrey lumbered toward him. Justine knew Bruce was the one who had drawn it. She had even tried to tell on him for it.

Raymond turned to face his teacher. "This isn't mine," he said, wadding the picture into a hard ball.

Miss Autrey held out her hand. "Then you certainly won't mind showing it to me."

Raymond stubbornly clung to the drawing for a moment before surrendering it. "It's not mine," he said again.

While all the students strained for a glimpse, Miss Autrey smoothed the wrinkles in the paper. "Then whose is it? Who's the artist?"

Raymond hesitated and then jerked his head toward Justine. "She knows—I mean, she knows I didn't do it."

Justine glanced toward Bruce's desk for just a moment and then threw up her chin defiantly. "Raymond did it."

Raymond jumped up. "Liar! You know that's not mine!"

"Sit down," Miss Autrey ordered in a cold voice. Her eyes dropped to Jackie Lee's red pen on his desk. It was the final evidence against him. "So whose is it, if it's not yours?"

There was absolutely nothing Raymond could say. If Bruce had been present, he probably would have confessed. As it was, Raymond hated to tell on him and get him in trouble. Besides, he had no evidence, and Miss Autrey certainly was not going to take his word without any proof.

"You may stay in at recess tomorrow and practice your

artwork," Miss Autrey said before heading back to her desk and taking the essays from Little A. She glanced at her watch. "We'll have time for several of you to read your essays."

There were groans from everyone except Justine. Miss Autrey ignored her raised hand until it became obvious no one else was going to volunteer. Finally she nodded at the girl and shuffled through the essays until she found one several pages thick and tied at one corner with a pink ribbon.

"That's mine," Justine said, walking proudly to the front. " 'What I Did This Summer,' " she read, smiling around at the class as if she had created the most original title in the world. " 'One of my most favorite experiences was going to visit my grandmother who has a lot of money and a great big house right on the beach in Florida.' "

"Oh, no," Wade muttered. "We have to hear about Grandma Moneybags again!"

Raymond would have laughed along with everyone else if he hadn't been so petrified at the prospect of getting up in front of the class himself. His shyness was never worse than when he had to stand in front of a large group all staring directly at him.

Miss Autrey restored order and jerked her head at Justine to resume reading. However, the class continued rolling their eyes at each other at every opportunity, and several of the braver ones yawned openly as Justine read about the wonders of swimming in the ocean and gathering seashells and sand dollars. By the time she got to her two weeks at Girl Scout camp, the book-reading club she had joined at the library, and the cross-stitched pillow cover she had made, Wade was pretending to be asleep.

" '. . . and from my baby-sitting I earned a total of thirty-five dollars and fifty cents,' " she finally read. " 'I am going to spend it all on Christmas gifts for people I like such as my grandma in Florida, my Girl Scout leader, and my teacher.' " Justine smiled at Miss Autrey. " 'The end.' "

"Thank you," said Miss Autrey. "Next?" She looked around the room and, seeing no hands, pulled a paper from the stack. "Sandra Lowery."

Sandra's essay was a mercifully short one on the wonders of training a parakeet to eat out of your hand and say "Jimmy is a good boy." Wade's was an only slightly longer paper about building a model airplane. Henrietta's was next. The class perked up when she told them about how her father was the first one to arrive on the scene of an automobile accident and how he saved one of the victims by using CPR.

The clock hands inched closer and closer to three o'clock. Raymond was beginning to feel sure he would escape reading when Miss Autrey pulled out a paper and called his name.

"One page," she said. "We should have time for this."

Numbly, Raymond slid from his desk and walked the thousand miles to the front, where Miss Autrey waited with his paper about how he had gone for long walks with his grandfather, and the time they had seen a hawk catch and pluck a blue jay. Could he possibly read that with everyone staring at him?

He took the paper and walked another thousand miles to the place off to the side of the teacher's desk where Miss Autrey had decreed they must stand. He stared at the floor, unable for a few minutes to look out at the sea of faces in front of him. They were so quiet that he could hear every sound in the hallway, and the school buses lining up outside. His heart pounded. His breath was tight. He stole a glance at the clock. Surely the bell would ring and save him. It didn't.

Miss Autrey cleared her throat. "Well, are you going to read?"

Somehow he found the strength to force his shaking hands to open the folded paper, but it was several seconds before he could make himself focus on the words before him and realize with horror what they said:

" 'The midsummer-night sky was filled with a thousand stars and reflected silver off Angelique's golden blond hair and Kevin's handsome profile. . . .' "

11

MONEY

"And you read it?" Bruce said to Raymond, dropping his side of the car seat they were half-carrying, half-dragging down the quarry road. "You actually read all that garbage from your sister's romance story!"

Raymond blushed at the memory. It had been three days, but none of the embarrassment had faded. "Just the first paragraph. Then the bell rang."

Convulsed with laughter, Bruce threw himself down on the seat and pounded the ragged upholstery until dust rose in clouds. "King Shoes, I ain't believing you! Now I wish I hadn't missed school these three days."

"That's not the worst!" Raymond said, dropping down on the small amount of seat left after Floppy had taken his place next to Bruce. "Jackie Lee heard them laughing about it on the bus and she got mad as blazes. She told Mom and Dad and they got mad, too." He shook his head miserably as Bruce continued to laugh. "It's not funny. Anyway, not to me."

Bruce tried to straighten his face. "Have your folks found out about the field glasses yet?"

"Not yet. But they will."

There was a long silence during which Bruce took to buckling and unbuckling Floppy's ratty-looking collar. He had found it along with a bunch of stuff for the hideout somewhere in Chatsworth. "I been thinking," he said at last. "I might find you some field glasses at one of the flea markets the old man goes to. Sometimes you can find stuff like that for nearly nothing. That's how I got my good knife."

Raymond brightened for a moment and then shook his head. "You'd never find any exactly like Grandpa Brock's. And if you did, I couldn't pay for them."

"Well," Bruce said at last, "look at it this way, your folks may never find out."

Raymond grunted his disbelief. "Sure! Fat chance."

"And as for school," Bruce went on, returning to their earlier topic, "what happens there ain't important no way."

Raymond felt like saying that to him it was, but he didn't think Bruce would understand, so he kept silent.

"You'll forget all that when I show you what all I got for the hideout," Bruce went on, jumping up and starting a game of tag with Floppy. He jumped the ditch and shinnied up a tree while Floppy circled and barked on the ground below. "Did I tell you about Floppy digging up that mole?"

"Only two times," Raymond answered.

Bruce laughed and jumped down beside his dog. "He got it pretty as you please! Didn't you, boy?"

Floppy barked his agreement. His coat was shiny from the bath Bruce had given him. The tomato juice seemed to have worked, for there was very little of the skunk stench left on him.

"He's a real hunter, too," Bruce bragged. "He goes after rabbits and you ought to see him tree squirrels. Even the old man had to brag about him today at Messer's store. Telling what all he's caught. Messer said Junior Elrod might want to buy him. But he ain't buying my dog, 'cause I ain't selling." Bruce rubbed Floppy's head. "He sure is one smart dog. Like today. If it hadn't been for him, I wouldn't have found this car seat."

"You told me," Raymond replied, but it did no good. Bruce told him again anyway.

"He barked like crazy when that truck stopped to throw it and all the rest of that garbage out on the side of the road a while ago. Can you believe someone'd dump a good seat like this 'un?"

Raymond looked down at a rip where cotton stuffing was showing and grunted something that passed for agreement.

The boys picked up the car seat and moved on down the road. It seemed to grow heavier and heavier and the sun hotter and hotter with each passing moment. "We're not ever going to get this thing to that shack," Raymond grumbled when they stopped for their next breather. "It's too heavy and too far. Why didn't you wait and haul it over there in the truck or car?" Then he remembered that several bushes and a bunch of good-sized pines blocked the road, and he amended himself. "I mean, as far as where the road cuts off of this one."

Bruce mopped his face. "Couldn't. The old man left in the truck and he's got the motor tore out of the Camaro. But don't worry, I've got a wagon we're gonna use. It's hid in the woods up here a little piece ahead."

"A wagon?" Raymond said. "A little kid's wagon?"

"It's big enough," Bruce assured him. "When I picked it up, I had in mind using the wheels for something else and I knew if I didn't hide it, the old man would have it sold like everything else he gets his hands on. Let's go."

They heaved up the seat once more and trudged on. Floppy trotted off a short distance ahead, sprinkling bushes and sniffing at the breeze. Sometimes he acted as if he wanted to cut off the road and pursue some interesting scent but could not quite bring himself to leave Bruce.

At last in the shade of an overhanging tree, Bruce dropped his side of the seat and announced, "The wagon's right over there."

Raymond fell down on the car seat in utter exhaustion. He wished now he had taken time to get more of a snack before he left the trailer park with Bruce. He rolled over, enjoying the shade on his hot face. But before he had really cooled, Bruce was back with the wagon in tow.

"Now we're gonna get somewhere!" he said.

Raymond sat up, looking at the wagon. Its wheels were crooked and wobbled as they rolled and only bits of the original red paint clung to the body. "You really think that thing will hold up this much weight?" he asked.

Bruce pulled the wagon up next to the seat. "Sure! Let's load up."

He was right. With Bruce pulling and Raymond holding the seat steady, the wagon managed to roll.

The quarry finally came into sight, looking as majestic as ever. Its sheer face of blue-gray stone glinted in the sunshine and dwarfed the pines, piles of rubble, and fencing at its base. Raymond looked at it and was amazed once more that Bruce had climbed it. He wondered again why he would want to.

A few hundred yards short of the gate, the road to the hideout cut off to the right, obviously unused for years. Even beyond the bushes and trees at its beginning, the road was barely noticeable in the sea of grass across which it wound. At the place where it entered the woods on the far side, there was barely a gap in the trees. Probably no one would notice the road unless they knew.

Bruce stopped a good distance short of the cutoff. "We're going to take the seat up here," he said, jerking his head to the steep bank on the right, "and then we'll cut across the field and get on the road."

Raymond stared at the high bank in disbelief. "Why should we try to drag this thing up there when we can do it so much easier down there at the road?"

"Simple," Bruce said. "If we drag it through the weeds there, we're gonna make a trail."

"So?"

"So anybody that comes along will see that somebody has been there. I want to keep this our secret."

"You don't think we'll make marks on this dirt bank?" Raymond argued. "Heavy as this thing is? It's gonna drag."

"Yeah, but in dirt we can wipe over tracks and hide them easy as pie." Without waiting for consent, Bruce pushed the car seat off the wagon and scrambled up the bank, pulling the wagon behind him. Then, just as Floppy began to complain, he jumped back down, leaving the wagon behind. Inspecting the marks he'd left, he made several swipes with his hand. "See, exactly like it was. Okay, let's get the seat into the ditch and stand it on end."

Floppy didn't like the looks of things any more than Raymond did. He whined as the boys tugged the car seat into place. He complained louder than ever when Bruce climbed up the bank and took hold of the top end.

"Hush, Floppy," Bruce ordered, looking at the dog affectionately. "You're nothing but a big crybaby." He turned to Raymond. "You push and I'll pull."

Raymond obeyed. They panted and grunted and strained while Floppy sat on his haunches, turned his nose skyward, and howled. The seat seemed to weigh a ton but finally they inched it upward. It was almost on a level with Raymond's shoulder when Floppy gave one final cry and made a lunge for the bank.

"What . . ." Raymond began as the dog clawed his way past him, bringing down a shower of dirt.

"No, Floppy!" Bruce yelled, but it was too late. The dog slipped and fell against Raymond's leg, throwing him off balance. Raymond grabbed for a new hold on the tilting seat and heard the upholstery rip, then something was fluttering downward around his head.

"Hold on!" Bruce yelled.

"Can't!" Raymond gasped. Leaping to one side, he fell over Floppy and watched helplessly as the seat crashed, bounced, and landed upside down. Then he saw somethng else. Something green. Money!

Bruce saw it, too. "Hey!" he yelled, leaping down and grabbing bills with both hands. "We're rich!"

Raymond jumped into the ditch beside him, picking up money as fast as he could. When the ground was clean, they ran their hands through the rips in the upholstery, finding several more bills, a nearly empty package of cigarettes, and a screwdriver.

"Heck!" Bruce said a few minutes later when they were sure there was no more money to be found. "Mine are all ones." He smoothed the wrinkles in his bills and stacked them. "Twelve dollars. How much you got?"

"A five and four ones," Raymond said. "Nine dollars. You got more."

Bruce looked at his money and then at Raymond's. He frowned. "I guess we could split fifty-fifty."

Raymond remembered the uncle with the horses and the money Bruce was saving to go there. He shook his head. "You keep yours and I'll keep mine."

Bruce grinned and shoved his money into his pocket. " 'S a deal!"

"How do you reckon this money got there?" Raymond said, kicking the car seat.

Bruce shrugged. "Someone musta hid it and forgot it."

"Probably a drunk," Raymond suggested. "Or maybe the person that hid it died."

"Either way, we didn't steal it. Those people dumped it out with all the rest of that garbage. It's ours now." Bruce's face lit up. "Hey! If I ever do find field glasses at a flea market, you have money to pay for them now."

"Yeah," Raymond said, looking at the money with a new interest. Then his face fell. "But I'll need forty more dollars if I have to order them from a catalogue."

"So, we'll earn more," said Bruce. "You can save your money with mine."

Before Raymond could answer, Bruce began tugging the car seat from the ditch. "I guess you're right about this bank," he admitted. "I reckon we'd better use the road. But just for today, while we get all our stuff hauled over there. What we're gonna have to do is find us some different ways of getting there so we don't use the same route all the time." He dropped his voice. "That way, if anybody watches us, they won't be able to figure out where we're going." He picked up the package of cigarettes. "You want these?"

Raymond shook his head, remembering his grandfather's long battle with giving up chewing tobacco. "I don't want rotten lungs myself. Do you smoke?"

"Oh, I have—two or three times." Bruce wadded the package and threw it back in the ditch. "But I decided I ain't going to waste my money on stuff like that."

The sun was behind a cloud when they approached the hideout. The small building looked like a gray ghost through the swaying pines, and the blackberries and kudzu seemed to press closer than ever. Floppy trotted ahead, nose to the ground, and waited on the porch as though welcoming them home when Raymond and Bruce arrived with the car seat.

"Welcome to the hideout," said Bruce, unlatching the door.

They lugged the car seat inside and fell down on it.

"This can't really be ours," Raymond said a few minutes later. "I mean, this isn't like a car seat that somebody throws away. Land has to *belong* to somebody."

"It does," Bruce replied, "the paper mill. I asked the old man about it and he says that's who owns it. They're trying to buy up all the land around here. That's why there are so many houses falling in. They don't care about houses. All they care about is how many trees they can get off the land."

Raymond had to admit the paper mill probably didn't care about the building. The mill his father had worked for in Tennessee wouldn't have cared. It seemed sad to him that this place where a family had once lived would someday be only forest waiting to be cut down. He wondered what would happen to the pear trees.

"Well," Bruce said, interrupting his thoughts, "are we going to get the rest of the stuff over here today?"

The next two trips went faster. They hauled all the jars and cans of food in one load, and in the next, went to the bus and loaded up the stuff Bruce was so proud of: a hammock, a broom, some planks, and a few tools. By the time they moved all this in, Raymond realized that it was getting too late for another trip.

"I gotta go," he said.

"Wait," answered Bruce from a back corner where he was tying a length of twine to the neck of a lidded jar. "Here, roll up your money and tie it with this string," he instructed. "Then put it in here with mine."

Raymond looked at the jar, puzzled. "Why?"

"So we can hide it, remember."

Raymond hesitated for a moment. He liked the feel of the money in his pocket. But on the other hand, it would be difficult to explain to his parents if it should be discovered. He shrugged and tied up his money.

"Let's go," said Bruce when the money was in the jar. "This won't take long."

Raymond did not ask where they were going until he saw the quarry wall looming ahead and, when he did, Bruce did not really answer except to smile. They entered by their usual route—the washed-out place under the fence—and made their way through the trees, around the rickety buildings, and past the tattered tent. The mattress still lay outside where they had left it, somewhat worse for wear and because of the rain they'd had one night. Bruce stopped just short of the gravel slides piled against the quarry wall and began tying the twine holding the jar to his belt loops.

"What are you doing?" Raymond asked.

Bruce made one final knot and left the jar dangling at his left hip. "See that hole up there," he said, pointing up the wall. "Nearly at the top?"

Raymond spotted the opening in the rock that Bruce must mean and nodded.

"That's it. That's the place I found to hide my money. Good place, ain't it?"

Raymond's stomach flip-flopped at the thought of it. "I guess nobody'd ever find it there," he gulped.

Bruce grinned proudly. "That's why I picked it. You keep Floppy calm while I put it up there."

Raymond pulled the dog down beside him while Bruce kicked off his shoes and scrambled up the rock slide. Floppy trembled and whined, seemingly sharing all Raymond's apprehension.

At the point where the pile of rubble met the wall, Bruce stopped. "Hey!" he yelled. "I forgot to tell you, I can't climb down. It's too steep. I have to go all the way to the top and go down the mountainside. Meet me at the big gate with my shoes."

Raymond nodded. His throat felt too dry for talk. Bruce began climbing. Seemingly without fear, he reached with first one hand and then the other, moving his feet in rhythm. He never stopped, never hesitated, never searched for the next footing, the next ledge to grasp. He seemed to know them all by heart.

"Hush, Floppy," Raymond whispered to the dog that was whining and trembling. "He'll be all right." He wished he could believe it. Raymond dropped his eyes and did not allow himself to look again until he heard Bruce's shout thin and high above him. When he looked, he saw the boy waving triumphantly and pointing to the dark crevice in the rock. Then he was moving upward once again.

Raymond did not head for the gate until he saw Bruce pull himself over the top. Then he ran. His legs felt as weak and his head as light as if he had climbed the quarry wall himself.

"All right, Floppy, all right!" Bruce said some minutes later when he arrived. "You don't have to lick me to death!" He pulled on his shoes and beckoned to Raymond, who lay on the grass. "You seen where I put the money, didn't you?"

Rayond pulled himself to his feet and started toward home. "Yeah."

"So if you needed to get your part, you could."

"Sure," Raymond lied. He knew that he would never, ever need money badly enough to make that climb.

They reached the cutoff to the hideout and Bruce pulled the wagon from the grass where he had concealed it earlier. "But you can't tell anybody else where it is."

"I wouldn't do that," Raymond said. He felt like adding that he couldn't think of anybody he would want to get killed, but he didn't. He only glanced at the sun hanging low in the sky and broke into a run. "Time to get home," he called over his shoulder.

"You want to work on the hideout tomorrow?" Bruce yelled after him.

"Sure. Okay," Raymond answered. Looking back, he saw Bruce standing by Floppy, one hand on the dog's head, the other raised in a parting wave, and a great big grin on his face. For the first time, Raymond began to see Bruce as a friend.

12

HENRIETTA
TAKES CHARGE

Bruce and Raymond did not meet the next day. A steady rain set in that night and wiped out Friday afternoon. Then on the weekend when the weather finally cleared, Bruce had to help his father with a house-painting job. Raymond used those days to draw up elaborate plans for shelves and tables and stools.

Unfortunately, school did not get any better. In fact, it seemed to get worse. Nothing Raymond did pleased Miss Autrey, and unless he counted Henrietta—which he wasn't sure he did—he still had no real friends other than Bruce. The only bright spot was that his week of clean-up duties was over.

Monday morning, Raymond arrived in Miss Autrey's room to find the place in more disarray than usual. The counter under the bulletin board was filled edge to edge with bottles and jars; there were big poster boards with charts and diagrams on them, and wooden boards laced with wires, light bulbs, and flashlight batteries. Some had faded prize ribbons attached to them. Miss Autrey hovered over them all like a mother hen.

"Science projects!" Wade whispered. "That big one over there with all the wires and switches was my big brother's. It got first prize."

"Ugh!" said Bruce, who, as usual, had entered the room several minutes after the bell. "My old man and me haul better stuff than that off to the dump every day!"

Several kids giggled and Miss Autrey glowered. "Bruce, did you bring that excuse for being absent three days last week?" she asked. She had been asking for it every day and making it clear she did not believe he had been sick as he claimed.

Bruce grinned and produced a wrinkled piece of paper. "We going to have Phys Ed today?" he asked, bringing up one of Miss Autrey's least favorite subjects. She did not approve of physical education taking away part of her class time and she did not approve of the young newly hired Phys Ed teacher with her modern ideas about teaching.

Miss Autrey threw Bruce's excuse down on the desk. "Have a seat."

"Miss Autrey, I love your science projects," said Justine, "and I can't stand Phys Ed."

"It's not time for science fair," ventured a skinny boy with thick glasses.

Miss Autrey looked up from her roll book. "My class does several projects during the year," she informed the boy. "Of course, this year with *Phys Ed* and all the other frills . . ." Her voice trailed off.

As soon as she could get lunch-money collection and absentee lists out of the way, Miss Autrey began telling them about the dusty collection on the counter, lingering especially on the ones that had ribbons attached.

"Why don't she tell us what she wants us to do and shut up," hissed Bruce into Raymond's ear.

Raymond silently agreed. He already knew what his project would be: a drawing of the solar system. He could do that in thirty minutes easily because he still remembered all the details from doing it in fourth grade.

"No drawings of the solar system, please," Miss Autrey said, as though reading his mind. "Anybody can do that. I expect better of my students."

Raymond groaned inwardly and turned his mind to other things. He wondered whether Bruce would be able to go to the hideout this afternoon. Maybe they could hang the hammock and start building shelves. Perhaps they'd have time to hunt for cans. He wondered how many hundreds of cans it would take to pay for field glasses.

"A project on electricity wouldn't be bad," Miss Autrey was saying, picking up one of the boards with a light bulb attached.

"Yeah," Bruce whispered against Raymond's neck. "We could build an electric chair and fry the old bat."

"Perhaps you'd like to stand and tell all of us what is so hilarious, Raymond Brock," Miss Autrey said, slamming the board down on the counter so hard that one of the projects on the edge teetered precariously. Jumping up to save it, Big A knocked over two other projects.

"Nothing," Raymond answered, leaning forward away from Bruce's voice.

The viewing of the relics finally ended and Miss Autrey began passing out photocopied pages. There was a chorus of moans as the class looked over the list. ". . . more than thirty topics here, class," she was saying, "and you don't have to use any of these if you can think of a better one."

As if anyone would dare suggest they had a better idea than she did, thought Raymond.

"I believe I'll do mine on number fourteen: 'maggots,' " Bruce drawled. A nervous titter ran around the class.

"For the benefit of those who can't read, students," said

Miss Autrey, "number fourteen says 'magnets.'" She slapped a sheet down on Raymond's desk.

Raymond leapfrogged down the list. "Motors," he read. Bor-ing. "Effect of light on plants." He rolled his eyes and sank down in his desk. "Tree rings," "pond water," "osmosis," he murmured.

"For this first project, we will work in groups," Miss Autrey went on. "No more than three on a team, please."

A hubbub broke out in the room at this bit of information. All the boys competed to get Wade on their team, while all the girls vied for a blond-headed girl named Marlene.

Bruce leaned forward. "Me and you'll work together," he said. "Which project do you want?"

"How about tree rings?" said Raymond, remembering some tree stumps near the quarry.

Bruce shrugged. "Fine with me."

"Order!" said Miss Autrey. "The class will come to order."

"Me and Wade are a team," said Big A. "We're gonna build a model of a volcano."

"No fair!" cried a boy named Steve. "Wade and me already planned to work together!"

"Wade and I," Miss Autrey corrected, picking up her notebook and pulling a pencil from behind her ear. "All right. Wade, Albert, and Steve are working on a volcano. Yes, Justine?"

"Pam and I are going to make a pressed-flower collection."

"Me and Raymond are gonna do tree rings," said Bruce.

Henrietta swung around in her desk. "Hey! Tree rings was mine!"

"Raymond, Bruce, and Henrietta—tree rings," decreed Miss Autrey. "Next?"

"Not with them!" said Henrietta. "I was going to work with Doylene Hill."

"Sorry, only three to a team," said Miss Autrey. "Yes, Ella Jo?"

"But . . ." Henrietta said, and then was drowned out by other voices.

A few minutes later as Miss Autrey was getting down the last of the project groups, Miss Ellis arrived, wearing shorts and a T-shirt. The woman cleared her throat. "Miss Autrey."

Miss Autrey did not turn. "Sandra Lowery, Marlene Shaw, and Edna Lowe. Pond water," she said, writing in her notebook. "And Chuck Morgan and Rickey Granger. Rock collection." She frowned and seemed to deliberately look everywhere in the room except at the doorway. "Anyone else?"

Miss Ellis took several steps into the room. Her round face had grown pink. "Miss Autrey, remember the schedule I gave you? It's time for your class to have Phys Ed. I let them skip last week, but I've got to start them on their program today."

Now Miss Autrey turned. She took in the shorts-clad young woman and sniffed in disapproval. "Phys Ed! When am I supposed to teach basic subjects around here when my students are constantly being pulled out for other things? *Phys Ed!*"

The woman stood her ground. "They'll only be gone for thirty minutes."

Miss Autrey ordered the class to line up at the door row by row. They had to do it a second time before she was satisfied and let them go.

Instead of taking them outside as the children had been counting on, Miss Ellis led them to the auditorium. Up near the stage with its tattered green curtains was a rickety table with a tape player on it. Grumblings and complaints rose from the crowd.

Wade voiced the general opinion. "Let's go outdoors."

"Yeah," chorused his supporters. "It's too hot to stay inside. Let's play ball."

"Or wrestle," suggested Bruce, grabbing and twisting a boy's arm.

"It's hot and stinky in here," Marlene added, wrinkling her dainty nose.

"Yes," the girls around her agreed. "It's stinky."

"We'll do outside things in a couple of weeks," promised Miss Ellis cheerily. She moved over to the table and plugged in the tape player.

Marlene pushed at her hair. "Well, what are we going to do?"

Miss Ellis clicked a cassette into the tape player and turned back. "Folk dancing."

Everyone, including Raymond, complained loudly. It took Miss Ellis several minutes to restore order. "*Mayim* is a Jewish folk dance," she told them when she finally got them divided into circles. "Its name means 'water.' "

"Water! Water!" cried Bruce, grabbing at his throat.

Miss Ellis pushed a button and lively music filled the auditorium. "These are the steps," she said, pretending to hold hands with someone on either side and going through the motions of the dance. "Now, join hands inside your circles and we'll try the steps."

A new wave of protests began as everyone realized with whom they would have to hold hands. Wade looked at Justine, who stood on his left, and pretended to throw up. Five other boys began gagging. The music continued and Miss Ellis moved from group to group, showing steps, singing directions in time with the music.

On Raymond's right was Henrietta, still puffed up like a bullfrog over the project assignment. On his left was red-faced Marlene, who had failed in her attempt to get moved next to Wade. Opposite him in the circle was Bruce, who was trying to see how many times he could step on his partners' feet.

"Circle, circle, circle," Miss Ellis sang with forced cheerfulness. "To the center, to the center. Hands up. Back out." The music swirled around them and seemed to force them to move to its rhythm. *"Mayim, mayim, mayim!"* sang Miss Ellis.

Raymond felt Henrietta's elbow in his ribs. "You dummy! I'll never make a good grade working with you and Bruce Manis. You heard me tell Doylene that we would do tree rings!"

Raymond glared right back at her. "I did not! And who wants to work with you anyway!"

Marlene shoved him on the other side. "Move on, clumsy!"

"To the center," sang Miss Ellis. *"Mayim, mayim, mayim!* Again! *Mayim, mayim, mayim!"* Bruce flew to the center with his hands so high that he had practically lifted his partners off their feet, and then he backed out so fast that he almost pulled them to the floor.

Miss Ellis shook her head when Raymond laughed, so he closed his eyes and let the music take him around the floor. He swirled around as if caught in a swift current, floating around and around, in and out, in and out. Big A's voice grounded him.

"Ain't that sweet!" the boy sang out in a falsetto. "Raymond just *loves* dancing."

Face blazing, Raymond opened his eyes just in time to catch Bruce's out-thrust foot and Big A's thundering crash to the floor. Big A took his partners with him, and then two people fell over their feet. Bruce threw himself on top of the heap.

Miss Autrey chose this moment of total havoc to appear in the door at the back of the auditorium, hands on hips and face like a thunderstorm. She stared at the students until they grew quiet, and then looked at Miss Ellis. The young woman seemed to shrink several inches. "We were folk dancing," she said in a small voice.

"I know," said Miss Autrey. "I heard you from my room. Are you ready for my students to line up?"

That afternoon when Raymond got on the bus, he was carrying a book on trees. Henrietta spotted it as they moved down the aisle. "Got the only good book on trees in the whole library, I see!" she muttered, dropping into a seat right behind the bus driver.

Raymond did not answer. He took a seat behind her that was already occupied by a timid first-grade boy. The boy drew up against the window, eyes large and scared. Raymond smiled at him.

The seats filled and then the aisles. The bus driver rose to do her daily routine. "On back," she yelled to be heard over the din. "Move on back."

At the last possible moment, when the driver had already reached to close the door, Bruce Manis jumped on board. "Wait for me!" he said. "I'm riding this bus."

"Not for long," said the bus driver. "Not if you don't behave yourself. I'm not going to put up with the kind of things Mrs. Tibbs took from you last year."

Bruce gave her a wide menacing grin and swaggered down the aisle. He shoved himself onto the seat with Raymond so hard that the first grader's head knocked against the window. The little boy took one look at Bruce and swallowed the protests he had started to utter.

The bus started up and jolted forward. "Guess the old man won't work me today," Bruce said, stretching out his arms. Kids in the aisle dodged. He leaned close to Raymond. "I know where we can get something else for the bank."

Raymond looked at him blankly. "The bank?"

Bruce elbowed him and looked quickly around. The only person who seemed to be listening was Henrietta, and she pulled back her head when Bruce scowled at her. "You know! The *bank!*"

Raymond jerked his head. "Oh, the bank. Yeah."

The bus braked and threw a boy in the aisle against Bruce. Bruce was up in an instant, giving the boy several quick jabs in the mid-section and dropping back into his seat before the bus driver looked back.

"What's the problem?" she called, looking into the rear-view mirror.

"Nothing," the boy in the aisle gasped, staggering toward the rear.

The first grader tried to disappear into the upholstery.

Raymond's thoughts were racing. What could Bruce be planning now? The way he was acting, it might be danger-ous, illegal, or both. And even if it wasn't, the very thought of where money had to be hidden afterward was enough to get upset about. Bruce might expect *him* to hide the money this time.

Raymond looked back to where Jackie Lee usually sat, half-wishing that his bossy big sister would start telling him all the things he had to do this afternoon. Then he remembered that today was the first day of her afterschool baby-sitting job. She had ridden a bus going toward Fuller.

Bruce nudged him. "It's gonna be easy money," he whis-pered.

Raymond turned, catching Henrietta's curious eyes as he did so. She had eased around in her seat and was peeking over the back. "B . . . but," he croaked, "what will we be doing?"

Bruce cut him off. "Later!" He was talking out the side of his mouth like a television gangster. "Wait till we're off the bus."

The bus jerked to a stop and the little boy next to Ray-mond squeaked, "My stop!"

Raymond swung sideways and the boy shot out like a flash.

When the bus stopped at the trailer park, Bruce piled out with Raymond and the other trailer park kids and headed for the Brock trailer, with Raymond still talking in hurried whispers. "We can work on the hideout, too," he was saying. "It won't take too long to—"

"You just stop right there!" Henrietta yelled. She had planted herself in front of them and danced from side to side when they tried to go around her. "I know what you're up to and you're not going to get away with it."

"What do you mean?" Bruce demanded.

Henrietta acted as if she had not heard him. "You're not going to leave me out. I'm in charge. You're going to do things my way."

Bruce's mouth fell open. "What things?"

"Yeah, what things?" Raymond repeated.

Henrietta narrowed her eyes. "The same things you and Raymond have been talking about all the way home. Only it's not going to be how you plan it. It's going to be how *I* plan it!"

Bruce stepped forward menacingly. "Oh, yeah?"

Henrietta didn't budge. "Yeah."

"You ain't got no say in this," Bruce said. "We thought it up first."

Her eyes flashed. "You did not! Raymond knows. He knows who thought of it first."

Bruce swung around to face Raymond, who shrugged elaborately.

"Don't you lie! You heard me tell Doylene Hill!" Henrietta stamped her foot and advanced on Raymond with fire in her eyes. "Then you grabbed the project we wanted and got me put on your team! Well, I can tell you one thing. You're not going to leave me out and you're not going to mess it up. I'm going to get a good grade. You're going to do it my way!"

"Grade? Project?" said Raymond, looking down at the book in his hands and suddenly realizing what she was talking about.

Bruce slapped Raymond on the back. "Ha-ha-ha-ha-ha! Project! She's talking about a project!"

Henrietta's anger dissolved into bewilderment. She looked from one boy to the other. "Well, I'm in charge," she said, backing toward home. "And we're going to begin work on it tomorrow. I'm going to ask my father to saw us some tree sections, and I'm in charge."

"Okay!" Bruce said, winking at Raymond. "But you know the one in charge does most of the work."

"I'm in charge," she repeated stubbornly, moving up the steps to her front door.

"Now," Bruce said as soon as she closed the door behind her. "Hurry up and get rid of that book. I found us the biggest stash of deposit bottles I ever saw. They're dumped just down the road from us."

Raymond went limp with relief. "Bottle deposits?"

"Yep! At ten cents on the bottle! Hurry up! We're gonna make us some money!"

13
FLOPPY SOUNDS THE ALARM

"Shut up, dog," Henrietta called to Floppy across the Manis yard. The dog was pacing restlessly along the bushes on the back side of the bus, keeping up a steady volley of yapping barks. Henrietta sighed with exasperation. "Dogs never know when to shut up. That's why I like cats."

"Oh, yeah?" said Bruce, wiping sweat from his forehead and picking up a bow saw he had borrowed from his father's storage shed. "Well, cats don't know *anything* and that's why I like dogs."

"Henrietta, which tree do you want sawed now?" asked Raymond, who was weary of listening to their arguing. He wanted to get through and go to the hideout. He had been taking turns with Bruce on the sawing and he was tired.

Henrietta frowned. "I guess this one right here. I want a thin cross section of this stump. It's pine and pines have better rings."

"Listen to the big expert," Bruce muttered to Raymond, who was carrying the circle of wood he had just cut over to a growing pile under a dogwood tree. "It's *pine* and pines have better *rings*," he mimicked. "I can't believe Bruce Manis is spending Friday afternoon doing school stuff!"

Raymond nodded agreement. The assignment was only days old, but Henrietta, who had become panicky when her father had said he didn't have time to help, had Bruce and Raymond working as if it was due tomorrow. So far, she had not been pleased with a single slab they had cut.

She probably wasn't going to like the display stands he had been working on, either, Raymond thought, bending to peer through the bushes. Something was bothering Floppy. The deposit bottles he and Bruce had hidden in the ravine, perhaps? They had stashed all forty-two of them there after Mr. Messer had refused to take them.

While Bruce sawed, Raymond ambled off around the bus, circling a bank of honeysuckle and a clump of blackberry vines. He still did not see anything, however, and he certainly couldn't hear anything with Bruce and Henrietta bickering and Floppy barking.

"Listen, girlie," Raymond could hear Bruce saying, "I don't know about you, but I got other fish to fry. Project or no project, I ain't going to stand around here all day sawing wood."

Henrietta folded her arms belligerently. "You promised. You said that I was in charge and that you would cut the wood I needed. Didn't he, Raymond?" she demanded.

Raymond, who was walking back toward them now, did not have a chance to reply. Bruce jumped in with his own answer. "Yeah, I promised! And I kept my word. You already got three or four good slabs. That's aplenty."

Henrietta shook her head. "We need a lot more samples. And anyway, most of these are no good. They need to be bigger around and you haven't been cutting them neatly enough. I told you I had to have straight-across cuts with no splinters and no jagged places."

"Listen to the big boss!" Bruce laughed and looked back at Raymond. "Why don't you try using this thing for a while? It ain't no power saw and I can't cut through a tree as big around as a bicycle tire with it. Another thing, my old man is going to be getting home any time now and he's gonna be plenty sore about me messing up the yard."

Henrietta glanced around the debris-strewn yard and for a moment appeared on the verge of laughter. Then she looked at Bruce and grew serious. "Well, I didn't want to cut here in the first place, remember. I told you we ought to go to the woods down there," she said, pointing toward the quarry. "In fact, I'll just ask my daddy again. I'll bet he . . ."

Bruce's face changed in an instant. Raymond knew why. Having her go to the quarry road and perhaps find the secret road and then the hideout was the last thing he wanted. "I'll cut another sample for you," he offered hastily.

In fact, he cut several more while Henrietta lined them up and inspected each one critically. Meanwhile, Raymond began gathering the sample pieces of wood Henrietta had decreed they should use. All the while he watched Floppy, who continued barking and sniffing in the same direction.

"What are you looking at?" Henrietta finally asked when she caught Raymond staring intently at the trees behind the bus.

"Nothing," Raymond replied, turning his attention to the wood samples.

Henrietta squatted next to the largest one and gave a cluck of satisfaction. "This is the best specimen," she said in her most know-it-all tone. "It has fifteen rings. I counted a while ago. That means it's fifteen years old."

Raymond put on a bored expression. "Everybody knows that." He wasn't about to let her think she knew more than he, though she probably did. He had not opened his book on trees yet.

"Look how narrow these rings are in the heartwood," she went on, pointing to the darker-colored center. "That means when it was a real young tree, it was in the shade and didn't get much water."

"Yeah, I know," said Raymond.

"The wider rings over here on this side show that the tree leaned in this direction."

Raymond yawned. "I could have told you that from the way the stump is leaning."

Henrietta traced several V-shaped markings in the rings. "This is where a branch used to grow and this over here is probably fire damage."

The sound of sawing ceased and Bruce headed toward them, carrying the latest slab of wood. His face was red and beaded with sweat.

"You call that thin?" said Henrietta, rising to inspect the piece of wood.

Bruce exploded. "I call it thin as I could get it, and I call it *thinner* than *you* can get them. You wanna try your hand?" He turned to Raymond. "I'm gonna cut her one more. You get the wagon. She'll need it to haul these home in."

"You mean you're not going to help me!" Henrietta demanded indignantly.

Raymond did not wait to hear the rest of the argument. He ran down the driveway as fast as he could go. For a moment he thought Floppy would go with him. The dog did trot after him a pretty good distance before stopping and returning to the yard.

Raymond was almost at the place where the wagon was hidden when he discovered the reason Floppy had been barking. In the meadow, hidden behind a stand of kudzu-draped pines, stood a green truck. Its windows were lowered and from its rearview mirror hung a pair of foam-rubber dice. On its bumper was a sticker saying DRINK

MORE BEER. Raymond moved closer and saw in the back some kind of cage contraption and in the rear window, a rifle rack. Both were empty.

Looking down, Raymond saw the tire tracks in the dust and then footprints, headed toward the quarry. He stopped for a few moments, listening and looking for some sign of the driver of the truck. There was none. He was hesitant to go after the wagon, yet reluctant to return without it. If he didn't get it, he and Bruce were going to be forced to help Henrietta lug all that stuff to the trailer park.

Suddenly Raymond made up his mind and ran for the woods. From the safety of a patch of huckleberry bushes, he looked at the truck again, alert for any noise, any sign of movement. However, only the distant cawing of a crow disturbed the peace. Finally he crept to the place where the wagon was hidden, grabbed it by the handle, and headed back to the bus.

Bruce had the three best cross sections of wood waiting at the quarry road when Raymond returned. Henrietta was still fuming about having to haul them home by herself, but Bruce was not listening.

"I'll come for my wagon later," he informed her. "You put it somewhere safe."

She snatched the wagon handle from his hand. "Maybe I will and maybe I won't."

"If you don't we won't help you anymore with the project," Bruce threatened. "You'll get a bad grade."

"You will, too."

Bruce laughed. "Yeah, but we don't care." He turned to Raymond. "Let me go put back the saw and get a hammer and nails and we'll be ready to go."

Raymond grabbed him by the arm. "Wait!" he whispered. "Down there in the field is a truck—hid behind those pines."

Bruce looked in the direction he indicated, though nothing could be seen from where they stood. "You sure?"

Raymond nodded. "Real close to the road. And I saw footprints headed toward the quarry."

Bruce swung back to face him, agitation plain in his face. "The quarry! I don't like that. You ever seen the truck before?"

Raymond shook his head. "It's an old green Dodge. Got a rifle rack. And it's got some kind of cages in back."

Bruce bit his lip and looked toward the bus. "I *thought* it was funny how Floppy's been carrying on."

"What are we going to do about going to the hideout?" Raymond asked.

Bruce thought for a moment. "We'll go anyway."

"We will?" Raymond said.

"Yeah. Only we won't go by the road. We'll cut across this field and go through the woods. We'll just keep an eye out while we're going." He started toward the bus. "I better put the old man's saw back in the shed. You run to the bus and get the hammer and nails. The hammer is on the table and the nails are on my bed."

On reaching the yard, Bruce grabbed up the saw with hardly a break in stride and headed for the makeshift shed to the rear. Raymond, on the other hand, slowed to a creep at the door of the bus. He had never been inside before and somehow, even with Bruce's permission and Peavy Manis's absence, he was a little reluctant to enter.

Slowly he eased up one step and then another until he was inside. He found the hammer right away but the bag of nails was another matter. The place was dim and crowded in back and he was reluctant to do too much poking about.

"What's taking you so long?" hissed Bruce, bursting in through the door and rushing past him. He threw the covers off the nearest of two cots at the rear of the bus, grabbed up a brown bag, and ran for the front. "We gotta get out of here."

Bruce was already running along the drive when Raymond reached the ground. Then the boy suddenly slid to a stop. "Tell you what, Raymond," he said in a loud voice. "Let's go help Henrietta haul that wood over to the trailer park."

Raymond looked at him in disbelief. "What? I thought you said . . ."

"We might as well help old Henry out," Bruce said, almost shouting now. He winked and jerked his head toward the woods behind the bus.

Raymond caught on at last. Bruce thought there might be someone back there. "Oh, okay. Sure. We'll go help her."

Together they ran down the drive, turned right, and ran until they were nearing the highway. Just short of the pavement, they cut off the road to the left and headed across the field to the woods. Only when they reached the shelter of the trees did they allow themselves to slow and look back. No one had followed and Floppy had stopped barking.

The cellar of the hideout was cool. Munching on pears they had picked on their way, Raymond and Bruce lay on the brick floor resting, the hammer and nails between them. Upstairs, Floppy was complaining as he always did when left behind, yet he still could not summon the courage to try the stairs. He did go so far several times as to set his front paws on the first step, but seemed unable to go farther.

Raymond finished his pear and looked over at Bruce. "You going to stay here tonight?"

Bruce studied the unceiled floor joists above his head. A spiderweb just over their heads trembled with the pacing of the dog. "I'd like to."

Raymond looked at the vine-shrouded window and then around at the gloomy stone walls. The shadowed area beneath the tablelike landing was spiderwebbed, too, and two big black crickets crawled up the stone wall beside it. At night, when no one else was here, this must be a scary place. He turned to Bruce. "You're not afraid to stay here by yourself?"

Bruce hesitated a moment before he shook his head. "Nah! I ain't afraid. But I better not stay tonight. Tomorrow's Saturday—the old man's flea market day. He may decide he needs me. He ain't told me yet." The boy looked around and smiled with satisfaction. "Thanks to you, we got this place pretty much fixed now."

Raymond grinned modestly, but he was pleased himself with how everything had turned out.

"I mean, those shelves are first-rate. And that table looks like it come out of a store!"

Raymond knew this was overstating the case, but he accepted the praise without arguing.

Floppy hung his head down through the trapdoor opening and whined. Bruce laughed. "Speaking of first-rate, what do you think about that protection we're getting!"

Raymond laughed along with Bruce and then asked, "So what are we going to do tomorrow? I mean, if you don't go to the flea market."

Bruce raised himself up on one elbow. "You want to ride in my canoe? I just about got 'er ready to go."

Before Raymond could answer, Floppy leaped up and burst into a volley of yelps that brought both boys to their feet in an instant. This was not a complaining bark, it was a cry of alarm.

"Somebody must be coming!" Bruce whispered, lunging for the steps.

From outside came a crackling sound, like twigs being crushed underfoot. Raymond immediately thought of that empty rifle rack in the truck. Bruce fell back against Raymond, almost knocking him down.

"What are we going to do?" said Raymond, looking up the stairway to where Floppy stood in the doorway barking with all his might. It was too late to close the trapdoor and he wasn't sure he would want it closed anyway. He retreated toward a corner, looking around the room wildly. No place to hide. No way to escape. Except . . .

He swung around toward the window at the same moment that Bruce did, but before either of them could move, a creaking sound froze them in their tracks. Someone swinging the door upstairs? He was afraid to go look.

"Let's get out of here," said Bruce, making a dash to the high window. He did not need to say it twice. Raymond was right beside him, grunting and sweating and trying in spite of his shorter stature to get a grasp on the window. It wouldn't budge.

"Need something to pull with," grunted Bruce, looking desperately around the room. Raymond was looking, too. His eyes fell on the shadowed nook beneath the landing. He tugged on Bruce's sleeve and darted in that direction. Paying no attention to crickets or spiderwebs, he dived headlong into the dusty corner and drew himself up small to make room for Bruce.

Bruce, however, had grabbed up the hammer and was jerking on the window with its claws, his eyes on the stairs. Abruptly, the window broke free and jolted to the side with a thud. Dropping the hammer, Bruce pulled himself up to the window ledge, paused long enough to motion for Raymond, and leaped out into the vines and briars.

Raymond made a move and then fell back as the creaking sound came again, louder this time, and was followed immediately by a crack that could have been a rifle shot. Raymond drew up into the corner, his heart hammering against his ribs. He seemed frozen to the bricks in the floor and the stones in the wall.

From outside came a muffled thrashing that had to be Bruce moving through the thick and tangled growth that hugged the building at the back. Then there came a period of total silence that seemed more ominous than all the noises that had preceded it. Even Floppy's frenzied barking had finally hushed. Had someone killed the dog and perhaps Bruce, too? Raymond bent to peer through the steps in front of his face, listening with his entire body. Then he heard the footsteps.

They went slowly and deliberately across the floor of the upstairs room while dust sifted downward and danced in a shaft of sunlight stealing through the window vines. They hit the first step and then the second. The entire staircase vibrated with them. Then on the step only inches from his nose, a foot appeared, *thump*. Another foot came into sight, *thump!* And then some kind of iron implement appeared, *thud!*

Suddenly a wild laugh erupted and the person on the stairs leaped out into the middle of the brick floor, brandishing the iron like a weapon. It was Bruce! "You ain't going to believe what that dumb dog was barking at," he said. "Guess!"

"I don't know," Raymond replied, crawling weakly from his hiding place. His knees were still trembly with fright.

"Oh, it was something real dangerous!" Bruce said. "It was a man-eater pine. You know that tree that was leaning over against that other one out front? Well, it broke, and Mr. Floppy Super Genius up there musta thought it was a bunch of thieves and cutthroats!" He rubbed his arms. "Thanks to that lamebrain dog, I scratched myself in three zillion places. I guess it worked out all right though, 'cause I found something in those briars that we need—a crowbar. I think I'll go use it on that dumb dog."

Bruce looked up at Floppy, who had his head hanging down through the trapdoor opening. Then both boys were laughing and racing upstairs. Outside, moments later, they were staging a mock battle with the two of them pitted against the dog. Around trees and stumps they raced,

Floppy letting out pretend growls at the two of them while the boys sneaked in tugs on his flapping ears and wagging tail. Finally all three fell down on the grass in front of the hideout.

"Life ain't half-bad," said Bruce when he had caught his breath.

Raymond squinted up through the swaying pine limbs to the cloudless blue sky overhead and for just a moment the burden of the lost field glasses and Miss Autrey lifted. "No, it's not half-bad," he said.

14

PINK-EYED PURPLE
HULLS AND
OTHER BAD LUCK

Saturday did not work out as planned. Shortly after breakfast, Mr. Brock's older brother, Otis, showed up. When
Raymond opened the door and glimpsed his uncle's fancy
chromed truck, he just knew his grandfather had come,
too. Gladness was quickly swallowed up by despair as he
thought of the empty place under Old Lizzie's seat.

Otis came up the steps laughing. "Don't strain your eyes,
Short Stuff. Your grandpa's not out there!"

Sure enough, Raymond could see that it was not a man
but a red-headed woman who sat on the passenger side of
the cab.

"Where's that football-hero brother of yours?" asked
Otis.

Before Raymond could tell him that Vance had spent the
night with Bunky and was going fishing with his friend that
morning, his uncle had gone on past him to greet the rest
of the family. Otis never paid much attention to Raymond
except to tease, which was one reason Raymond did not
like this uncle very much.

"Can't stay, can't stay," Otis said, sweeping off his cowboy hat and refusing the chair he was offered by Mr. Brock. Taller and heavier than Raymond's father, he seemed to fill the family room and overflow into the kitchen. His checked cowboy shirt and high-heeled western boots made him appear even larger in both directions than he actually was. His tanned face was damp with sweat. The morning already promised a hot day.

Mr. Brock looked out the window. "So you didn't bring Dad to get Old Lizzie?"

"What with this heat, Dad didn't feel like coming. But I'll be bringing him next Sunday sure." Otis shook his head to the steaming cup Mrs. Brock offered. "No time for coffee! And I'm in a hurry anyhow. Edna Earl and me are on our way to the Sandhop stock car races." He jerked his head toward the woman in the truck. She waved and then began to apply fresh lipstick to already red lips. Mrs. Clendenin, who had come out of her trailer on the pretense of sweeping her steps, was staring in open curiosity at the truck in the Brocks' yard.

"We need to get on over to Sandhop if we're going to find us good seats at all," Otis went on, heading back outside. "We don't want to miss the monster trucks and the demolition derby." He waved his hat toward the back of his truck as he went down the steps. "Dad wouldn't be satisfied until I brought you some Tennessee peas to put up, Millie. He sent you several bushels of purple hulls."

While Otis performed introductions, Raymond wandered to the back and looked at the collection of grocery bags with dismay. There were at least a dozen of them all stuffed with the peas his grandfather said were the very best in the whole world. It didn't look as if there would be any canoeing for him today.

From the very edge of her yard, Mrs. Clendenin was looking, too. "Fresh peas, huh?" she said, adjusting her glasses. Her usual frown softened. "Sure do look good." No one paid the slightest attention except Raymond, and he pretended not to hear.

Otis leaned on the side of the truck. "Dad picked 'em yesterday."

"Well, bless his heart," said Mrs. Brock. "Some purple hulls sure would be a good change from store-bought vegetables."

"Sure would," agreed Mrs. Clendenin, moving over to stand by Raymond.

Raymond didn't think they would be good. At least, not good enough for the trouble they'd be. He knew from experience what that many peas would mean—a whole day of splitting purple shells and pushing out brown peas until his thumbs ached.

Jackie Lee knew what it meant, too, and hastened to remind her mother that she was already committed for an entire day of baby-sitting. "Mrs. Nickols is depending on me, Mother," she said.

"Count me out, too, honey," said Mr. Brock. "I've got to go see about getting the car fixed and I don't know how late I'll be getting back." He didn't sound too sorry about it.

Mrs. Clendenin cleared her throat. "I never did mind shelling peas myself."

Mrs. Brock smiled briefly at the woman and then turned to her daughter and her husband with an impatient frown. "Well, I have a lot to do today, too."

Raymond took hope when he saw his mother was wavering. "And Vance has gone fishing with Bunky," he reminded her.

Otis shrugged apologetically. "I could just throw 'em away, Millie." He adjusted the silver steer-head buckle on his belt. "You're too tired to fool with—"

"Throw away pink-eyed purple hulls!" said Mrs. Clendenin, waddling past Raymond and on around to the truck cab. "What's this world coming to? I'd be glad to lend a hand. Miz Brock, me and your boys'll set over here under one of my shade trees and shell 'em while you can 'em." She waved aside Mrs. Brock's protests. "I'll just take a portion of the peas and that's pay enough."

"But, Mom," Raymond began, but Mrs. Brock smiled and the deal was made.

As if afraid they might change their minds, Mrs. Clendenin rose on tiptoe and reached for the nearest bag. "We'll finish in no time," she was saying. "With three pairs of hands—"

"*Two,*" Raymond corrected her, staring reproachfully at his mother. "Vance isn't here to help."

"That's no problem," said Mrs. Brock. "You can go get him."

"But I don't know where he is," Raymond protested. "You know Vance never lets me go anywhere with him, especially to his secret fishing place."

"Bunky's father will know where the boys are," said Mr. Brock.

A short while later, Raymond was plodding down the highway toward the creek, kicking rocks and muttering darkly. The prospect of pea shelling all day long with Mrs. Clendenin made him feel sorry for himself and angry at his mother. He was also mad at his father and Jackie Lee, who had escaped all the work, and at Vance, who might escape if Raymond did not find him.

He squinted into the sunlight and looked ahead. There was no traffic in sight now, and the Garmon house was quiet. In the hush of morning the bees working a nearby scattering of goldenrod seemed loud. Somewhere a dog barked and then fell silent.

A few yards short of the bridge and off to the right, he

found the path that Amos Potter had told him to take. With his eyes, he followed it down the steep bank, under the tree-lined fence, and across the pasture. Black cows and white cattle egrets moved lazily about the thickets that dotted the creek bank. There was no sign of Vance and Bunky, or anyone else, under the trees along the stream. But Mr. Potter had not been sure how far the boys would go before dropping their lines. "Just follow the trail till you find them," he had instructed vaguely.

"So I'll walk along the creek," Raymond muttered. "And if it takes me two hours to find Vance, it won't be my fault! Mrs. Clendenin can just shell by herself!" There was another dog bark as Raymond started down the bank. It sounded quite near this time.

"*Psssst!*" a voice called.

Startled, Raymond stopped and looked quickly about.

The voice came again. "Hey! Over here! I've been waiting for you."

A grin spread over Raymond's face as he spotted Bruce and Floppy crouching in the grasses just to the right of the bridge. "Hi!" he called, running to meet them.

"Sh-h-h-h-h!" Bruce hissed, beckoning him to come on. "I don't want nobody to see us!"

Raymond dropped to his knees and followed the boy under the bridge to a concrete ledge, trying to avoid Floppy's wet tongue and wagging tail. "Who are you hiding from?" he asked. "Is somebody after you?"

"Not that I know of. I just didn't want the old man to find out I got a canoe."

"Oh," said Raymond. "I was just thinking about that truck . . ."

Bruce shrugged. "I ain't seen that truck today. When the old man left for the flea market, I went down the road looking. It was probably just a hunter. Look down there." He pointed down to a warped metal object half-hidden by bushes. The thing was so dented and bent out of shape that Raymond was at first uncertain what it was.

"Your canoe?" he blurted.

"Yep!" Bruce smiled proudly. "Ain't she a beauty?" Fortunately, he did not wait for an answer but started explaining how he had knocked out dents, stopped up holes, and propped up sagging seats to get the wreckage to its present state of perfection.

"And you and me are going to take the first ride in it this morning before we go over to the hideout," he finished up.

"I can't," Raymond answered, explaining about the peas and his orders to find Vance.

"Doggone it, King Shoes!" said Bruce. "Your family makes mine look like a prize. With them folks of yours, you can't hardly go to the toilet! Who's going to try out my canoe with me?"

Raymond laughed. "You could go ask Henrietta. She was out gathering leaves in the trailer park a while ago."

"Let me guess. She's going to put together a model of a real tree. Right?"

Raymond laughed. "No. She said we'd need a display on tree leaves to go with the rings, only she said 'foliage' instead of leaves."

"She *would!*" Bruce said, spitting at a dragonfly. "I guess she'll want tree limbs and roots next. Maybe a coupla stumps." Settling back and propping his feet on a bridge support, he returned to the subject of his canoe, explaining in detail what else he planned to do to it. "I might just end up selling it and getting something bigger," Bruce said at last.

Before Raymond could reply, Floppy gave a low growl and moved toward the road bank. The boys followed right behind him. "Quiet, Floppy," Bruce whispered, holding the dog by his collar. Crouched in the grasses, they looked down the highway.

"Henrietta!" said Raymond. There the girl was, a magazine under one arm and a pencil behind one ear, starting down the bank toward the pasture. She stopped just short of the fence at a persimmon tree and pulled off several splotched leaves. One by one, she flattened them between pages of the magazine.

"Heck!" said Bruce. "You know what she's going to do? Before this thing is over with, she's going to end up going down the quarry road."

Raymond nodded and crawled back under the bridge with Bruce. "So what are we going to do?"

Bruce thought for a moment and then grinned. "We'll help her," he said, sliding down the concrete ramp. "Get some leaves off that tree over there and I'll get some off these over here. We'll move the canoe out ahead of her and act like we've been out gathering leaves like crazy. I'll tell her I've already got a bunch at home for her—one off every tree in the woods around where I live."

"Like I told you, I got to go hunt Vance," Raymond said, following him down the ramp.

"We'll look for him, too," said Bruce.

Raymond hesitated. "I don't know . . ."

"You ain't scared of my canoe, are you?"

"No," Raymond lied. "But . . ."

"Well, come on then," he said, handing the leaves to Raymond. He grabbed his canoe and eased it into the water. "You're going to have to be quiet now," he said to Floppy, "like I trained you." Bruce seated himself in the canoe and picked up the paddle. It was really only half a paddle, the handle being mostly broken off, but he managed to use it to anchor the boat next to the shore.

Raymond looked at the inch or so of water sloshing about in the bottom of the boat and did not feel reassured.

"Nothing to worry about," Bruce said, seeing his hesitation. "You always get a little water in a canoe. And this creek ain't deep nohow."

It didn't appear deep, now that Raymond saw it close

up. The creek wasn't all that wide and waterbugs were skating around its edges as if it were a mere puddle. Making up his mind, he climbed in. Floppy, however, still had reservations. He stood on the bank whining and only when Bruce began pushing off did the dog make a flying leap into the center of the canoe. Raymond clung to both sides as water splashed and the boat rocked.

Bruce laughed. "That's one of the tricks I learned him."

Gradually the boat steadied and was caught by the current. The bridge and its traffic sounds dropped away. The plaintive mooing of the cows was all they heard. The boys watched the pasture glide by, but, to their relief, caught no sight of Henrietta anywhere along the bank.

"Soon as we gain some distance on her," Bruce said, "we'll get out and head back, gathering leaves fast as we can."

"Okay," Raymond agreed without thinking, his eyes darting from one plugged hole to another. Each one was seeping water.

The blackberry thickets gave way to forest and the cattle sounds faded into bird twitterings. The water in the canoe continued to rise, and Raymond was relieved when, just short of a boulder-strewn bend in the stream, Bruce announced that it was time to head for shore. He had no sooner begun to turn, however, when the sound of voices and splashing up ahead stopped him.

Forgetting his worry about leaks, Raymond strained to see something around the bend, but all he could make out beyond the cluster of rocks immediately in front of them was that the stream seemed to widen into a rippling poollike area. The voices came again. "Vance and Bunky," Raymond said, putting a hand on Floppy to quiet him.

Bruce nodded and aimed the canoe toward the rocks just ahead and off to the right. Despite the tug of the water that whooshed like rapids through the gaps, Bruce managed to turn the canoe and edge it longways against the largest of the boulders. Raymond cringed for a moment as the sides scraped with a noise that seemed louder than the rushing water.

"See anything?" Bruce whispered when Raymond raised himself by grabbing hold of the nearest rock.

"Not yet," Raymond answered, trying to hold the canoe steady by tightening his hold on the rock and bracing his knees.

Bruce shifted about impatiently. "Now?"

Raymond nodded back to Bruce, who was laying the paddle across the canoe and moving to hold the dog. Then he turned back to the scene ahead. Where were Vance and Bunky? They had to be here. He had heard them. And besides, there were two piles of clothing on the bank—one of them topped with a red T-shirt. "It's them," he whispered, his eyes sweeping over the banks and the rippling surface of the water. He took in an overhanging tree at the water's edge and a rope that dangled from one of its limbs. He noticed that the trunk was wet and the rope was swaying back and forth.

"Well, what are they doing?" asked Bruce, impatience making his voice sharp. Getting no answer, he moved to stand up.

"Sh-h-h-h-h!" said Raymond as the canoe rubbed and scraped against the rocks.

"I wanna see, too," said Bruce, reaching for one of the other rocks.

At that moment two heads bobbed gasping and sputtering to the surface of the water beneath the rope swing. "I beat you," Vance bragged. "I stayed under longer."

"Huh-uh!" gasped Bunky. "We stayed under the same length of time."

"Some fishing they're doing," Raymond whispered to Bruce, shifting about. His feet were becoming quite wet, but he hardly noticed in his delight at the trouble his brother was about to be in. "Vance's going to have some tall explaining to do when he shows up at home with wet hair. Mom told him no swimming."

Bruce did not answer. He was reaching back with one hand to grab at Floppy, who was becoming uneasy.

Meanwhile, Raymond could hear Vance continue bragging. "How'd you like that flip I did a while ago?" he said.

"Probably a belly flop," muttered Raymond.

"It was good," admitted Bunky, heading for the bank, "but I can beat yours!"

Vance started after him. "Bet you can't!"

"I'll show you," Bunky declared, pulling himself out of the water and scrambling up the leaning tree. Vance was right behind, scuffling for first position. Bunky laughed when he caught the rope first and swung out over the water. Turning loose at the height of his swing, he grabbed his knees and ducked his head, hitting the water with a tremendous splash that even sent a spray of water over Raymond and Bruce.

"Still didn't make a whole turn," Vance yelled when his pal surfaced. "Watch me!" He grabbed the rope and shoved off with a mighty kick on the tree trunk. High in the air, he turned loose, hugged his knees, and tucked his head. Raymond held his breath as his brother spun and dropped. He had to admit his performance was impressive.

"Hey!" Bruce said, abruptly turning loose from the rock and the dog. The canoe lurched.

Raymond swung around and immediately saw the source of Bruce's alarm. Their paddle was gliding downstream. Without thinking, Raymond gave up his hold on the rock to make desperate grabs at it, bringing in water with each swipe. But it was too late. The paddle was already rushing between the two big rocks through which water sluiced like a spillway into the pool.

"Grab hold of a rock," whispered Bruce, and Raymond

tried. But they had already moved too far from the ones where they had been, and the ones rushing past now were either too small, too slippery with moss, or too far away. Besides that, the canoe was just plain moving too fast. Channeled by the rocks into a narrow stream, the creek was rushing and bubbling on all sides and batting the canoe about like a toothpick. Floppy's desperate pacing was making their plight even worse. As the water in the boat grew high, the whine in the dog's throat became desperate.

"Use your hands," said Bruce, throwing himself to his seat and backpaddling with his hands. "We gotta get to shore."

At that moment they heard Bunky yell out, "Hey! Where'd this paddle come from?"

Floppy chose this time to desert ship. Jumping off the side with a leap that rocked the boat and brought in more water, the dog made for shore. Raymond groaned as Vance and Bunky turned to look first at the dog and then at him. The water in the canoe was now halfway to Raymond's knees.

"What are you doing here?" demanded Vance, moving toward them just as the canoe turned sideways and braced itself firmly against the last two rocks between them and clear water.

"Yeah, what are you doing here?" Bunky echoed.

Raymond would have been delighted at the surprise and dismay in his brother's voice if circumstances had been different. As it was, he put all his energy into grabbing hold of the rock on his end and trying to help Bruce turn the boat.

"I said, what are you doing?" Vance demanded again.

"What do you *think* we're doing, dummy?" Bruce grunted, pushing at the rock on his end with all his might and only succeeding in bringing in more water. "We're taking a canoe ride. How about helping us?"

Vance laughed and began throwing water. "Oh! A canoe! I thought it was a bathtub."

"Or a submarine!" shrieked Bunky, joining in the water barrage.

"Stop it!" Bruce screamed. "Help us get it loose."

Still laughing, Vance and Bunky grabbed the canoe and rocked it back and forth, bringing water with each dip.

Bruce kicked at their hands. "Not that way, you idiots!"

"You better quit it, Vance," Raymond said. "Mom sent me to get you! Uncle Otis brought some peas— "

Suddenly Raymond's words ended with a rip of metal and a *glub-glub-glub* as the canoe went under the water, taking him with it.

Raymond bobbed to the surface in time to see Bruce thrashing across the creek after Vance and Bunky. "You low-down, sorry scum-bums. I'll teach you to sink my canoe!"

Raymond went under again and bobbed up an eternity later, to hear Vance shrieking, "Thank you, but we already know how to sink canoes!"

When he surfaced again, weighing a thousand pounds in his waterlogged clothing, Raymond found to his great relief that his feet touched solid bottom, and he dragged himself to the bank behind Bruce, who had apparently given up on catching the older boys. Behind them, Vance and Bunky were crowing triumphantly.

"Serves you right!" Bunky yelled.

"Yeah!" Vance agreed. "Teach you to snoop on us!"

Bruce pulled himself to the bank, where Floppy welcomed him with a spray of sand and water he was shaking from his fur. Bruce ignored the dog and turned back toward Vance and Bunky, his face red with a fury that matched Raymond's own. "Well, now I'm going to teach you two smart alecks something! Four can play this game, can't they, Raymond?" He ran toward the piles of clothing, with Raymond right behind him.

"No! Wait!" yelled Vance and Bunky together, the laughter suddenly gone from their voices.

Bruce did not listen. He did not even slow up. Grabbing a pair of shoes in each hand, he waved them in the air while Raymond gathered up the clothes remaining on the ground.

"Don't!" yelled Bunky, swimming for shore.

"Raymond, don't you dare!" Vance screamed.

Raymond hesitated for a moment as Bruce threw the shoes, one pair at a time, far downstream, and then he began to throw the things he held. A pair of jeans sprawled crazily across a tangle of briars, another caught and hung from an overhead tree limb, and both shirts sank in a stand of reddish-green leaves Raymond recognized as poison oak.

"Over here!" Bruce bellowed, kicking off the top of a huge fire anthill against a nearby stump. "Put the undershorts over here!" Raymond dropped the shorts on the boiling mass of furious ants and headed through the woods after Bruce.

"Just keep on coming," Bruce said, running backward and motioning the boys on. "You're about to be in the open. The pasture's right up here!"

The boys did keep on coming, with Floppy barking right at their heels.

Then Raymond remembered something. "Hey! You better go back," he yelled. "There's a girl up here."

"Aw, why'd you tell 'em?" said Bruce.

Vance and Bunky looked at each other. Bunky shook his head. "Ain't nobody up there."

Vance licked his lips. "You're lying, Raymond!"

Raymond shrugged. He'd done his duty. "Come on then," he yelled. "I don't care."

"Yeah," Bruce said. "Just don't never say we didn't warn you!"

Vance's eyes turned on Raymond. His face was a mask of fury. "I hate you!" he said.

"I hate you, too," Raymond shot back. "I didn't do a thing to you until you sank the boat!"

"We tried to help you get it loose!" cried Vance.

"Liar!" said Bruce.

"And anyway, it serves you right for spying on us."

"I did not spy on you!" Raymond said. "You're always saying that, and it's not so. I haven't followed you a single time since I went to the Hinkles' that once. For your information, Mom told me to get you. You have to go home and help shell peas that Uncle Otis brought."

That message seemed to get through to Vance for the first time. His shoulders sagged. "Peas?"

Raymond nodded, gloating at his brother's misery. "And you're going to be in trouble when Mom sees your wet hair."

"Look who's talking!" Vance shot back. "You're wet all over!"

Unable to think of an answer to this, Raymond turned and sloshed toward home.

15

NEVER IS
A LONG TIME

Sunday afternoon when the Brock family was finishing lunch, Henrietta knocked on the front door.

"Guess what, Raymond!" she said as soon as Jackie Lee let her in. "We're going to be able to get all the rest of the leaves for our tree project today."

Raymond pushed back his chair and got up from the table. "I thought we already had plenty," he answered carefully, stealing a glance at his mother, who only last night had given him a serious talk about improving his schoolwork and his grades. "We gave you a bunch yesterday. I'm not working on that project today. Bruce and I are going to . . . well, we have plans." He and Bruce had agreed after they left the creek to go through the dumpster at Messer's Store and then to haul some more things to the hideout that afternoon.

Henrietta's face fell. "You've got to! I promised Mrs. Clendenin. I already got it arranged."

"Unarrange it."

"I can't. You see, Mrs. Clendenin is going to get pine needles to put on her flower beds and she said we could help her and then we could—"

"I told you, I'm not going."

Henrietta folded her arms. "Raymond Brock, you and Bruce both said I could be in charge. And I want us to get a good grade on this project."

"What's this?" asked Mrs. Brock from the sink, where she had begun stacking dishes. It was her turn to clean up the kitchen. "Is this something for school?"

Henrietta smiled in her direction. "Yes, ma'am. For science."

"Well, then, I think you'd better go, Raymond," Mrs. Brock said.

"Yes," agreed Mr. Brock, moving into the family area and picking up the Sunday funnies. "It's the least we can do after Mrs. Clendenin helped us shell those peas yesterday."

"Huh!" Raymond grunted, wishing he dared protest the use of "we" and "us" when it really had been only he and Vance who had shelled. He chose to forget that his mother had washed and canned the peas.

"Yeah!" said Vance, agreeing with Raymond for once. He held out his right thumb, which was as stained with purple as Raymond's. "We don't owe Clangdang any favors."

Raymond sent his brother a grateful look, but Vance ignored it. He was still angry about the incident at the creek the day before. His sneakers were not dry yet, and every time he looked at them he muttered dark hints about a plan he had for getting even.

Henrietta headed for the door. "Bring some magazines to press leaves in, and hurry."

"You better not use any of *my* magazines," said Jackie Lee.

Raymond was trapped.

A few minutes later, he found himself loading rakes, a pitchfork, and plastic bags into the trunk of Mrs. Clendenin's car while Henrietta loaded up enough magazines to press a thousand leaves. In addition, she had all kinds of books from the Fuller library identifying trees. Raymond was closing the lid when Vance and Bunky passed, their arms loaded with racquets, aluminum poles, and a net. They were on their way to play badminton with the Hinkle twins.

Filled with resentment at seeing his brother headed off for an afternoon of fun while he had to work, Raymond forgot the good feelings he had had toward Vance a few minutes before. "Your shoes are still making that squishy sound," he said, making sure he spoke low enough so that his parents could not hear. He was no more anxious than Vance to have Mr. and Mrs. Brock start questioning them about yesterday's events.

"That's all right," Vance retorted. "My shoes *look* a whole lot better than yours."

"*Squish-squash, squish-squash,*" Raymond answered.

Vance's ears lit up. "Bet he'd like to know what I know," he said to Bunky. "But I'm not telling him a thing."

Raymond picked up a pebble and drew back his hand.

"Whoa!" said Mrs. Clendenin, who had chosen that moment to make her appearance wearing bright-green knee-length pants, a flowery smock, and a straw hat tied on with a bright-orange scarf. "Let's don't get that started again. You two threw enough pea hulls yesterday to last a while. Let's don't begin on rocks today." She turned back toward her trailer, where Tosche could be heard barking. "Be quiet, you bad boy!" she yelled. The dog only barked louder. "Minds good, don't he?" she said, searching through her huge purse until she found her car key. "Well, let's get that mulch for my flower beds."

"And leaves for our project," said Henrietta, jumping onto the front seat.

Raymond frowned at both of them. "I don't see why you

have to get pine needles now," he said, climbing over Henrietta's junk to sit on the backseat. "Winter's a long way off."

"That's what you think!" Mrs. Clendenin walked around the car and heaved herself into the driver's seat. She was so short that she seemed to look through instead of over the steering wheel. "I admit hot weather is hanging on mighty stubborn this year. But fall and winter are coming. They always do." She started up the engine and moved down the drive at about five miles per hour.

She stopped at the highway, looked both ways twice, and then pulled out in front of a speeding truck. There were screeching brakes and a screaming horn before the truck found an opening in the oncoming traffic and whipped out and around them. "Crazy driver," muttered Mrs. Clendenin. Slowly accelerating to twenty miles an hour, she leaned forward and clutched the wheel as if she was racing.

"By the by," she asked, catching Raymond's eyes in the rearview mirror, "What are you and your brother fussing about?"

Raymond shrugged and looked back nervously at the cars collecting behind them. There were already three of them. "Nothing."

She grunted. "Folks don't usually argue that hard about nothing. So what are you fussing about?"

It was too big a question to answer. Raymond did not want to try to explain all the ways Vance made him feel stupid by always being larger, faster, smarter, and stronger. He sure didn't want to talk about the day at the Hinkles when their serious troubles had begun.

"I used to argue with my sister Bootsie," she went on, "but it sure wasn't over nothing."

"Bootsie!" Henrietta laughed. She didn't seem to notice the cars behind them. "Bootsie?"

Mrs. Clendenin chuckled. It was the first time Raymond

had ever heard her laugh. "Her real name was Betty, but nobody called her that after I nicknamed her Bootsie. It took her forever to forgive me."

"I don't blame her," Henrietta murmured.

"We argued over *big* things, like the time Bootsie gave Mama and Daddy my love notes that Byron Ethridge wrote me." Mrs. Clendenin ran her right front wheel off the pavement and then swerved across the center line when she pulled it back on, almost sideswiping a car that was pulling around them. Unaware, she kept right on talking.

"And then there was the time Bootsie inherited the piano from Aunt Viola and wouldn't let me touch it."

"That was mean," said Henrietta as yet another car zoomed around them.

Mrs. Clendenin nodded. "Then Bootsie bought herself piano lessons with money she earned clerking at a dime store and every time we had company she showed off. I'd about die of jealousy every time people started raving about how talented and smart she was."

"Yeah," said Raymond. He understood that. It was the way he felt when everyone praised Vance.

"I guess I got even—" she began and then broke off as they approached Rosanna Garmon's house. "That's where the old Lewis place used to be when I was a girl," she said, putting on her brakes and craning her neck to stare disapprovingly at the sign with the hand. There was a honk from one of the cars behind them, but Mrs. Clendenin paid no heed. "Charlie Lewis used to try to court me."

"So how did you get even with Bootsie?" Henrietta prodded her.

Mrs. Clendenin returned to the story. "Well, I didn't mean to, but nobody ever believed me. I got punished like it was on purpose."

Raymond was overcome with curiosity. "What did you do?"

"Spilled a can of paint on the keyboard," she said, turning onto the quarry road without giving any signal. Raymond closed his eyes. There were sounds of screeching brakes all around them, but thankfully no collision occurred and presently he felt the welcome bouncing-jolting movements that meant they had reached the quarry road. "Bootsie said she'd never forgive me, but she did. And I forgave her for everything she did to me. I want to tell you kids something I learned a long time ago: Never is a long time when you're talking about not forgiving your folks. You have to forgive when it's family."

Floppy came running when they pulled up in front of the trailer, and then moments later, Bruce came from around back.

"Come on, Bruce," Henrietta called to him from the window. "Mrs. Clendenin is going to take us to a real good place to get the rest of our leaves, and we're going to help her get some pine needles for her flower beds."

Bruce turned questioning eyes toward Raymond.

Raymond hunched his shoulders. "Henrietta arranged it." It was all the explanation he could politely offer in Mrs. Clendenin's presence.

Henrietta smiled at them both. "That's right. I'm in charge, remember?"

Bruce threw up his hands and headed for the car. Floppy trotted right behind him.

Mrs. Clendenin frowned. "You can't bring that dirty dog in my car."

Bruce looked down at Floppy and drew back. "My dog ain't dirty!"

Mrs. Clendenin refused to budge. "Looks it to me. Besides, the car is full already. And it'll be running over when all the bags of pine needles are loaded up."

Bruce turned away, then swung back to look at the woman through narrowed eyes. "How much you paying?"

"Pay!" She sniffed. "The way I figure, it's a fair trade.

You get leaves for your project and I get pine needles for my flower beds."

"Huh! Figure again! I can get plenty of leaves right around here."

There was an uncomfortable silence during which Raymond was sure he and Henrietta would be the only ones helping with the pine needles. Then Mrs. Clendenin looked at the bus, the blue car off to one side of it, and the crude shed at its back, and her face softened. "Well," she finally said, "I reckon I could go a dollar each, providing you work hard. But that's my top offer."

Bruce grinned. "All right, it's a deal." He pushed Floppy back and climbed into the car beside Raymond. "No!" he yelled out the window to the dog. "Paw'll be here in a little while. You stay here and wait!"

Floppy chased the car to the quarry road, crying and carrying on all the way. However, he finally turned back, tail drooping, and headed for the bus.

Back on the highway, Mrs. Clendenin resumed her meandering progress, frequently slowing to point out landmarks and remains of landmarks while traffic stacked up behind them once more. "The old Hollis place was over there," she said presently, waving her hand toward a bunch of trees off to the left. "That's where my man friend Garner Hollis grew up."

That must be the man with the beard, Raymond thought. The man who helped her with her flower beds and sometimes went shopping with her.

Bruce sniggered. "Man friend? You mean, you date?"

"Oh, you think I'm too old?"

Bruce gave her a straight answer. "Yes."

Raymond agreed, but he wasn't going to say so.

"I guess you think I'm too old for square dancing, too, huh?" She turned to frown at Bruce and ran two wheels off the pavement this time.

"Too old to drive, too," Bruce whispered in Raymond's ear.

"Well, I'm not too old to dance, and I'm not too old to get married, either. And I might just do that. For your information, me and Garner are only in our seventies."

"Seventy's not old," Henrietta said, managing to keep a straight face.

It was more than old, thought Raymond. It was ancient. Then he remembered that his grandfather was in his seventies. There must be different ways of being old, he decided.

Mrs. Clendenin went on to tell them all about how Garner used to play football a thousand years ago when he was in high school and how he was still the best square dancer— even better than the late Mr. Clendenin—not to mention the best banjo picker, whatever that was. She interrupted herself when the road to Miss Autrey's house came into sight.

"That's Autrey land," she said.

Henrietta leaned to look down the road. "Miss Autrey, our teacher?"

Mrs. Clendenin nodded. "She lives in the old homeplace, they tell me. All by herself. Used to have that crazy father of hers living with her, but I think he finally died. He used to spend every dime he got his hands on putting up fancy buildings and buying fancy breeds of cows. Thought he was a cross between an architect and a cowboy, I guess. Some said he was dangerous."

"He was bound to be dangerous—and mean—if he was Miss Autrey's old man," said Bruce.

"Really?" said Mrs. Clendenin, looking surprised. "I've always heard what a wonderful person Rosemary Autrey was, and several people I know say she was the best teacher they ever had."

Raymond grunted with disbelief. As far as he could tell, Miss Autrey didn't even go out of her way for good students like Henrietta and apple-polishers like Justine. As for students like himself and Bruce, she only found ways they could improve. Hundreds of ways. Okay, he thought, recalling her bull, Buster, maybe she is good to animals and maybe she was kind to her father. But he was never going to see her as a good teacher.

"The Bonners used to own the land next to the Autreys," Mrs. Clendenin went on. "Fact is, they used to own the land where the quarry is now. They say the Bonner homeplace fell in years ago."

Raymond and Bruce exchanged glances. Raymond longed to ask questions, but he did not want to give away any information about the hideout.

Mrs. Clendenin chattered on until finally she pulled onto a dirt road with a huge pine forest planted in rows on one side and a forest of mixed trees on the other. Then the work began. Raymond and Bruce piled up the needles with rakes while Henrietta and Mrs. Clendenin scooped them up and bagged them. When every spot in the trunk and part of the backseat was filled with bags stuffed full, they went leaf hunting. They didn't need the books Henrietta had brought along. Mrs. Clendenin was a walking encyclopedia.

"This is black gum," she said, pointing out a small tree on the left. "We used to make toothbrushes out of this. And this over here is ironwood. Don't never try to saw any of this down. It's hard as a rock." She identified three kinds of oak, a sassafras with its three different kinds of leaves, and hickory while Bruce and Raymond gathered leaves and Henrietta took notes.

By the time they started home, Mrs. Clendenin declared herself too tired to spread any pine needles that day. "You can all help me tomorrow after school," she said when she turned on to the quarry road. When Bruce spoke up to protest, she added, "And I'll pay you when we're finished, of course."

She pulled to a stop in front of the bus. Peavy Manis's

truck was back now, loaded with new-looking lumber and roofing tin, but the man was nowhere in sight. Bruce got out of the car, looking around for Floppy, and Raymond followed him. "Tell my mother I'll be home in a little while," he called to Henrietta as the car backed up over a small bush and turned.

Bruce whistled. "Here, Floppy! Here! Here! Here!" He grinned at Raymond. "Must be after a squirrel. He's the huntingest dog you've ever seen. I was telling Mr. Messer about that squirrel he treed the other day and Mr. Messer said it sounded to him like I had a real hunting dog." Bruce cupped his hands to his mouth and whistled and called in several different directions. "Here, Floppy! Here!"

Peavy Manis appeared from behind the bus, lugging a saw and dragging a ladder. "Quit bellering," he said, dumping his equipment in the back of the truck. "The dog ain't here." He headed behind the bus again.

The happiness drained from Bruce's face. "What do you mean, Floppy ain't here?" he demanded, running after his father.

Raymond hung back, wanting to hear and yet not wanting to, either.

Peavy was back in moments with a box of tools, which he set in the truck next to the lumber. He would not meet his son's eyes. "Just what I said. He ain't here and he ain't coming back."

Bruce looked about wildly. "Where is my dog?"

Peavy spat and headed for the truck cab. The usually slow-moving man seemed in a hurry to Raymond. "Back home, I guess," he said.

"Home is here," Bruce said, his voice becoming sharp.

"No, it ain't. That dog trainer Junior Elrod come by here while you was gone."

Bruce looked stunned. "Junior Elrod?"

"Yep. Said he lost a squirrel dog he was starting to train a few weeks back. Messer told him about the dog we had.

Elrod took one look at it and said it was his." Peavy got into the truck and slammed the door.

Bruce let out a bellow. "But that ain't so! Floppy didn't have no collar. All those hunters use collars and tags on their dogs."

Peavy shrugged. "Musta come off. Elrod give me ten dollars reward, loaded the dog up in that cage of his, and left."

"Floppy ain't his! He's not," Bruce yelled as the truck started up. Raymond retreated, but Bruce moved along with the truck as it backed up, still arguing with his father.

"It was just a dog, and we don't need one noway," Peavy said, changing gears and moving forward. "See you tomorrow sometime. I got a job to do in Hazelton." The truck speeded up and moved away.

Bruce would not give up. He ran out in the road, screaming, "Wait! Where does Elrod live?" though it was obvious by this time that his father could no longer even hear him over the sound of the motor.

"I hate Elrod," he screamed, bending to scoop up and sling a handful of rocks, "and I hate you!"

As Raymond heard the sound of rocks clanging against the metal, he drew back, chilled both at the words and the thought of what Peavy Manis's reaction would be. But apparently the man did not notice. The truck kept on going and soon disappeared in a cloud of dust.

Even when the truck was gone, Bruce was scooping up more rocks and throwing them. He threw them at the bus, the Camaro, and the metal shed. His face red with fury, he picked up a piece of pipe and headed for the bus.

"No!" Raymond cried, but it did no good. Bruce pounded several dents before throwing it down and heading for the door.

"Don't!" Raymond yelled as Bruce overturned the concrete-block steps. Gathering his courage, Raymond caught him by the arm as he headed for the storage shed. "Hey, don't do this! Man! You're going to be in trouble!"

Bruce fell against the metal building, shaking with exhaustion and fury and taking in rasping gulps of air. "Who cares! Floppy's gone, and he ain't Elrod's!"

Raymond nodded, though he really wasn't positive about this. Wouldn't the man know his own dog?

"Elrod just heard from Messer what a good dog he was and decided to claim him."

This seemed a good possibility to Raymond, but before he could say so, Bruce went on. "If Floppy was his, how come Elrod had to put him in a cage?"

"Yeah," said Raymond, glad that he could find something with which he heartily agreed. Bruce certainly would not have to cage Floppy to take him somewhere.

Bruce turned his eyes toward the trailer and then to the grease-marked spot where his father's truck had been parked a few minutes before. "I hate him!" he said in a low voice. "I hate the old man for this, and I ain't going to never forgive him!"

Raymond recalled what Mrs. Clendenin said about never being a long time when it came to not forgiving someone in your family, but he did not think this was the time to repeat it. Instead he asked, "But if your father thought the dog was Elrod's, didn't he have to let him take it?"

Bruce shook off the question as if it had no merit, but he had no immediate answer.

"I mean, Floppy *might* be Elrod's."

Eyes flashing a warning, Bruce stood and straightened his shoulders. "Don't you say that! Floppy's mine and I'm getting him back." He started around the bus in a determined, purposeful stride.

"How?" Raymond whispered. The whole thing looked pretty final to him.

"I don't know how yet," Bruce answered, jamming his hands into his pockets, "but I am." Suddenly he took off running down the road. Raymond did not try to follow.

16
KING SHOES AND CLOWN POCKETS TO THE RESCUE

"Oh!" cried Henrietta as Raymond dropped the "Common Tree and Foliage" poster board on the counter beneath the bulletin board in Miss Autrey's room. Her voice echoed impatient and shrill in the early morning stillness. "Now see what you did! You broke off part of the oak leaf!"

"Oh! A broken leaf! How terrible!" Vance mocked, knocking the circle of tree trunk he carried against a desk and Raymond's wooden stands under his other arm against the counter.

It was the Friday following Floppy's departure and it was also project-judging day. At Henrietta's insistence, Mrs. Lazenby had hauled everything to school, arriving there even before Miss Autrey. Vance was there because he had been ordered by his father to help lug everything in.

"I'll open the windows," Raymond muttered, heading across the room. His brother's voice followed him.

"Why isn't Bruce Manis helping with this instead of me?"

he demanded as Raymond jerked open the first window. It was the same question Henrietta had asked several times during the week. Raymond had no answers. Bruce had said very little to him during the past four days. Absent from school several days, he had been sullen and untalkative when present, and after school, Raymond had been unable to find him either at the bus or the hideout.

Raymond opened the second window just as a car pulled up out front. "Miss Autrey!" said Henrietta. "Hurry! I want everything set up before she gets in here."

Raymond didn't hurry. Plodding to the next window, he watched his teacher unload a pile of things from her car. He smiled when one item tumbled to the ground and bounced, and laughed out loud when another, a paper construction of some sort, was caught in the breeze and blown across the driveway before the woman was able to run it down and pin it to the ground with one big foot. Whatever the thing was, it was crushed flat when she picked it up.

"Tree section right here," Henrietta was saying to Vance, "Diagram of a Tree Cross Section poster here. Set the stands up! Hurry!"

"Gladly!" Vance threw the tree cross section up on the counter, plopped down the stands, and started for the door. "Raymond, Mrs. Potter is picking up Bunky and me after school," he said, "so I'm not going to help you take this stuff home today."

"We don't want you to," Henrietta called after him. "These will be on display for days."

Raymond didn't answer. He was watching Miss Autrey close her car door with one hip and begin trudging toward the front steps with a teetering mountain of objects. Still smiling, Raymond moved on to the last window and reached to open it.

"*Psssst!*"

Looking out the window, Raymond sobered instantly.

Bruce was outside, crouched in the boxwood that pressed close to this part of the building. Quickly, Raymond looked from Miss Autrey to Henrietta, who was still busy arranging the display, before opening the window and whispering, "What are you doing?"

Bruce put a finger to his lips. "Climb out the window and come on," he hissed. "I'll tell you all about it when we get away from here!"

Raymond darted another glance in Henrietta's direction. Out in the hallway, Miss Autrey's voice sounded. The woman was offering advice to another teacher. Raymond turned back to Bruce. "Go where?" he asked, playing for time while he thought it over. "You talking about skipping school?"

Even as Bruce nodded, Raymond was being tempted to do this thing that he had never done before. The thought of escaping the stuffy schoolroom and Miss Autrey was almost too appealing to resist.

Bruce saw his hesitancy and pounced on it. "Nobody'll ever know you were here if you keep your mouth shut. I heard your brother say he wouldn't be home after school. And your sister has that afternoon job. Come on," he said. "I need you!"

"Need him for what?" asked Henrietta.

Raymond swung around to find the girl right at his elbow. "Nothing!" he said, trying to keep her from looking out the window. It didn't work, and, besides, Bruce kept right on talking.

"I found out where Junior Elrod lives. The man that took Floppy last Sunday."

"What?" said Henrietta, pushing by Raymond and leaning out the window. "Floppy's gone? What are you talking about, Bruce Manis? Who'd want that mangy dog of yours?"

Bruce ignored her. "You going to come or not?"

"No, he's not," Henrietta answered and then turned to

Raymond, hands on hips. "You're not going anywhere! You're going to stay right here and help me give the report!"

Suddenly Raymond's hesitation was swallowed up by anger. "I don't have to mind you and I already told you that you had to do the report by yourself!"

"Yeah," Bruce agreed. "You ain't his boss! He'll come if he wants to. Come on, Raymond."

"I'll tell," Henrietta threatened as Raymond lifted his knee to the window ledge. Heavy footsteps were echoing down the hallway.

"I could tell something, too," Raymond began, seeing in the girl's face that she was thinking of the curtains Chester had torn up. Then he thought of a different approach. "How would you like it if somebody had taken your cat off?"

Henrietta let out her breath. "All right, all right!" she said. "I won't tell."

Raymond slid out the window in a flash and dropped into the shrubbery beside Bruce. Moments later they were tearing across the deserted playground to freedom.

Raymond's joy did not last long, however. Before they had crossed the meadow, doubts were nagging at him. By the time they stopped for breath at the edge of the woods, he was pretty certain he had made a mistake. As Bruce rattled on about all the ingenious things he had done over the last four days to track down Junior Elrod, Raymond was casting his eyes back in the direction of school, reconsidering his hasty actions.

He watched a yellow bus pull into the distant school yard, and then another. Suddenly the school yard was not empty anymore. In fact, as the minutes passed, it was getting more and more full. He still might be able to go back without being seen. He could probably get into class without being caught. Maybe . . .

"So what do you think?" Bruce was asking.

Raymond looked at the boy blankly. He had no idea what the question was.

"I mean, maybe we don't even have to see the man. Floppy's going to know my voice. He'll come to me."

Raymond nodded slowly. "Yeah. If he's not penned up."

Apparently Bruce had not considered this. He bit his lip. "Well, could be nobody's home. And if they ain't, I figure taking my own dog ain't no crime."

Raymond hesitated. This was getting more and more serious. "Yeah, but . . . What if someone *is* home?"

Bruce shrugged. "Well, then we'll just have to work out a trade."

"Trade?"

"You know, swap something with him. I'll get something out of the old man's shed. Something he won't miss. Or—or maybe we could do some work for Elrod."

Raymond was not too happy with the use of "we." "You could use your money," he suggested. "You could buy—"

Bruce cut him off. "No way. That's what I'm saving for getting away."

"But what if this man won't—"

Bruce didn't wait to hear any more negative possibilities. "He will," he said, starting on again. "Over this way's Hogan Road," he said, pointing. Raymond saw only trees. "Which ties on to Kelly Bottom Road, and that dead-ends on to Alpha Springs. I figure we better stick to the woods and dirt roads where we won't be likely to meet up with somebody that'll ask why we ain't in school."

Raymond nodded. He was all for that. He cast one last look back toward the white stucco building. The place was swarming with students now and the parking area was full of teachers' cars. Then, even as he watched, the children all headed toward the building. He knew even though he had not heard it that the bell must have rung. No turning back now. Not without being caught. He turned to follow Bruce.

The woods quickly swallowed them up. Most of the trees were pines, but there were some hardwoods, too, as well as a multitude of stumps from trees cleared out in the not-too-distant past. Henrietta could have gotten plenty of tree sections here, Raymond thought.

Bruce cut through them all as if he knew where he was going. Raymond tromped after him for what seemed like hours while the sun rose higher and higher in the sky. They stopped once in the middle of a field for some squashed candy Bruce dug out of his pocket and another time for water from a clear spring. Again they stopped and waded a creek and shared a box of raisins Bruce produced. Just as Raymond despaired of ever seeing another sign of civilization, a road appeared.

They looked both ways along the narrow winding road before jumping down onto it. It was only a little wider than the quarry road and had almost as many washed-out places. "We'll hide in the woods when we hear somebody coming," Bruce said.

Raymond hoped there'd be nobody from whom to hide. His wish was granted. There were no cars or trucks until they reached the road Bruce identified as Kelly Bottom. A wider, better-kept road than the first one, Kelly Bottom was bordered by more fields than woods, and there were several run-down houses and fading trailers squatting along its banks.

The boys speeded up. They held their breath each time they passed a trailer or a house, especially those where people seemed to be at home. Three different times they hid while trucks and cars passed, and once for an interminable length of time while a huge cotton-spraying machine inched its way past. Finally they saw where the road dead-ended up ahead.

"You let me do the talking if anybody's home," Bruce said.

Raymond nodded vigorous agreement. He sure didn't want to do any of it.

"We don't want to act too anxious now," Bruce went on. "The other day Elrod acted to my old man like Floppy wasn't one of his best dogs. Said he was just beginning to train him. But maybe that was just so he could get away with a measly old ten-dollar reward."

The sum did not sound measly to Raymond.

" 'Course, Floppy ain't *his* dog anyhow," Bruce went on, kicking at a rock, "and even if he was, Floppy was mine after I found and fed him for as long as I did."

Now Raymond went back to his earlier question. "What if he won't make a deal?"

"He has to," Bruce said with quiet determination.

"But—"

"He will. He has to. If he's there, I mean. Bet he's not there."

They saw the house and fell silent. It was a concrete-block building, once painted white but now graying and mud-splattered. The mailbox was painted blue, with the name "Elrod" scrawled across it in red paint that had dripped and run in several places.

To Raymond's surprise, Bruce seemed as reluctant as he to actually approach the house. His steps grew slower and slower as they neared the mailbox, then halted altogether when a green truck appeared beyond a stand of concealing shrubbery. It was the same truck Raymond had seen parked just off the quarry road the day they had helped Henrietta cut the tree sections.

Bruce's face sagged with disappointment. He studied the truck and the yard for a moment and then motioned Raymond to follow him to the kudzu-covered road bank off to the right. From the vines, they surveyed the yard, the truck, and the house for several minutes. Though they saw no one, Raymond was certain someone was there. Smoke drifted from a fire somewhere in back, and there was the unmistakable smell of food cooking.

Bruce cupped his hands to his mouth and whistled. Raymond sank into the grass as not one but a whole chorus of barking dogs replied. It sounded like fifty of them, all yelping at once. Minutes passed and none of the dogs appeared.

Bruce was dismayed. "Heck!" he whispered. "They must be penned up, like you said."

"Yeah," Raymond answered, relief in his voice.

Bruce stood. "Could you tell if one of them barks was Floppy's?"

Raymond almost laughed and then caught himself. "No."

"Me, neither." Bruce eased down the bank and headed for the house.

Raymond pointed out the cagelike contraption on the back of the truck and Bruce ran to look in it. "Empty," he said, running up the steps to the house and pounding on the front door. Raymond peered through the screen door into a room filled with old furniture. The walls were covered with overlapping photographs that curled at the edges. Raymond nudged Bruce and pointed to a large one showing a bald-headed man squatting between two dogs.

"Shoo!" said Bruce, pinching his nose. "This place pure stinks." Raymond turned away. From somewhere out back, a rooster crowed and then another. Several dogs barked.

Turning on his heel, Bruce jerked his head and ran down the steps. Raymond followed him past a garden with the remains of dried cornstalks, bean poles tied together tepee style, and skeletons of dead tomato plants. In the backyard, a foul odor masked the smell of food from the house. It did not take them long to figure out the source of it. Cages. Four cages, all filled with rabbits, each with a large accumulation of waste below the wire-bottomed enclosures.

To the right along a foot-worn path leading to the woods was a pen filled with clucking chickens. Then came roosters, more than a dozen of them, each tethered to its own small house, each strutting about its tiny yard or perched on its roof, crowing and making a show of itself.

It was at that moment that the barking started up again. It seemed to be coming from beyond a barnlike shed up ahead. When they rounded the shed a few minutes later, they found three large pens—two of them filled with dogs. Like the roosters, they seemed to each have their own little house, for there were lines of overturned oil drums along the chain-link fencing. The dogs were reared up against the fence. All of them were some combination of black and brown and all their ears were long and droopy.

"Floppy!" Bruce called, running from one side of the fence to the other, examining the animals, bending to look into the dog-houses.

"He's not here," Raymond said, looking back the way they had come, but Bruce paid no attention.

"He's gotta be," he said. "I heard his bark."

"Hey!" someone shouted. "What you doing?"

Bruce and Raymond jumped up to see a bald-headed man in overalls coming from the woods. He led a dog on a leash with one hand and with the other, he carried some kind of board with an animal skin attached to it. This dog had perked up ears instead of the big droopy ears of the dogs in the pens. As he drew closer, the boys realized that the man was barefoot and frowning. "What you boys doing?" he repeated.

Raymond gulped. "Nothing."

Bruce didn't look any too brave, either. "You Junior Elrod?" he said.

"So what if I am?" the man asked.

"We just happened to be passing by and decided to look at your dogs," Bruce said. "Thinking about buying one."

"Yeah," Raymond said when the man's eyes cut around to him. "We like dogs."

"You can't afford mine," the man snapped, opening the empty pen and shoving the leashed dog inside. The dogs were barking more loudly than ever. "And I don't like getting 'em riled up. Messes up their training." He locked the pen and turned on them with narrowed eyes. "Who are you?"

"Uh, Bill," Bruce replied, almost shouting to be heard over the noise of the dogs. He moved on around the shed, looking quickly this way and that. "I'm Bill Smith and this is Ray Jones," he said, jerking his head toward Raymond. "You got any more dogs besides these?"

The man ignored the question. "Smith and Jones, huh?"

Raymond winced at the fake-sounding names. He fell back behind Bruce and considered ducking around the out-buildings and running. It was then he caught a glimpse through the partly open doorway of the shed and spotted a dog rearing up against a rope. However, this dog was familiar. Brown and white in color, it had one pointy ear standing up, while the other flopped down.

Meanwhile, Bruce chattered on, still retreating with Raymond toward the rows of rooster houses. "You are Junior Elrod, ain't you?" he said.

"That ain't none of your business," the man replied. "What you want anyway?"

"I want a dog. Sort of a present. Yeah, a present for my old man. Somebody told me you really know how to train dogs, and I'm willing to make you a good trade for the right one."

A horn sounded and two men appeared in the yard behind the house. One of them was tall and skinny and the other was very stout. Neither of them looked too clean and neither was smiling.

"Hey, Junior! We're here to do business!" the stout man shouted.

Junior started toward the house and then stopped. "Get outta here!" he said. "You boys can't afford my dogs! I ain't even going to give you a price. No deal."

"But—" Bruce protested.

"Can't you understand English! I said, no deal!"

The men at the house were growing impatient. It was the tall one who called this time. "Hey, Junior! You gonna do business or not?"

"Coming!" said Junior, taking Raymond by the shoulder and grabbing for Bruce.

"Oh, all right," said Bruce, to Raymond's relief. "We'll go." He took several steps toward the house and then stopped, looked around, and patted his pockets. "Uh oh! My knife!" he bellowed. "I lost my old man's pocketknife! I musta dropped it back there. Please let me go back and find it before I go!"

"Junior, we ain't got all day," called the stout man.

"My old man'll wear me out!" Bruce blubbered while Raymond looked on in disbelief and Junior Elrod started toward him with a flushed and angry face. "And he'll bring me back over here this afternoon and make me hunt till dark," Bruce sobbed. "It was his best one!"

Junior stopped and cursed. "All right, get your blasted knife and get out of here!"

"Yes, sir!" Bruce said as the man turned and stomped toward his house. "Thank you! You wait here," he said to Raymond. "I know right where I dropped it."

Raymond waited. He watched Bruce disappear around the side of the shed and listened to the dogs tune up again. In the other direction, he saw Junior talking to the two men, their heads close together. They started up the steps once, and then Junior jerked a thumb in Raymond's direction and stopped.

"Found it!" Bruce shouted a few minutes later, running down the path toward Raymond, a pocketknife in his upraised hand. Raymond ran with him past the rooster cages, chicken yard, and rabbits.

"Thanks, Mr. Elrod!" Bruce sang out as they passed the three men moments later. "I found it!"

They rounded the house and Bruce slowed long enough to hear the voices start up again. The back door slammed as the boys passed between the old green truck and the newer blue one parked beside it. Bruce smiled and broke into a run once more. He did not slow until they rounded a bend in the road far ahead and found a grove of trees. There he climbed a bank and hid himself in the grass.

Raymond lay in the grass beside him and tried to decide whether or not to tell the boy about Floppy being tied up in the shed. He felt sorry for the dog and for his friend. But what good would it do for Bruce to know? Elrod obviously was not going to give up the dog and might even hurt Bruce and Raymond if he caught them around his place again.

While Raymond fought with himself, Bruce said quietly, "He was in the shed."

Raymond sat up. "Who?"

"Floppy. Elrod had him tied in the shed."

So Bruce had seen him, too. Raymond groaned inwardly. Now Bruce was going to want to do something foolish and dangerous. Something in which Raymond was not going to want to have any part. He took a deep breath and made up his mind to speak. "I'm not going to go back there," he said.

"Don't have to," said Bruce. The boy rose to his knees and parted the weeds to look down the road. "All we gotta do is wait."

Raymond looked through the bushes, too. All he saw was a dirt road. "Wait? For what?"

Bruce grinned. "For Floppy. When I went back to the dog pen a while ago, what I really did was go around back of the shed and crawl through a window. Man! Floppy just went crazy, jumping all over me, licking me. He nearly had that old rope chewed in two already. I got my pocketknife and worked on it a little in the place he had gnawed on the most. It won't take him any time to get loose. All we have to do is wait here a little while and . . ."

Raymond shook his head. "Elrod will catch him."

"Not if Floppy hurries and chews through while they're in the house. And with Floppy's nose, he'll pick up our trail in no time."

"Elrod hasn't forgotten where your father lives," Raymond said. "He'll come back after him, and if he catches you there, he's gonna know . . ."

Bruce bit his lip. "I thought of that. I'm gonna lie low. I'll tie Floppy up over at the hideout for a while. Wait till Elrod has had a chance to come asking and the old man has told him he ain't seen his dog. Then I'm gonna use some of Rita's old hair dye—she used to buy every color in the world—and dye his fur before I let him go back to the bus."

Raymond shook his head. "It won't work. That stuff will wear off. Besides, Elrod's gonna know . . ."

"Well, if nothing else works, I'll just have to take my dog and go live with Rita."

"Your mother?" said Raymond, only now realizing how desperate Bruce was. "I thought you said—"

"I'll do what I have to do to keep my dog, even if it means living with her," Bruce said. "The only friend I have is that dog. I can't count on nothing else. But Floppy loves me no matter what. I don't aim to let nobody take him away from me."

At that moment the sound of happy barking broke into their conversation. Looking through the weeds again, Bruce smiled and held out his arms to receive an armful of yipping, lapping dog. It was Floppy all right, still dragging the remnants of the rope from his collar.

Raymond watched as boy and dog, dog and boy rolled over and over in the grass, paying no heed to briars, rocks, or pinecones. Bruce was laughing and Floppy was letting out little yips of joy. So absorbed was he in watching that at first Raymond did not notice the yells from somewhere down the road, but as they drew closer and closer, he heard—and so did Bruce. Even Floppy raised his head and perked his ears.

"Hector!" a man was yelling. There was no doubt about the voice. It was Junior Elrod. "Here, Hector! Here! You come back here, you sorry mutt!"

Bruce was up in an instant and streaking through the woods with Floppy on his heels. Hoping they knew where they were going, Raymond followed right behind.

17

ON THE RUN

Bruce pulled Floppy close and looked up and down the highway before digging into his pocket for coins for the pay phone outside Messer's Store. Raymond looked, too, keeping up his vigilance after Bruce hunched over the phone and began dialing. Suddenly he saw something appear around a distant bend.

"The school bus!" he yelped, feeling both surprise that the day had gotten away so fast and alarm at the possibility of being spotted by a classmate or perhaps even Vance if Mrs. Potter had not picked him and Bunky up as planned. He punched Bruce, but the boy only shrugged him off and kept on dialing.

Raymond edged himself past a soft-drink machine and around the corner of the building, where he found absolutely nothing nearby behind which to hide. The usual scattering of customers' cars was missing at the moment and noises from the rear of the building warned him away from that area.

He continued his survey. The large green trash dumpster at the edge of the parking area was swarming with flies. The meadow was too far away and the grass too short to hide in. With a groan, he flattened himself against the brick wall and tried to become invisible. Floppy, rope still dangling, joined him as Bruce began to speak in a low mumble.

"Hello. Rita?" he was saying. "I want to speak to Rita. Rita Manis . . . er, LaSalle, that is. Rita LaSalle. Well, where is she? I'm Bruce Manis, her son, and I have to talk . . ." There was a long pause. "She did? Well, when will she be back?" There was a another, longer pause. "But she's got to . . . she told me . . ." His voice broke. He cleared his throat and went on gruffly. "You got her address? She musta left an address. Well, okay. Sure. Sure. Yeah, sure, lady."

The bus of noisy children rumbled by at last and suddenly Bruce was bounding around the corner. "Hide! *She's* coming!" he said, looking around desperately.

"Who? Who's coming?" Raymond asked, poking his head around the building just in time to glimpse a familiar-looking black car coming from the same direction that the bus had come from—school.

"Miss Autrey!" he uttered, skimming over the parking lot after Bruce, who was headed for the trash dumpster. Before Raymond realized what was happening, the boy had heaved Floppy up and into the dumpster and was scrambling up himself. Without stopping to think of the flies or the odor, Raymond followed, pulling himself over the rim and landing with a plop into a collection of plastic milk jugs, old newspapers, and rotten vegetables. Floppy found a bone to chew on while Raymond clamped his nose firmly between thumb and forefinger and looked around for Bruce.

"Of all the dumb hiding places!" he whispered when Bruce emerged a moment later from a large cardboard box picturing a TV set.

For some reason, Bruce chose not to reply. He was ripping one sleeve off his shirt. Before Raymond could ask why, the sound of a car pulling off the highway silenced him.

A horn beeped and an indistinguishable woman's voice called out something. A man's voice answered, "Just a minute, ma'am. Be with you soon as I take care of this."

Both boys drew up small and Floppy looked up from his bone as footsteps crunched across the gravel. Then suddenly what seemed like a truckload of garbage was raining down on them. Floppy was in heaven. Dropping his bone for the moment, he rolled over and wallowed in the mess. The footsteps crunched away and finally there came a sound of a distant door opening and then closing.

"Stinking garbage!" fumed Raymond, pulling himself over a carton of crushed eggs and making his way toward the top of the dumpster.

"Nobody made you get in here," hissed Bruce from behind him.

"Shut up!"

"Shut up yourself!"

There was an angry silence as they peeked out. The coast was clear. Raymond leaped to the ground.

"To the hideout, the back way," Bruce ordered, jumping down behind him. "Go across the meadow to the pasture." Trailing bits of garbage and swatting at flies, Raymond went, looking back only once, to see Bruce jerking Floppy out of the dumpster.

Caught! Caught! Caught! The words echoed in Raymond's brain each time his foot struck the ground. What-ifs buzzed in and out of his mind like the flies around his face. What if Henrietta had blabbed after all? What if Miss Autrey went to the trailer park? What if Vance and Jackie Lee were both, through some trick of fate, at home? Worse yet, what if his mother had left work early today?

"We'll go to the creek and wash up," Bruce grunted, catching up as Raymond rolled under the barbed wire into the pasture.

Raymond did not give the sharp answer he would have given a few minutes before. His anger had been swallowed up by his fears now. "Fine with me," he said.

Encouraged, Bruce continued on. "Then we'll go the back way to the hideout."

Raymond jerked his head in agreement. That, too, was all right. Anything to keep him away from home. Anything to delay finding out how many of his frightful what-ifs had come true.

It was at the creek while he was stripping off his clothes that Raymond realized the reason for Bruce's ripped-off shirt sleeve. It was wrapped around the boy's right hand. A bloodstain showed in one place.

"Hey," Raymond said, reaching out.

Bruce thrust the hand behind him. "Just a scratch," he said.

"Where—" Raymond began, but Bruce cut him off.

"Some glass in that TV box. It ain't nothing."

Raymond felt his throat tighten. "Hey, man. There must be a thousand germs in that trash. Let me see—"

"No!" Bruce's voice was sharp. "I told you it was just a scratch."

Raymond shrugged and waded into the water where Floppy was already frolicking. After all, he told himself, he had enough problems of his own without worrying about Bruce's scratches. He looked downstream, and seeing no sign of either the bridge or Madame Rosanna's place, he gave himself up to the delicious coolness of the water.

He was finished scrubbing and was floating when Bruce finally got his clothes off and waded in. Rayond tried not to see the boy holding his right hand up while washing himself with his left. He tried to think only of how good the water felt and how wonderful it was to be clean.

But later when he began to scrub his clothes and scrape his shoes, it was not so easy to dismiss his friend's injury, not when he noticed how awkwardly Bruce pulled on his clothes, or how the bloodstain had spread.

"I guess you heard me talking to Rita a while ago at the store," Bruce said, breaking a long silence.

Raymond concentrated hard on the tying of his shoes. "Uh, yeah." If Bruce wanted to pretend he had actually talked to his mother, it was all right with Raymond.

The boy squared his shoulders and started in the direction of the quarry road. " 'Course she wanted me to come stay with her, same as always."

"Yeah?" was all Raymond could think of to say.

"Yeah. But I told her, 'Listen, this ain't gonna work.' I mean, while I was talking to her, I figured that out."

"So what you going to do?" Raymond asked.

Bruce slung the hair out of his eyes and put on a false-looking grin. "I got it all figured. I'm going to let you keep Floppy."

"Me?"

"Yeah. Elrod would never think to hunt for him at the trailer park and I could go over to see him every day and . . ."

Raymond shook his head. "He wouldn't stay. He'd be back over at your place before you got home."

"Not if you tied him."

"Yeah, and then we'd have Mrs. Clendenin fussing at us about him howling. Besides, my folks wouldn't allow me to keep him in the first place. I told you how they made me leave my dog Butch in Tennessee. You'll just have to keep him at the hideout."

Bruce frowned. "That ain't going to work, neither. I thought about it, but something might hurt him—maybe a bigger dog or a snake or something, and him tied up so he can't defend himself. Besides, if he's over there in the woods by himself, you talk about howling! There's got to be another way."

They walked on at a slower pace now, thinking. Floppy was the only one of the three who seemed happy. While Bruce frowned and hunched his shoulders and Raymond struggled to find some way out of his mess, the dog pranced on ahead, coming back frequently to lick Bruce. He seemed to sense the injury and want to help.

They reached the quarry road and paused. Something did not seem right somehow. Then Raymond figured out what it was. There were fresh-looking tire tracks on the little-traveled road, several sets of them, and in the air a dust cloud hung like a light fog. Bruce frowned and pointed to a cigarette butt in the ditch just below. A curl of smoke rose from it.

Presently, Floppy lifted his head and perked his ears in the direction of the quarry. At that moment the sound of a motor sent both boys into hiding. Bruce only managed to pull the dog down into the bushes beside him and order him to be silent before Junior Elrod's green truck appeared.

Raymond pressed his face into the grass and closed his eyes for a moment. First Miss Autrey and now Junior Elrod. Who else was going to take off after them?

The truck inched forward slowly, a head hanging out either side. They heard Elrod's voice before they could make out the face of the man himself. Still wearing his overalls, he was leaning out the window, yelling with an obviously forced cheerfulness, "Here, Hector! Here! Come on, boy."

Floppy was not deceived. Keeping low in the grass, he showed no inclination toward obeying.

Only when the truck drew even with them did Raymond

realize the man in the passenger seat was Bruce's father. "Four wasted trips," Peavy Manis yelled to be heard over the motor. "But if it'll make you feel any better, I'll have my boy Bruce look again when he gets home from school." He spat. "Like I told you, though, I ain't giving back your money. A deal's a deal."

The truck stopped and Junior Elrod got out and looked across the field along the opposite side of the road. Raymond and Bruce flattened themselves to the ground as the man called, "Here, Hector! Here! Here! Here!" Finally they heard him say, "I don't want money. I want the dog. He was supposed to be a squirrel dog, but I ain't been able to keep hold of him long enough to find out if he knows for sure what a squirrel is."

There came the sound of a door slamming and then the truck moved on. When it was out of sight, Bruce leaped up and jumped down to the road. He was headed toward the quarry. "You heard him," he said grimly. "He ain't going to stop. Not until he finds my dog."

"So what are you going to do?" Raymond asked.

"Stay out of sight until I can get out of here," Bruce replied, looking over his shoulder and breaking into a run.

Raymond considered turning toward home, but he hated to leave Bruce alone to run from the man. Besides, Miss Autrey might be waiting for him at the trailer park at this very moment. He caught up with his friend again as the road to the hideout came into sight. "Where are you going? Your mother is already . . . I mean . . ."

Bruce stopped and turned on him. "I told you I ain't going to her! I'm going to my uncle."

"How? Bus tickets cost a lot of money, and they wouldn't let Floppy ride."

"I know that." Bruce ran on. This time he did not stop until he reached the turnoff. Even then, he only paused long enough to glance one more time at the road behind.

"How?" Raymond asked again when the road had finally been swallowed up by the woods. "How are you going to your uncle? It's too far to walk."

"By train."

"Train?" Raymond asked, looking at Floppy. "Will they allow dogs . . ."

Bruce laughed. "The way I'm going, they will."

Raymond realized at once what he meant. "You can't do that," he exclaimed. "You could get hurt—or arrested. My grandpa says sometimes escaped convicts hop trains!"

Bruce put on his bravest face. "Floppy will stick up for me, won't you, boy?"

The dog, which was several yards ahead, turned as though he understood the question, barked an affirmative, and trotted on.

Bruce laughed. This time it sounded real. "See? It's like I tell you, I can count on my dog."

"You heard Junior Elrod," Raymond couldn't help saying. "Floppy isn't really yours."

Bruce swung around to face Raymond. "He *is* mine! I was the one that fed him and took care of him when he was nearly starved to death. And I'm the one he wants to stay with. He could've gone to Elrod a while ago if he had wanted to."

Raymond had to admit Bruce was right on both points. Perhaps Elrod had mistreated the dog. Certainly he did not love Floppy as Bruce did. So thinking, Raymond pushed his doubts aside.

They were nearing the pear trees when Raymond next broke the silence. "When will you leave?" he asked.

Bruce did not answer until he started around the ruins of the old house. "Tomorrow."

Raymond's mouth went dry. "Tomorrow?"

Bruce nodded and ran past the barn and downhill toward the hideout. The dog ran on ahead. "I got to get out of here. Elrod is going to get Floppy if I don't. And you heard my old man. He'll make me give him back—especially if Elrod comes across with more money."

Tail wagging, feet prancing, Floppy was waiting for them on the porch when they arrived. Raymond lifted the latch and threw open the door. Bruce headed for a shelf and grabbed a rag that looked none too clean. When Bruce unwrapped his hand, Raymond caught his breath at the sight of a gash running across three fingers. Before he could get a better look, however, Bruce had rewrapped his hand and thrown himself down on the hammock. He stared at the rafters and the roofing tin above it.

"I'll sneak over tomorrow after the old man leaves for the flea market," he said, thinking out loud, "leave a note saying I'm going with Rita. He'll believe that. Then I'll get my money and go to the railroad siding to wait for a train."

The silence stretched out long. "Hey, I'm sorry," Raymond said at last, wishing he could make the boy understand how helpless he was. "I'm sorry about everything."

Bruce turned his face away. "It's all right."

"But like I said, I can't take Floppy. My folks wouldn't allow—"

"I told you it's all right. Listen, this place'll be yours from now on. You can have all my stuff."

"Thanks," Raymond said, feeling the need to match his friend's generosity, even though most of what was left would do him little good. "I'll come see you off in the morning," he finally offered.

Bruce smiled slowly and Raymond realized it had been the right thing to say. "It'll have to be early."

Raymond busied himself catching a cricket that hopped across the floor. "I always get up early on Saturday."

Bruce swung his legs off the hammock and stood. "You . . . well, I guess you're the only real friend I ever had—besides Floppy, I mean."

Raymond dropped his head. The compliment warmed him but embarrassed him, too. He stepped outside. "I could take the note to your father," he said. "I'd leave it in the mailbox."

Bruce rose to follow. "Nah, I gotta get a few clothes. Thanks anyway. But there is something . . ."

"What?"

"Well, about the money . . . Will you . . ." Bruce hesitated.

It came to Raymond what the boy wanted. He wanted Raymond's share of the money. For a moment Raymond resisted the idea of giving it. After all, the car-seat money represented a beginning toward replacing the field glasses. Raymond had to struggle with himself several moments before finally nodding.

Bruce's face was instantly transformed with a smile. "You will?"

"Sure." Raymond shrugged off the gratitude in the boy's voice, stepped off the porch, and swaggered up the hill, feeling pretty good about himself.

Bruce followed after him. "Great," he said. "I don't think I'll be able to climb up there with my hand being sore and all."

Raymond lost his swagger. Open-mouthed, he swung around to stare at Bruce. "Climb?"

Bruce frowned at his bandaged hand. "You need two hands when you go up that quarry wall."

"Quarry wall," Raymond repeated, shaking his head. "I thought—I mean, I didn't know . . ." he began, trying to think of a graceful way out of this mess. Before he could, Bruce ran uphill and grabbed his shoulder with his good hand.

"I ain't never going to forget this," he said. His eyes glowed with gratitude.

"But I . . . " Raymond began again.

"Be here real early, now," Bruce said.

"All right," Raymond said at last and turned away and headed for home. His feet were as heavy as his heart.

18
THE QUARRY WALL

It's funny, Raymond thought the next morning at breakfast, how most of the things you worry about never happen. Then something you don't think of at all, something you don't dream of, happens in its place and turns out to be ten times worse. Apparently Miss Autrey had not come to the trailer park yesterday to find out why Raymond had skipped school. If so, she had not talked to his folks. But now here he was, trapped into doing something that had given him bad dreams all night and now filled his stomach with dread. He forced down a bite of eggs and looked around the table at his family wondering whether he dared confide in one of them, wondering whether he dared ask for help, and wondering most of all who'd be most likely to give it, if he did.

"Dad," he said in a low voice a few minutes later when his father left the kitchen.

Mr. Brock patted him absently on the shoulder. "Not now, son. I'm going to be late." He looked over Raymond's head to Mrs. Brock, who was carrying glasses to the sink. "The boss said I'd probably get five or six hours' overtime today."

Mrs. Brock gave him a quick smile that softened the lines in her face and made her look younger. "I may not be here when you get back. Jackie Lee and I have a hundred things to do in town."

The man with whom Mr. Brock rode had picked him up and left before Raymond found courage to tackle his mother. He gathered up dirty plates from the table. "Mom . . . " he began, sliding the plates on to the narrow counter next to the sink.

His mother let out a squeal as the half-full orange juice pitcher tipped and spilled. "Raymond!"

Raymond grabbed a dish towel. "I'm sorry!"

Mrs. Brock let out her breath and reached for the bottle of dish detergent. "It's all right. What did you want?"

"Nothing," he replied, turning away.

"Maybe you'd like to go to town with Jackie Lee and me," his mother called after him. "I could get you some new shoes."

Raymond shook his head. Somehow, new shoes did not seem important right now.

"I'm busy, Raymond," Jackie Lee said to him a few minutes later when he tried to talk to her. She was applying long fake nails on top of her real ones and having a hard time of it.

Vance was outside under a shade tree, working on Bunky's motorbike. Bunky was nowhere in sight right then. Raymond watched his brother for a few moments in silence, being careful not to bother the bike.

Just as he was about to speak, Henrietta went out her front door carrying a litter box and a bottle of disinfectant. Raymond turned away from her curious eyes.

"Gimme some elbowroom," Vance said, shuffling through the wrenches in Mr. Brock's tool chest.

"That wrench there is the one you need," Raymond said, giving his brother a friendly smile.

Vance scowled. "Just because you helped Grandpa all the time, I guess you think you know everything about fixing things," he said, deliberately choosing another wrench.

Raymond pretended not to notice that the wrench did not work. "Hey, Vance," he said, "I need to talk to you."

Vance threw the wrench back into the tool chest and snatched up the one Raymond had pointed out earlier. "Yeah? What about?"

Raymond licked his lips. "Well, what would you do if you had to do something you were afraid to do?"

Vance looked up. "What are you talking about? What are you afraid of?"

Raymond hesitated, not sure how much to tell him, and while he tried to make up his mind, Bunky arrived. "Here are the new parts," he said.

Vance smiled. "Great!" He turned back to Raymond. "So what is it you need? We're busy." Impatience was written on his face.

Raymond moved away. "Nothing," he called over his shoulder. "Forget it."

Vance apparently already had, for as Raymond walked away, he heard him saying, "Bunky, hand me those pliers."

From the corner of his eyes, Raymond was aware of Henrietta coming toward him as he started nearing the end of the trailer park, but he pretended not to see her.

"Wait!" she called behind him as he broke into a run.

Raymond looked over his shoulder to find the girl right behind him. Vance and Bunky were laughing. He wasn't sure it was directed at him, but it irritated him anyway. "Don't have time!" he yelled at her.

She kept right on coming. "I got something to tell you," she said moments later, grabbing him by the arm.

Raymond stopped and swung around. "What?"

"Miss Autrey liked the wood sections you and Bruce cut. I told her you did that part and got most of the leaves and that since I was in charge, I did the report."

"Thanks," said Raymond.

Henrietta grinned. "She liked your stands, too. She gave all three of us *A*'s."

Ordinarily this news would have interested Raymond a lot, but not now. "All right," he said, turning to go. "Great."

"Stop!" Henrietta said, falling into step beside him. "What's going on? What did you and Bruce do yesterday? Did you get the dog?"

Raymond kept walking. "I gotta go," he said.

"You better tell me what is going on, Raymond Brock!" she said, raising her voice so loud that Vance looked toward them.

Raymond turned on the girl. "Hush! My mother is going to hear you! And if she does, I'll . . . I'll . . . "

"Don't you try to blackmail me!" she said. "I've never seen anybody so hard to be friends with. I'm trying to help you. I'm not like Justine Weaver, going around telling on people for the fun of it."

Grudgingly, Raymond conceded that point. She was no tattletale. "All right, all right," he said. "But there's no way you can help. Yesterday I went with Bruce to get his dog back from this man who took it."

"I know that. But—"

"And we got him," Raymond said, answering the next question before she could get it out.

"So where are you going now?"

"To the quarry," he answered before he thought.

Henrietta's eyes grew large with excitement. "Your field glasses! Madame Rosanna said they would be around stone!"

"Ha!" said Raymond. "No, the field glasses wouldn't be over there. They're not anywhere! They're gone and tomorrow when Grandpa Brock comes for his truck, he's going to know about it. My folks are going to kill me and Grandpa Brock is going to be disappointed in me."

"So why do you want to go to the quarry?"

"I don't *want* to!" Raymond burst out. "I've *got* to! That's all I'm telling." Turning away, he darted around the end of a trailer and cut across a yard. The pasture fence was just ahead. He heard Henrietta yelling as he crawled through the fence and more faintly as he tore off across the pasture, but he did not answer. Why bother? She couldn't help. And probably wouldn't if she could.

When he neared the Manis place, he slowed long enough to determine that all seemed quiet and deserted around the bus. Undoubtedly, Peavy Manis was gone to one of his flea markets. Raymond hurried on. It was later than he had realized, he decided, looking at the sun glinting through the trees. Perhaps Bruce had given up on him and gone on without the money. The possibility pulled him two ways. That would mean he did not have to climb the quarry wall, but it would also mean he had let his friend down.

A better thought came to him a little later as the quarry wall came into full view: Bruce's hand was better. So much better that Bruce had gotten the money himself. He had probably left a farewell note in the hideout. He proba-bly . . . That did not satisfy him, either. He wanted to be able to tell Bruce good-bye.

A familiar yip broke into his thoughts and Bruce Manis arose from a clump of bushes on the road bank. He was cradling his right hand in his left. "Why are you so late?" he demanded. "I bet I've been here an hour." Without wait-ing for explanations, he jumped down to the road. Hoisting a burlap bag over his shoulder with his good hand, he jogged toward the quarry. Raymond had no choice but to follow.

They entered the fenced area and Bruce set his bag down. Floppy spotted a rabbit and took off in hot pursuit. While the two boys made their way past the place where the tent had once been pitched, the dog yipped his way through the thick bushes and pines at the far end of the enclosure.

"Sounds like Floppy's got something," Raymond said, hoping for a reprieve. But it did not work.

"Yeah, he *better* learn to feed himself," Bruce said with a grim face. He was headed straight for the rubble-strewn base of the quarry.

Raymond looked up and bit his lip. It looked like a thousand miles to the top.

Bruce looked up, too. "You can just throw down the jar. Don't matter if it breaks. Throw it over here where it's cleared out, so the money will be easy to find." He pointed to an area so stony and pebble-strewn that it supported a bare minimum of grass. "Best pull off your shoes," he instructed. "Easier to climb that way."

Raymond obeyed dumbly.

"This way," Bruce continued, approaching the rubble at the base of the wall of stone. "Go up right over here. Remember where I put the jar? Just over to the right of that little ledge. Straight down from that oak tree on top. You'll be able to use it for a marker 'cause part of it sticks out over the edge."

"What do you think you're doing here?" a voice demanded right behind them. The boys swung around to find Henrietta.

"You," Bruce exploded. "Why do you always have to show up where you ain't wanted? Get out of here and go home! You're the one ain't supposed to be here!"

"Yeah," Raymond agreed, but his heart wasn't in it.

"You're trespassing!" the girl accused them.

Bruce advanced on her with a menacing frown. "And what about *you*, Miss Busybody?"

Henrietta held her ground. "I only followed you to find out—" She broke off as her eyes dropped to Bruce's hand.

Dried blood showed on the makeshift bandage. "What's wrong with your hand?"

"None of your business!" Bruce thrust the hand behind him. "All right, you're here. You ain't going to bother us none. Come on, Raymond."

Raymond only nodded, mostly because his throat was suddenly too dry for talk. He began to clamber gingerly over the sharp-edged rubble along the cliff, Bruce accompanying him and Henrietta tagging along behind, still demanding an explanation while both the boys ignored her. They reached the top of the pile of rubble and Bruce pointed out the best place to begin the climb.

"Climb?" Henrietta panted. "What are you talking about?"

Raymond reached for his first handhold. "Don't look down," Bruce instructed. "Not till you're ready to drop the jar."

"Jar?" Henrietta asked. "What jar? What are you going to do?" She looked from one boy to the other and then, as if for the first time, at the jagged cliff in front of them. Then her eyes went to Raymond's hand, which was already grasping a ledge of rock. "You're not going to . . ." she said. "You're not . . ."

"He ain't scared," said Bruce.

"Scared!" yelled Henrietta, turning on Bruce. "You dummy! He's terrified!"

"I am not," Raymond managed to croak. It did not sound convincing.

Grinning, Bruce clapped him on the shoulder with his good hand and pushed him forward. "I knew you weren't, King Shoes."

"You idiot!" Henrietta screamed as Raymond turned to the wall and began to place his hands. "You jerk! Don't you go up there."

Now Raymond couldn't back down. He hoisted himself

up to the next handhold, and then the next, while below him Henrietta continued to yell.

"You're a natural," Bruce called out, and it did seem to Raymond that his hands and feet were moving as if they knew what to do, as if they belonged to somebody else, somebody who climbed all the time and wasn't afraid. Gradually the girl's screams subsided.

"I can do it," Raymond whispered into the silence. His knees scraped against rough edges. Powdery grit grated like sandpaper against his fingers and toes. He looked upward and reached again, then again. He squinted at the bit of green floating against the sky far, far above. It must be the oak tree.

"Don't look down," he told himself, and then, "faster, I gotta go faster. Get it over with."

Straining his neck backward, he put his whole mind and body into finding the next place to grasp, and the next. Not that one. Too far off to the right. Gotta go straight. Not that one. It's not wide enough. Right hand up, right foot up, left hand, left foot. The wind blew, and sand and pebbles sifted down like rain. His neck began to ache. His eyes began to sting. Right hand, left, right, left. Muscles in both arms and legs began quivering as though about to cramp. Perspiration made trails down his forehead and stung his eyes. Salty grit collected on his arms and face. Minutes that might have been hours crept by, and far away, as if from another time, a dog barked. Vaguely he realized it must be Floppy.

"You're nearly there," Bruce yelled at last.

"Yes," Raymond whispered, recognizing the niche just above him. Moments later he reached it, thrust his hand inside, and, yes, there was the jar. He grabbed it, twisted around, and threw it off to the left. As the jar left his hand, he gasped in terror. The ground was a million miles away. Bruce and Henrietta were bugs, Floppy a mere speck. Head swimming, heart pounding, Raymond hugged himself against the stone wall. The sound of breaking glass came back long moments later.

Bruce yelled something from down below and then Henrietta. Raymond didn't try to figure out their words. He hugged himself more tightly than ever against the wall. It was as though he could not breathe, could not move. Why had he done this foolish thing? He was so scared that he would never be able to move another inch. He was going to fall to those rocks far below and he would never, ever live after such a plunge. He closed his eyes tightly and wished this could be a dream. If only he could wake up safe in bed.

Bruce yelled again and Raymond forced himself to open his eyes and look down. "Climb on up!" Bruce was calling between awkwardly cupped hands. Henrietta had her hands twisted together as though in prayer.

Raymond didn't even try to answer. He only let out a low moan and squeezed his eyes shut again. The wind moved across the face of the cliff. He pressed his face against the rocky wall and squeezed his fingers and toes tighter against the stone. Minutes passed.

"Climb on up!" Bruce yelled.

"He's too scared to climb!" Raymond could hear Henrietta scream. "I told you! I told you!"

"He is *not* scared!" Bruce yelled back at her. "Get moving, Raymond!" he called again. "I hear a train coming. It may go on the siding. We gotta go."

Yes, far in the distance, Raymond heard it, too. But it was of no importance to him. He couldn't even remember why it was important to Bruce.

"Climb on up," Bruce screamed again.

"Can't, can't, can't," Raymond whispered against the rock.

"Climb up," Henrietta yelled. "You can make it!" Raymond could hear the uncertainty and fear in the girl's voice.

She knew as well as he did that he could not do it. She knew he was going to fall. Even now, his fingers and toes were beginning to slip a little. He tried to squeeze them tighter against the rocks, but they would not obey.

"You rested long enough!" Bruce yelled. "If you don't climb up right now, I'm leaving you!" Sure enough, when Raymond forced himself to open his eyes, Henrietta was already gone and Bruce was moving away. Suddenly Raymond felt total fear engulfing him like darkness. It would be completely unendurable to be left alone.

"No," Raymond called down in a voice that sounded too tiny and weak to be heard. "Don't leave!"

"Well, start climbing then! You're nearly all the way to the top."

"I am?" A tiny ray of hope penetrated Raymond's despair. Nearly at the top. Was it possible? He squinted upward. The tree still floated above, reddish-yellow leaves mixed with green, all outlined against a blue cloudless sky. Suddenly he realized that he had not been able to see individual leaves a while ago. He must be getting close! Eagerly he examined the irregularities of the rocks above him. Maybe . . . Hope shot through him like liquid fire. Just maybe . . .

Quickly he darted his right hand upward, then the left. Gritty rock chips ate into his flesh, but he hardly noticed. His pants ripped against a sharp-edged rock, but he kept on moving. Inch by inch he climbed, not permitting himself to look upward, not allowing himself to think. Handhold by handhold he moved upward, and then suddenly a dark head was outlined against the oak leaves! It was Henrietta. She hadn't left after all! She had gone around and climbed up the mountainside. Her hand stretched downward toward him. Minutes later Bruce was there, too, reaching his good hand down. Then they were both grabbing him, one on each side, and hauling him over the edge.

Raymond broke loose and ran several yards, whirled

around and around, and then threw himself to the grass, hugging himself to earth as if he were afraid someone might jerk it away. Safe! Safe! The soil smelled good. He had never noticed that before. The grass was so green and cool and lovely. Floppy seemed to catch his mood. He, too, rolled on the grass, barking as he went.

Bruce bent over Raymond. "Hey, you all right?"

Suddenly realizing how foolish he must look, Raymond jumped up and became very busy, brushing himself off, hunting for dusty places on his legs. "Sure!" he said in a voice that was shaky in spite of his best efforts. "Did you get the money?"

Henrietta jumped in before Bruce could answer. "Humph!" she snorted, throwing his shoes and socks down at his feet. "I tried to tell you! But, no! You had to climb up that wall and get him that dumb money, which you were crazy to put up there to begin with, and you nearly got killed when you got scared— "

"He was not scared!" Bruce informed her.

Raymond pulled on his socks and shoes. "No, I wasn't scared," he said, but he could not meet her eyes.

"Oh, yeah! Then why did you freeze up there for an hour and a half?"

"He was resting!" said Bruce. "Weren't you, Raymond?"

Squirming in embarrassment, Raymond nodded his head. He couldn't admit how terrified he had been, especially when Bruce believed in him. "That's it. I was resting. Did you get the money?"

"Nearly all. Oh, and this is your part." He held out a wad of bills.

Raymond pushed the money away. "You keep it."

Bruce hesitated, looking first at the green bills and then at Raymond. "You sure?"

Raymond nodded. "I want you to have it. You need it more than me, and it's not enough to buy what I wanted anyway."

"Thanks," Bruce said just as the train whistle came again. "You going with me?"

"Sure," Raymond said, though he could tell this train was going too fast to be stopping.

Henrietta ran after them as they started downhill, bombarding them with questions. "Are you going to get on a train? Where are you going? What about your hand, Bruce? Are you going, too, Raymond?"

Bruce and Raymond ignored her and kept on running. The train came louder and louder as they raced downhill, and by the time they retrieved Bruce's burlap bag and headed around the mountain toward the railroad tracks, the clacking of the wheels was clearly audible. However, as Raymond had suspected, this particular train was not stopping.

Henrietta fell back, but she kept hollering questions as the boys headed into a tangle of underbrush. "What about your hand?" she called as they were almost out of sight. "Don't you know about infections? You might get gangrene. You might have to get it amputated."

Bruce hooted with laughter. "Well, just as long as they don't cut it off!"

Henrietta said no more. Shrugging elaborately, she turned toward home.

19

LEAVING

"Reckon Henrietta's gonna tell on you?" Bruce asked Raymond as they picked their way alongside the railroad bed where a rough road made the walking easier. He seemed worried about that. It was the second time he had brought it up since the girl had left.

Raymond shifted the bag he had volunteered to carry to his other shoulder. It was much heavier than he had expected. "Nah," he answered with an assurance he did not feel. He looked down the pair of tracks that stretched through a seemingly endless tunnel of tall trees until they converged and disappeared. "Nobody'll be home to tell. Mom and Jackie Lee were going to town, Dad's at work, and Vance'll probably be gone with Bunky."

"You don't have to stay with me," said Bruce. "I may have to wait a while for a train going in the right direction to pull on the side tracks. Old Flop here'll keep me company, if you need to go." He reached to pat the dog that trotted along by his side.

For a moment Raymond was tempted. The burlap bag was getting heavy. And he wasn't really sure his mother would be gone when Henrietta returned. Neither did he feel certain the girl wouldn't tell. But, on the other hand, he couldn't leave his friend alone to manage the bag now that he realized how heavy it was. "I'll stay until you leave," he finally said. "I wanted to see you off."

Bruce seemed relieved and glad. "Great!" He stopped suddenly and looked around. "You know, Miss Autrey's place is probably just over this way." He gestured down the railroad tracks with his good hand.

Raymond looked where he pointed. There seemed to be no houses, just forested countryside, and yet now that he thought about it, mentally placing the quarry and estimating its distance from her home, Bruce had to be right. The train whistle had been clear and close that day in her shed.

Bruce pointed to a gap in the woods. "Look there. I bet that chimney is one of hers."

Raymond squinted at the smudge of red brick. "Could be."

Bruce laughed. "Maybe I oughta swing by there and see if I can get my other knife before I go."

"Yeah," Raymond replied, shifting the burlap bag again, "and miss your train."

"You're right," Bruce agreed. "Ain't worth that."

"Besides, you'd never find something as little as a knife in all the junk she has."

"That's a fact."

The land dropped into lower, marshier area, and as it sloped, the mound of slag on their left became a wall. The boys fell silent, each lost in his own thoughts. For the first time, Raymond realized how very lonely he was going to be without Bruce. Without him, there would be no fun in going to the hideout, nothing to do during the long and lonely afternoons after school. Miss Autrey's class would be intolerable without him to liven things up. And Floppy . . . He looked at the dog trotting out ahead. Even though Floppy was Bruce's, Raymond felt that he was part owner.

Bruce seemed to share his thoughts. "We sure have had fun," he said, his voice cracking a little on the last word.

Raymond nodded. "We sure have. Wish you didn't have to leave."

Bruce cleared his throat. "Me, too." He looked up ahead. "Up there where the tracks go over that creek is a good place to wait."

Reaching the stream, Raymond put down the burlap bag and found a place to stretch out full length. Bruce sat down, pulled a plastic jug from the bag, and turned it up to his lips. "You want some water?"

Raymond shook his head and looked toward the bridge. The area beneath it was a spooky place, deeply shadowed and devoid of grass. Support posts painted with black creosote lined with hundreds of fingerlike dirt-dauber nests marched across the bare creek banks. Mysterious markings in the sand told of animals that had been here under cover of darkness. Nose to the ground, Floppy ran to investigate.

Turning back to his friend, Raymond asked Bruce a troubling question that had just occurred to him. "How do you know you won't end up in New York City or something?"

"Easy," Bruce said. "I ain't going to get on no northbound train." He pointed up the track with his good hand. "I'll be headed *south*." He slung out his injured hand in the other direction and hit a pine-tree limb. Groaning and cursing, he doubled over the hand.

"You all right?" Raymond asked.

Bruce did not answer, but as soon as he could speak again, he continued what he had been saying. "Then I'll get off in Birmingham, hop an eastbound freight to Georgia. Any more questions?"

"Yes, what are you going to do about that cut?"

"Nothing. It's nearly well."

"How about food?"

"Simple!" He jerked his head toward the burlap bag. "I got plenty of peanut butter and crackers in there."

"I wouldn't like peanut butter three times a day," said Raymond, who had grown tired of having it for a snack every afternoon since his mother had gone to work and stopped baking cookies.

"I like it fine," said Bruce.

"What about Floppy?" asked Raymond, nodding toward the dog, which was now sniffing his way into the woods, tail up and ears perked. "You got food for him?"

Bruce looked troubled for a moment. Apparently he either had not considered this or had not been able to make provisions. "Floppy can eat peanut butter and crackers, same as me," he finally said, getting up to follow the dog. "At least until we get where we're going."

Raymond followed, wondering how to word his next question. Finally he just blurted it out. "What if . . . what if you run into somebody who tries to hurt you?"

Bruce swung around to face him. "Listen, I ain't like you. I ain't had four or five people looking out for me."

Raymond had never thought of it like that before. He had thought of himself as being bossed around by the rest of his family, not as being looked after.

"I've had to learn to take care of myself," Bruce continued. " 'Course, now I have Floppy to stand up for me."

Floppy sure didn't look like much protection to Raymond, but he hesitated to say so. Instead he shifted to another bothersome angle. "This uncle of yours . . . What if . . ."

Bruce turned away before Raymond could finish the question, and started after the dog. "Let's see what Floppy's after."

Floppy led them up a small slope to the right and then

stopped in a room-sized clearing encircled with large trees. The spot was as free of underbrush as though cleared by hand and was lightly carpeted with leaves and moss. Several rocks were scattered about as though planned for seating. Bruce sat down on one. "Ain't this pretty?" he said.

Raymond nodded. It was more than pretty. It had a quiet peacefulness about it and a feeling sort of like he had in church sometimes. The sunlight streaming through the leaves in ribbons, the whispering of the wind through the trees, and the gurgling of the nearby stream all combined to give it a feeling of enchantment.

"This is where I'd like to live," Bruce said. Floppy wagged agreement. "Here with all these . . . What kind of trees are these, King Shoes?"

Raymond shrugged. "Poplars?" He wasn't sure.

Bruce laughed. "We need Henry and Clendenin here to tell us."

Raymond remembered Henrietta's news. "Hey! Guess what? You got an *A* on that science project. We all did."

Bruce's laughter faded. "No kidding? Well, what do you know? An *A*."

"I guess that's Miss Autrey's good-bye gift," said Raymond, surprised at the pleased expression on his friend's face.

"Speaking of presents," Bruce said, reaching slowly into his pocket. "Here's something I want you to have." He pulled out his knife—the one with the fancy white handle and all the different blades—and placed it in Raymond's hand.

"I can't take this!" Raymond protested. "Not your special knife."

Bruce laughed. "You have to. 'Cause I'm giving it to you."

A distant train whistle cut off Raymond's thanks. Bruce leaped up and headed toward the railroad tracks. "Which direction?" he yelled over his shoulder.

"Don't know," Raymond yelled back. It was too faint to tell.

Minutes later Bruce broke out of the woods and scrambled up the graveled bank to the tracks. Loose slag tumbled down with each foothold and sent Floppy whining back to the spot where Raymond waited.

The whistle came again and Bruce smiled. "South!"

Raymond's heart flip-flopped. Until now, Bruce's leaving on the train had not seemed real. Now it was real and sad and scary and Raymond wished he could find another solution for his friend.

Bruce did not seem worried. Laughing, he slid down the embankment in an avalanche of gravel. "Now, if it'll just stop on the siding!"

Long minutes passed. The whistle sounded again, closer this time, and the clackety-clacking of its wheels became clearly audible. Bruce was jubilant. "It's slowing!"

And it was. Even Raymond could tell. By the time the beaming headlight, piercing even in sunshine, appeared around a far bend, the locomotive seemed to have slowed to a creep. But its engines still roared as powerfully as ever. Raymond counted four gray-green diesels before Bruce jerked him into the bushes. Floppy did not like the noise, which seemed to spread until it enclosed the woods on either side and the ground beneath their feet. Whining low in his throat, the dog paced back and forth, looking frequently at his master for reassurance.

The train came closer. Through limbs and leaves, Raymond made out a man in overalls leaning out the window of the front engine.

"Down!" said Bruce, reaching to pull Floppy out of sight. "Don't want him to see us and get suspicious."

Raymond pulled himself so low he could only barely see the train. There were several tense moments as the engines passed, going slower and slower by the moment; but then the hoppers appeared, followed by a couple of rattling gondolas, some rack cars filled with new automobiles, and then at last the boxcars. They stretched back almost as far as the eye could see, interspersed only here and there with flatcars and hoppers, refrigerated cars and tankers. Several had open doors. Raymond could not help wondering whether other people had sneaked into them, perhaps into the one Bruce would choose. They might be there now, waiting.

The train grated to a halt, still roaring. "Now!" Bruce said, not bothering to keep his voice down. The diesels with the engineers were far ahead. He stepped out from behind the bush and ran to the place where the burlap bag lay.

"How do you know which boxcar to pick?" Raymond asked, his eyes taking in the several open cars. None of them was close by.

For the first time Bruce looked uncertain. "I'll take that red one down there," he said, and tried to lift the bag one-handed.

"I'll carry it for you," Raymond said, heaving the sack to his shoulder. He started after Bruce, who was already heading for the red car.

The train whooshed like a giant horse and the clanking grated on Raymond's ears. Plumes of gray diesel smoke rose into the air and acrid fumes stung his nose. Floppy liked it even less than Raymond. The dog was nervously running ahead and then returning to Bruce.

Bruce turned back. "I think I hear the train this one is waiting for. That means this one will be moving soon. Let's go!" Now he ran along the sloping wall of slag, looking for the best route up. Just short of the red boxcar, he found it and began climbing. Dodging the gravel Bruce was knocking loose, Raymond was first climbing and then crawling up after him.

"Come on, Floppy!" Bruce yelled, for the dog had refused to follow.

"I'll get him after I get your bag in," Raymond said, wondering even as he spoke whether he had the strength to do it.

Then above him, Bruce let out a cry of dismay. "Oh, no! It's too high!" Raymond looked up to find the boy at the open doorway of the boxcar. Sure enough, the wide boxcar hung over the steep embankment so far on this side of the tracks that the floor of the car was too high for Bruce to jump inside. The boy bent to look beneath the train and, for a horrible moment, Raymond thought his friend was going under the train, but Bruce looked at Floppy and shook his head. Then as the whistle of the northbound train split the air, he ran down the graveled slope.

"I gotta take it on the other side where I can get to a level place to climb in from!" he gasped. "We'll go under the bridge and when this train passes, I can go up there!"

Bruce hit the road and began running, with Floppy right behind. Raymond followed, but just as he was about to run under the bridge, he caught a movement from the corner of his eye. He turned to see Vance coming on Bunky's motorbike—and behind him sat Henrietta. Both of them were waving and hollering.

"Wait!" Vance yelled, stopping the bike in a cloud of dust. "Wait!" His voice was barely audible over the sound of the approaching train.

Raymond ran after Bruce. He splashed through the creek and out into the sunshine again, the burlap bag bouncing up and down on his back. Vance caught him as he turned right alongside the railroad bed.

"Are you crazy? Don't do this!" Vance yelled, swinging him around.

Raymond looked toward Bruce. Seemingly unaware of Vance's arrival, he was poised to climb the bank. He had to have the bag! "Let me go!" Raymond cried, jerking loose. Vance grabbed at him again and this time caught the burlap bag. The bag tore from Raymond's clutches and emptied crackers, peanut butter, water jug, and clothing all over the ground.

"Stupid!" Raymond yelled, gathering up crackers and clothing.

Now Henrietta got into the act. "I had to tell!" she said. "I had to tell even if you did get mad!"

"Shut up!" Raymond yelled at her, grabbing up the bag and running to catch Bruce. The boy was already making his way up the gravel slope. The end of the northbound train was in sight.

"Listen!" Vance said as Raymond started up the embankment. He managed to get out in front of Raymond and block the way. "I know why you're leaving and I'm sorry. I shouldn't have done it, but you made me so mad!"

Kicking and shoving, Raymond managed to get around his brother just as the gravel gave way beneath Vance's feet and sent him rolling into the brambles at the bottom.

"Stop, you little creep, and I mean it," Vance yelled from the tangle of briars. "I risked getting myself in big trouble riding that motorbike on the highway just to come get you, so you'd better stop and listen to me."

Raymond scrambled to the top of the gravel bank, leaving Henrietta to help his brother.

The departing whistle of the northbound train sounded as he reached the top and the clanking of the one headed south began almost immediately. Bruce was far down the track. Apparently having forgotten his bag in the excitement of the moment, he was trotting alongside of the open doorway of the red boxcar, his hand extended pleadingly toward his dog. Floppy hung back, keeping even with his master but refusing to approach the moving train any closer.

Raymond ran down the railroad track, too, eyes on Bruce and Floppy. "Go on!" he pleaded with the terrified animal. Bruce was going to get hurt if he waited much longer to get in. The train was picking up speed by the second.

Then in one smooth motion, Bruce darted out, grabbed up the dog, and ran back to the boxcar. He set the animal in and as the train began a slow clackety-clack, he tried to get himself on board. Raymond held his breath as the boy attempted to vault himself up once, then twice, failing both times.

The train went faster. So did Bruce. Now he was jogging, still furiously trying to haul himself into the train car. Meanwhile, in the boxcar, Floppy was desperate. Pacing back and forth, he alternately prepared to leap and then pulled back.

Then it happened. Just as Bruce finally managed to throw himself into the train car, Floppy chose to leap out. Stunned, Bruce lay in the doorway of the boxcar, holding on with one hand and reaching out with the other while his dog crashed into the slag. For one horrible moment, Raymond was sure Floppy was dead. But, no, he was up moments later, running furiously after the car where his master, now standing, beckoned him to *jump! jump!*

Floppy ran, looking up at Bruce while the train moved faster and faster. Finally he did jump: one mighty leap that almost took him through the door of the boxcar. But then he fell away, appearing to knock against the wheels before tumbling limply to the rocks.

Bruce leaped from the train car, screaming *"No-o-o-o-o-o!"* For a moment the boy's wail and his angular body seemed to float suspended in air. Then his cry became one with that of the onrushing train and his body with the gravel. It wasn't for several seconds that Raymond realized that he himself was screaming, too.

20

A SECOND CHANCE

The southbound train passed in a roar and as the caboose rattled by, Raymond saw with a flood of relief that up ahead Bruce was pulling himself unsteadily to his feet. Though dazed and bloodied in a number of places, he was alive.

"Floppy?" Bruce said, blinking and looking about. Only now did Raymond remember the dog. He was lying where he had last fallen—a limp and crumpled heap of fur. Floppy's eyes were staring, his legs sprawled, and his head lay at a strange angle from the rest of his body.

Just behind him, Raymond heard Henrietta give a little cry and Vance shush her. But it was too late. Bruce had found the dog, too, and he was already limping toward him, hands outstretched.

"Floppy!" he wailed, throwing himself to the gravel. "Don't be dead, boy," he was begging as Raymond reached his side. "Don't be dead! Please!"

Henrietta nudged Raymond. "Check for a heartbeat."

"Fat chance," muttered Vance, kicking at a railroad tie.

Raymond could only stand in helpless silence while the pleading gave way to sobbing. He could only watch Bruce flounder there on the rocks and feel the sadness and loss swelling up in himself. He had never before fully realized that death could take those he loved. He bit his lip to hold back the tears.

Bruce let out a howl of grief, and Vance and Henrietta drew back. Raymond wanted to do the same but he knew that as Bruce's friend, he had to be the one to do something, the one to say something. But what? He reached out his hand and touched the boy's shoulder. "I'm sorry."

Bruce leaped up as though struck. "He's dead!" he cried, looking at Raymond with wild unseeing eyes.

"I'm sorry," Raymond repeated, reaching for his arm.

Bruce threw off the hand. "Dead!" he screamed, lurching backward. "He's dead!" He turned and bolted down the steep embankment.

"Wait!" Raymond yelled after him. "Come back!"

"Somebody needs to see to those cuts of yours!" shouted Henrietta.

Bruce gave no reply. Still screaming, he limped across the road and plunged into the woods.

Vance shook his head. "He's gone crazy!"

"I gotta stop him!" Raymond said, scrambling down the embankment and running across the road. He was only vaguely aware of Vance and Henrietta following after him. He was intent on finding Bruce, who had now completely disappeared in the trees. Following his friend's broken cries, he crossed a narrow stream and circled around a tangle of fallen trees. Finally, as the land began to rise and the trees to thin into meadow, he spotted Bruce. Then he saw something else—Miss Autrey. She had on overalls and carried a bucket instead of a purse, but it was unmistakably her. Raymond pulled back at the sight.

"Uh-oh," said Vance. "He's done for. Alligator Autrey has him now. Let's get out of here!"

"I'm not leaving," said Raymond, starting on. "Bruce is my friend."

"What on earth is going on?" Miss Autrey demanded in a loud voice. "What's all this commotion about?"

"He's dead!" Raymond heard Bruce cry.

Walnuts went rolling as Miss Autrey threw down her bucket and ran to grab Bruce by the shoulders. Her frown was replaced with an expression of alarm. "Who? Who's dead, child?"

Bruce fought to free himself. Trying to tear loose, he pounded the woman's arms and butted against her with his head, but she would not turn him loose.

"*Who's* dead?" she demanded again, her voice rising.

Bruce collapsed against her. "Floppy! My dog. He's dead and it's my fault."

For a moment Miss Autrey's arms became a kind of embrace. Then she looked over Bruce's head and spotted Raymond, Vance, and Henrietta. She beckoned them with a jerk of her head.

"Run to the house," she said to Henrietta. "Get the first-aid kit out of my bathroom at the end of the hall. You'll find it in the cabinet next to the bathtub. Meet me on the front porch." She turned back to Bruce, examining his wounds, bending to feel his legs and arms, and asking rapid questions. "I guess you're able to walk?" she finally asked.

Bruce jerked his head in an affirmative.

"Well, I don't think anything is broken," she said. She turned to Vance. "You pick up my walnuts over there, put them back in the bucket, and take them on to the house for me." Vance mumbled something about the motorbike and going home, but she did not listen. Her attention had shifted to Raymond. "Now, young man, you are going to tell me what happened."

Raymond told the whole story while the three of them walked across the meadow to her house. He would have left out some parts if he had been able to think fast enough and if he hadn't been afraid Henrietta would fill the gaps later. But it was probably just as well to be honest, he decided. Miss Autrey seemed to know all the places to probe, all the right questions to ask. By the time she settled down on the front porch to doctor Bruce, she had the whole story and allowed Raymond to flee to the shade of a large oak.

Henrietta remained on the porch. "I'll help you, Miss Autrey," she volunteered. "My mother is a nurse, remember."

To Raymond's surprise, Vance showed up a few minutes later with the bucket of walnuts. Raymond had expected his brother to get the motorbike and go home as soon as he was alone. Henrietta must have expected the same thing, for she looked up curiously when Vance appeared and then left her post and moved partway down the steps as he set the bucket down at the corner of the porch and joined Raymond.

"Thanks," Raymond whispered.

Vance did not look at him but turned a walnut in his hands, examining its rough surface as if to discover some secret. "For what?" he asked.

Raymond struggled with himself for a moment. It was hard to put into words how grateful he was that Vance had not deserted him. "For staying with me, I guess." He hesitated and then rushed on. "And for coming after me when you thought I was the one leaving on the train."

Vance's eyes widened. "You mean you weren't? I thought . . ." His voice trailed off.

Raymond shook his head. "No, just Bruce. Anyway, thanks."

Vance shifted about uncomfortably, bouncing the walnut

up in the air and catching it several times. " 'Course I was going to come after you," he said in a gruff voice. "You're my brother."

They suddenly became aware of Henrietta's presence. She was now standing only a few feet away. "You going to tell *him* what you told me a while ago?" she demanded. Her sharp little chin was thrown out and her arms were folded across her chest. Apparently Henrietta was speaking to his brother. It was Vance her eyes were riveted on.

Vance blushed. "I was going to, Miss Busybody," he muttered.

She smiled and dropped her arms. "That's good. I was only checking." She turned and ran back up the steps to retrieve a box of bandages Miss Autrey had just dropped.

Raymond swung around to face his brother. "Tell me what?"

"I was going to give them back," Vance began. "I shouldn't have done it, but I was mad."

It was the same thing Vance had said at the railroad tracks earlier, and it didn't make any more sense now than it had then. "Give what back?" Raymond asked.

Vance looked toward Henrietta and bit his lip. "The field glasses."

Raymond blinked in bewilderment. "The field glasses. How . . ."

Vance sucked in a deep breath and then spoke hurriedly. "I found them. That day at the store, I went around the back way and I found where Bruce had hidden them. I was going to give them back before Grandpa came, honest. I just figured I'd let you worry some. I was about to give them back to you, and then last Saturday at the creek you made me mad all over again."

It was as if a huge burden had been lifted from Raymond's chest. The field glasses were not gone after all! They would be back under the truck seat when Grandpa came tomorrow. He was so relieved that he could forgive Vance everything.

"They're hidden under the Potter trailer," Vance was saying.

The Potter trailer, with its aluminum underpinning painted and shaped to look like stones, Raymond thought, remembering Madame Rosanna's words. He almost chuckled before Vance's words brought him back.

"I guess I was getting even for a bunch of things. I mean, I'm older, but you've always been Grandpa's pick."

"Why should you care about that?" Raymond asked, surprised at the sound of envy in his big brother's voice. "You're the one *everyone* likes. You're the one good at sports. You're the one who makes good grades."

"Yeah, but I didn't get to drive Old Lizzie and go fishing. I didn't get to help Grandpa build the doghouse and the shed. He's always bragging about how you can fix things and build things. I remember that time he said, 'Vance, you sure you know which end of a hammer to take hold of?' "

"He was just joking when he said that," Raymond said, quickly going to the defense of his grandfather.

"Yeah, like Uncle Otis is joking when he calls you 'Short Stuff.' "

Raymond nodded slowly with reluctant understanding. "Yeah, that kind of joke's not funny." Not even when it's Grandpa doing the joking, he added to himself.

Vance continued on in a calmer voice. "Anyway, I'm not mad anymore."

"Me, neither," Raymond said, and was glad to realize that it was true.

Vance pulled himself slowly to his feet and started toward the porch. Now he was throwing the walnut far up in the air as he walked. He didn't miss it a single time because he was just naturally good at things like that. For the first time ever, Raymond wasn't envious. *He* was good at some things, too—like using tools and building things. And if he had a choice, he suddenly realized, he would rather be good at them than at throwing and catching. All at once, for the first time in his whole life, he was satisfied with being Raymond Brock. It was a good feeling, he decided as he followed his brother across the yard.

"Just cuts and scrapes," Miss Autrey was saying to Bruce as Raymond and Vance reached the steps. "But you may not be so lucky next time. Of course, there'd better not be a next time." She handed the tape to Henrietta, who added it to the other supplies in the first-aid box. "I'm sorry about the dog," she went on in a somewhat softer tone.

"Floppy," said Bruce in a sharp voice. "His name was Floppy."

Surprisingly, Miss Autrey ignored the rebuke and resumed the lecture. "But all this was totally unnecessary. You and Raymond skipping school, climbing quarry walls . . ."

Raymond hunched his shoulders as Vance swung around to look at him.

". . . and trying to hop trains," Miss Autrey continued on. "If you had come to me . . ."

Bruce got up from his chair. "What good would that have done?" he snapped.

"What good was your way?" she countered. "Seems to me, the dog would be better off alive with Junior Elrod than dead with you."

Bruce's entire body seemed to sag as the truth of her words sank in. He lowered his head.

"If you had come to me," she repeated, "there might've been things we could've done."

"Like what?" said Bruce, asking the question in Raymond's mind. It would never have occurred to him that Miss Autrey could or would help.

"Well, for one thing, I could have talked to Junior. He was one of my students a few years back. Something might have been worked out."

Bruce grunted his disbelief. "Huh!"

"I know a little about hunting dogs," she went on. "Enough to suspect that Floppy was probably pretty much ruined for squirrel hunting by the time you'd had him going after rabbits, moles, and everything else that moved. Junior's not the brightest person around, but he would've figured that out soon enough. And when he did, that dog would've been for sale—cheap."

Bruce let out a sort of groan and moved stiff-legged down the steps. "My fault," he mumbled, looking across the yard.

Miss Autrey followed, reaching out her hand toward him and then slowly pulling it back. "No good blaming yourself. You meant it for the best, and it's done now. But next time . . ."

"There won't be a next time," came Bruce's strangled reply. "I ain't going to have another dog."

"I'm not just talking about a dog. I'm taking about whatever it is you have problems with. You don't run away. You confide in somebody. You ask for help."

Bruce looked her in the eye. "Who? I got Raymond here, but when the old man decides to move on again, I won't have him. I don't have no mama." Miss Autrey flinched. "All I could count on was my dog, and now he's gone."

There was a long silence during which Bruce stared across the yard toward the hedge. The vines there next to the driveway trembled as if moved by a wind and the chickens that scratched nearby suddenly squawked and moved off.

Miss Autrey cleared her throat. "I know you don't see it now, but you do have people who care about you—relatives, friends . . ."—she paused—"teachers."

Bruce did not seem to hear. His entire attention was on the hedge.

Apparently giving up, Miss Autrey sighed. "Well, I think we need to bury the dog."

"I'll do it," Raymond forced himself to say.

"I'll help," Vance offered.

"Floppy?" said Bruce.

"Yes, Floppy," replied Miss Autrey in stern voice. "No use putting off what has to be. You might as well face it. What's done is done. Floppy has to be buried."

"We have to, Bruce," Raymond pleaded, wanting his friend to understand.

"*Floppy!*" cried Bruce, limping across the yard toward the hedge.

"Bruce, you come back here!" Miss Autrey said, starting after him. "Didn't I just tell you that running away doesn't solve anything?"

Bruce did not answer. Throwing himself on the ground, he was elbowing under the hedge. By the time Miss Autrey and Raymond reached him, however, he was on his way out, and in his arms was a dirty, blood-matted brown-and-white animal.

"Floppy?" Raymond whispered in disbelief.

"But it can't be!" said Vance. "He was dead."

Indeed, he did look more dead than alive—with one eye swollen nearly shut and the other with a great gash over it. He held one leg in a strange way and each time Bruce moved him the slightest bit, he yelped.

"I told you to check for a heartbeat," said Henrietta smugly, but for once it did not bother Raymond that she had been right.

Miss Autrey took over. "Get my first-aid box," she ordered Henrietta. "Get the cushion from the porch swing," she said to Raymond. Moments later she was helping Bruce move the dog to the cushion. "Easy, easy," she murmured. Then her large hands were moving over the animal, lingering on his sides and one of his legs. Finally, she sat back on her heels and let out a long breath.

"He gonna be all right?" Bruce asked anxiously.

"He'll need to see a vet."

"That's all right," Bruce answered quickly. "I can pay." He looked at Raymond.

Raymond nodded. "You can still have my money."

"Thanks, King Shoes!" Bruce turned back to Miss Autrey. "So, is he gonna be all right?" he repeated.

"I think so," she answered slowly. "But you know we are going to have to talk to Junior Elrod."

Bruce dropped his head.

"We've got a second chance here," she said. "We're going to do things right this time." She didn't state it as a question, but it sounded like one anyway and she waited for Bruce's answer.

He closed his eyes for a space of time and then squared his shoulders as though taking on a burden. "All right."

For a brief instant, Miss Autrey appeared to be on the verge of smiling, then she caught herself and became all business again. "If Junior agrees on a reasonable price for the dog, I guess I could loan you a little money to pay him."

"You would?" Bruce's face lit up. "I'd pay you back."

She pulled herself to her feet. "I'd count on that. But I want more. An agreement is what I want"—she turned to include Raymond—"with both of you boys. I expect you both to promise there'll be no more shenanigans like you two have been pulling the last few days—no more playing hooky, no more hopping trains, no more climbing cliffs."

Those were easy promises for Raymond to make. He was nodding his head before she had finished the list.

Bruce held back, studying the woman's face. "You expect a heck of a lot," he finally said.

"I certainly do," she said. "That's why I'm a good teacher."

"You ain't one to run yourself down, are you?"

Miss Autrey shrugged. "The truth's the truth. Do we have a deal or not?"

"Well, all right," he said at last, solemnly holding out his hand. "You got a deal."

For a moment, as she shook the bandaged hand, Miss Autrey's face seemed to soften. For a second time Raymond thought he saw a ghost of a smile. Then she was her usual self, barking orders right and left and then bustling around the house as though marching off to battle. "I'll bring the Jeep around. We had better get Floppy to a doctor," she called over her shoulder.

Henrietta jumped up and ran for the front door. "You're going to need help, Miss Autrey. I'll call Mama and see if I can go with you. She understands about emergency medical situations."

Raymond and Vance looked at each other and burst into laughter. *"Emergency medical situations!"* they hooted in unison. It felt good to be laughing together, Raymond thought, especially when they could laugh together instead of at each other.

Several minutes later when the Jeep was coming around the house, Raymond felt a hand on his shoulder and heard Vance say, "I guess I'd better get the bike and head home." He hesitated. "You want to go with me?"

Surprised, Raymond swung around to look at his brother. Vance would not meet his eyes. He became busy with the walnut, bouncing it up and catching it. Then, lifting it high in the air, he sailed the nut across the yard and into the walnut bucket.

"Maybe you could play football with Bunky and me or something," he continued, dusting his hands. His voice was casual, as if it were just an ordinary thing he was offering.

It was Raymond's chance. His brother was offering to include him, to treat him like an equal. Then Raymond's eyes dropped to Bruce, whose happy bandaged face was bent over Floppy. He looked toward Henrietta, who was on her way down the steps with a smile that said her mother had agreed.

"Thanks anyway, Vance," he said. "I guess I'll stay with my friends. Okay?"

A look of surprise crossed Vance's face. "Sure. Okay. We'll do it later. We can do it anytime." He grinned the kind of grin he usually reserved for his pals. "See you later."

"Later," Raymond agreed. Smiling, he moved across the yard to join his friends.